The
Mythology
Bible

The
Mythology
Bible

The Definitive Guide to Legendary Tales

Sarah Bartlett

STERLING

New York / London
www.sterlingpublishing.com

STERLING and the distinctive Sterling logo are
registered trademarks of Sterling Publishing Co., Inc.

**Library of Congress Cataloging-in-
Publication Data Available**

10 9 8 7 6 5 4 3 2

Published by Sterling Publishing Co., Inc.
387 Park Avenue South, New York, NY 10016

First published in Great Britain in 2009
by Godsfield Press,
under the title *The Mythology Bible*,
a division of Octopus Publishing Group Ltd.
2–4 Heron Quays, London E14 4JP
© 2009 by Octopus Publishing Group Ltd.

Distributed in Canada by Sterling Publishing
℅ Canadian Manda Group, 165 Dufferin Street,
Toronto, Ontario, Canada M6K 3H6

Printed in China
All rights reserved

Sterling ISBN 978-1-4027-7002-9

For information about custom editions, special
sales, premium and corporate purchases, please
contact Sterling Special Sales Department at 800-
805-5489 or specialsales@sterlingpublishing.com.

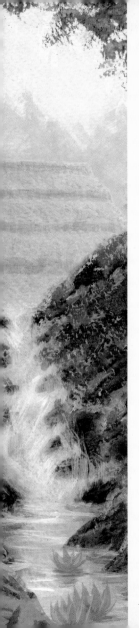

Contents

INTRODUCTION

Gathered from around the world, the major myths of love, heroes, creation, and adventure mirror our own heartfelt human stories. Offering a stunning insight into the most well-known gods and goddesses of each civilization, this book brings to life the magic of mythology. Not only are there familiar and beautifully retold tales from Greek, Norse, and Roman myth, but also from Asia, the Americas, Oceania, and Africa.

How to use this book

This book is a guide to the myths, gods, and goddesses that are evocative of our greatest visions throughout time and across cultures and civilizations.

You can use this book to source individual deities or simply to read about one particular civilization's pantheon of gods or mythological beliefs. Discover the wonders of the Dreamtime in Australia, read about the Egyptian belief in the afterlife, or get to know some of the Greek or Norse gods. Then in the second part of this book you can see how many myths from diverse cultures and timelines have similar themes. There is also a time chart on page 26—a reference point for comparing the timelines involved in world mythology.

The Introduction explores mythology both generally and comparatively. How did it all begin, and why? What does world mythology have in common, and what is the importance of myth in literature and art, as well as its relationship to psychology and modern interpretations? Part 1 then subdivides mythology by its geographical locations and/or civilizations.

Diversity and themes

The vast array of myths and deities from Greek, Norse, Egyptian, or Indian mythology alone could each fill a separate book. In the mythology of each of these civilizations, there is an initial creator god or supreme being, who is then joined by higher gods and their consorts, and subsequently by the lesser gods. The most important roles from these ancient cultures, such as fertility or love gods, or deities of war or harvest, are included in this guide. There are also three "family trees" which help to explain the relationship between the major gods of the Egyptian, Greek, and Norse pantheons. These can be found at the beginning of the relevant chapters.

This book also looks at the most evocative or significant myths from the indigenous peoples of America, Africa, Oceania, and the rest of Asia. Again, the most important deities or characters from each culture's mythology are outlined. The hunter-gatherer peoples of North America are mostly concerned

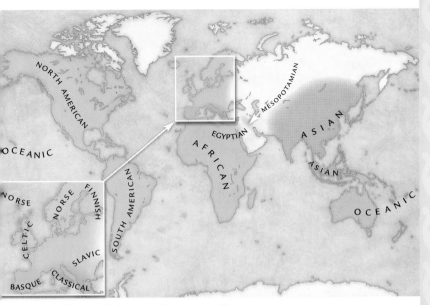

Part 1 of this book looks at mythology categorized by geographical locations and civilizations.

with local conditions or how the first man and woman were made. Meanwhile, the Inca, Aztec, and Maya civilizations of Central and South America are more structured and provide the basis of their own religious and ritualistic beliefs.

Meanwhile, the mythology of Africa (apart from Egypt) is fragmented; there is little connection between the diverse deities. However, great distances in Oceania, with its vast expanses of ocean separating islands inhabited by tiny groups of people, have not prevented certain gods from appearing in many different islands' belief systems.

Finally, we consider that the perennial interaction of experience, environment, and aspiration of the human mind often produces similar themes, whatever the culture base, geography, or timeline. This is covered in Part 2, *Themes in Mythology*.

What is myth?

Sacred stories of diverse cultures and civilizations make up the mythology of the world. Myth is the core element of many belief systems and religions—not only giving meaning and purpose to people's lives, but enabling them to understand the world around them.

Collective dreams are caught in our personal reality through myth, just like in a dream-catcher, holding our secret dreams.

"Myth" comes from the ancient Greek word *mythos*, which simply means "word," "narration," "tale," or "speech." To the ancient Greeks it was the antithesis of *logos*, the word for an objective way of describing an event, following the specific rules of logic. Philosophers would, in general, try to arrive at the truth through *logos*, while poets, historians, or artists of any kind would try to arrive at the truth via *mythos*.

Over several thousand years the word "myth" has gone through an etymological metamorphosis and it is now often used to describe a lie or stupid belief. "It's a myth" is a way of saying something isn't true, when in fact "myth" is "truth." People have been telling these sacred stories for thousands of years, not only to understand themselves, but to make better sense of the world and of the meaning behind existence.

Myth as reflection

Myths are very different from fables or legends. The latter often deal with aspects of morality in a certain society or culture, and are more concerned with values intrinsic to a particular ethos, civilization, belief system, or era. They are often connected to historical fact or arise out of a real-life person's adventures, deeds, or achievements.

Myths, on the other hand, are stories that concern our inner relationship with the divine or the "unknown." They are reflections of our own individual and collective desires, needs, and fears. Like mirrors, they remind us of who we are, and also of how little we as humans have changed since ancient times. Myths were recounted long before the advent of writing and form the basis

American professor of mythology Joseph Campbell re-established the power of myth and its shaping of our beliefs and values.

of most of the world's religions, philosophies, literature, and art. They reveal the powerful expression of the human imagination through a narrative form to create a universal language.

Public dreams

Myths are sacred stories that use symbols to tell their truth. They not only describe our perceptions of the world, but offer a key to questions such as "Who am I?", "How do I fit into my culture/society?", and "How should I live my life?" In fact, myths are the timeless expression of both the collective and individual imagination and of our need to understand who we are in the universe. As the famous American mythology professor and writer, Joseph Campbell, wrote, "Myths are public dreams; a dream is a private myth."

Introducing mythology

Mythology is a vast subject. Rather like history, it is not easy to encapsulate or contain it. Sacred stories from around the world are numerous, and huge bodies of stories make up the complete works of a culture or civilization's belief system.

Most of these sacred stories were originally transmitted in narrative form, passed orally down the generations, evolving and developing through time until they became the foundation of many religions. Those myths that have been passed down in written form are usually found in highly organized civilizations. Examples of these records include the stone tablets and hieroglyphics of Egyptian and some Mesopotamian mythology, the Rig Vedas of pre-Hindu mythology, as well as the vast literature of the ancient Greeks.

Egyptian hieroglyphics found on stone tablets reveal the sacred tales of more than three thousand years ago.

Universal themes

The 20th-century Swiss psychologist, Carl Jung, famous for his theory of the collective unconscious, believed mythology reflects the memories and images shared by all humankind. It reveals common themes, such as how the universe began, explanations of the forces of nature, the origins of people, personal quests and behavior, social rules and beliefs, as well as personal and collective psychological growth. Mythology is diverse in its detail due to local geography or local needs of the people, but the parity of imagery and ideas spanning huge geographical and time scales is extraordinary, too.

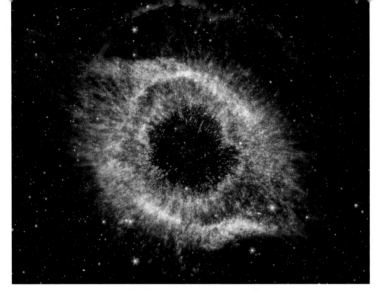

At the heart of most myths and belief systems is a creation story of how the universe began.

For example, the universal or cosmic egg appears in many creation stories, as do agents of transformation, such as birds like the Bluejay; horned gods such as Pan, the Minotaur, and Pashupati were all associated with the wildness of nature. Mythology also answers questions such as "How did the world or universe begin?" and "Why are we mortal?" Many cultures believed mortality was a punishment from the gods for human transgressions or for our ability to be corrupt. Similar themes and ideas that appear in vastly different locations may have traveled across continents like trade goods, as did the Indo-European languages that lie at the root of most of our "modern" European tongues.

Many of the tales and deities, with their virtues and vices, touch us profoundly at a "mythic" level. We still look to the ancient myths as parallels to our own life stories and can easily identify with the many different threads or concepts within the narratives, whoever the characters are and whatever the behavior or outcome of the tale. These myths capture the heart of the human dilemma—whether it be the lonely heart or the quest to prove oneself.

The purpose of myth

The personification of the natural forces as gods and goddesses was a way of explaining everything from the Sun, Moon, stars, and Earth, to thunder, rain, fire, and wind.

Essentially, gods and goddesses have "archetypal" potential—in other words, they evoke feelings, images, and experiences to which we can all relate. They are suggestive of various experiences in our own lives, such as power struggles, good versus evil, or the choices we have to make. The symbolic world of mythology can be viewed as a mirror of our own inner landscape.

Many cultures have long since lost their belief in such gods and goddesses. This, ironically, comes at a price. If we are wise and open enough to see that mythology is a wonderful mirror of human nature, a whole world into which we have projected our own fears, doubts, feelings, ideas, and desires, then it can offer a potent container for individual self-awareness and collective inspiration.

Many civilizations created mythical beings to explain the elements, such as gods of thunder, storms, and the sky.

Spiritual disconnection

The loss of mythology, particularly in Western society, has created a sort of spiritual disconnection. We are separated from the part of ourselves that is connected to something other than the material world. As Jung pointed out, "since the stars have fallen from Heaven and our highest symbols have paled . . . Heaven has become for us the cosmic space of the physicist." However, decades after Jung wrote this, we are returning to this symbolic network as a source of both spiritual and psychological nourishment. What the scientist is now discovering is what the ancient story-teller always knew.

Many scholars have tried to find a rational purpose for myths. One theory is that myth-makers were

Some believe that ancient myth-makers were primitive astrologers, looking to the heavens for answers, just as astrologers do now.

primitive scientists who wanted to explain how the world came into being. Myths were also used to explain the rituals and ceremonies concerned with the cycles of nature among ancient peoples. Societies created law and order through the oral traditions of mythology, and one hypothesis is that myths were created so that humans could ascend, or try to ascend, to the level of the gods themselves.

But it was probably Jung's breakthrough in thinking that explains our reawakened awareness of the purpose of myths. These sacred stories are simply the voices of our ancestors and, therefore, our own inner voice. Through myth we can reconnect to the universal nature of ourselves. No matter how separate we believe ourselves to be as individuals, it is mythology that reveals the underlying thread weaving us into a tapestry of wholeness that is the universe, which permeates all things.

Shared themes

Throughout world mythology the most common themes
involve the creation of the world and its first peoples. There is
often a creator god or a cataclysmic event that destroys the
first race of mortals and then the world is repeopled. For
example, there are flood myths from Sumer and Babylonia,
the Maya of Central America, and the Yoruba of Africa.

Death and rebirth were obviously important themes, as was the juxtaposition
between the Underworld and upper world. Creation myths satisfied the need
for a sense of where we come from, our roots and beginnings; fertility myths
were generated by a need for economic stability and the ongoing assurance of

*The Yoruba people of Africa celebrate their ancestors'
return from the dead at the Engungun ceremony.*

Similar themes appear in the most disparate parts of the world. Sky gods and creation stories prevail throughout.

life on Earth; hero myths provided models for human behavior. Some cultures were only interested in myths that explained their own people or culture. For example, the Yoruba had a structured explanation for their sacred city-state, as did the Navajo for their spiritual journey upward through four worlds.

Seasonality and creation

Most cultures had myths concerning the cyclical nature of the seasons, the development of agriculture, or a move from a more savage to a more civilized way of living. The children of the Sun were led to Cuzco by the Inca gods Mama and Manco; the story of Demeter and Persephone in Greek myth is both a powerful explanation of the seasons and forces of nature and a highly complex cyclical myth.

It seems that the ancient mind and the modern one have been working toward the same conclusions about how it all began. Whether it is the world egg that hatched, the cosmic man who split into many parts, or the Big Bang theory of the scientists, the cosmos was set in motion somehow. Creation myths offer basic answers to fundamental, yet profound questions. Creator gods create other gods, conflicts arise, and these give rise to heroes and their adventures. Dramatic love stories and heroic quests define the nature of humanity both for the collective and for the individual.

The gods and divinities, whether in human or animal form, throughout the world are "anthropomorphic"—in other words, they act, think, and speak as human beings. Some gods are sympathetic or concerned with the progress of mortals, as in Greece, India, Egypt, and North America. However, others are indifferent to human fate, as in the mythologies of Babylon and Sumeria.

The hero

Heroes and their missions are hugely important and become sacred icons for every culture, providing a useful basis or formula for the perpetuation of customs and beliefs. Heroes often teach humanity how to fish, heal, or hunt, or how to destroy the demons or monsters that threaten their communities. Heroes lead their people to a wonderful new world or give them fire and demonstrate new rituals.

It seems that the hero became a separate individual in his or her own right after the dissolution of the Great Mother or Great Goddess worship. This probably occurred near the end of the Bronze Age around 2500 BCE and near the beginning of the Iron Age around 1250 BCE. These hero myths came during a time of patriarchal emphasis in civilizations, during the development of agriculture as well as the establishment of empires and citadels.

Flaws and tests

Hero myths have much in common. The hero is usually the offspring of a divine being and a mortal. If not of divine parentage, then the hero is usually fostered by someone divine, as in the case of Odysseus by Athena, or acquires divine status as a result of his achievements and success.

The hero is rarely perfect, but he must always have a mission. In fact, because he has human weaknesses, it is easier for us to identify with him. His imperfections are as often as enlightening as his heroic qualities. As he is subjected to trials and tests, this process of the hero's journey symbolizes the gradual awareness of unused psychological potential in oneself. It also represents the development of consciousness and inner growth, and the very journey of one's life.

Theseus is a good example of a great hero who had divine parentage and a mission to pursue.

A hero's quest would involve many tests of strength and courage, such as meeting a dreaded sea monster.

Mission impossible

As the hero faces the monster, saves the tragic princess, or descends to the Underworld, he eventually wins over evil and either ascends to Heaven or is deified by the gods. Heracles is a fine example of a hero who faces a whole array of monsters during the course of his labors. The oracle at Delphi foretells his immortality as part of the Olympian pantheon, but only if he can complete all the labors successfully. Heracles manages to accomplish his tests, ascends to Heaven, and is married off to Hebe. Ironically, Hebe is the daughter of Hera, who hates Heracles because he is the product of her husband Zeus's affair with a mortal woman, Alcmene; it is actually Hera who is responsible for his nearly impossible mission.

The Great Flood

Another common theme in world mythology is the Great Flood, which generally destroys the human race so that a god or creator can cleanse the world of its corruption and start fresh. There are also flood stories based on geographical necessity and the yearly inundations near rivers such as the Nile and Euphrates. Flood myths are found right around the world from continental Europe to Peru, where the Inca creator god Viracocha destroyed his first race of giant-like humans with a flood and turned them all to stone.

In Greek myth, Deucalion was told by his father Prometheus, who was chained to Mount Caucasus, that Zeus was about to destroy all of life by sending a great flood. Prometheus told him to build a boat, fill it with food and live in the boat until the waters had subsided. Afterward, Deucalion and his wife Pyrrha stepped out onto Mount Parnassus into a totally deserted and barren landscape. They begged Gaia to replenish the Earth and suddenly trees sprung up and birds began to sing. To create humans they tossed stones and pebbles on the Earth, which turned to men and women.

Boat-builders

Utnapishtum was an ancestor of the hero Gilgamesh and the only human to survive the Great Flood sent by the angry gods to destroy humanity. Forewarned by the god Enki, he filled a cube-shaped boat with plants and creatures of every kind, then set sail with his family as the waters rose. After a week he sent out a dove to look for dry land, on the eighth day he sent a swallow and then on the ninth a raven. When the raven didn't come back, he set off in the same direction, found dry land, freed all the animals and planted the plants. The gods rewarded him for his kindness by giving him and his wife immortality and they became the ancestors of the new human race. Needless to say, this myth bears more than a striking resemblance to Noah's Ark from Genesis in the Old Testament of the Bible, and later in the Koran.

Other flood myths include the stories of the Chinese god Yu, the Egyptian Hapi, and Nu'u in Polynesian myth, who, upon hearing that the god Tane was going to swamp the world in a tidal wave, built a hut on a ship and stocked it with pigs and coconuts. He was eventually beached on the top of a mountain.

Floods were a common theme in many cultures, usually as a creator god's validation for cleansing the evils of humanity.

Indo-European culture and influence

Linguists, ethnologists, and mythologists have argued for many years about the origins of Indo-European languages and the subsequent effect on the mythologies of Europe and parts of Asia.

Some scholars believe the Indo-European culture descended from an ancient people once referred to as the primitive Aryans, now more commonly known as Proto-Indo-Europeans. These peoples lived around 4000 BCE.

But it was the Lithuanian-American archaeologist Marija Gimbutas (1921–1994) who studied the cultures of the Neolithic and Bronze Age peoples, combining linguistics with mythology to show how similar ideas, words, beliefs, and symbols could have been common motifs due to the widespread expansion of Indo-European cultures throughout Europe and Asia.

Kurgan model

The Pontic-Caspian Steppe is a vast area of treeless plains which lies between the Caspian Sea and the borders of Kazakhstan to the west. Once known as Scythia in Greek and Roman times, this steppe region was considered by Gimbutas to be the homeland of the Kurgan culture, the earliest Proto-Indo-Europeans. Gimbutas traced the migration of these peoples between 4000 and 1000 BCE and created what she called the "Kurgan model." This is a map of huge linguistic and mythological importance, which attempts to prove that these early people from the heart of the steppe lands spoke a language that is the etymological root of many Indo-European languages.

According to Gimbutas, Kurgan culture gradually expanded until it encompassed the entire Pontic-Caspian Steppe, and the expansion beyond the steppes led to hybrid cultures such as the proto-Greeks, the warring Indo-Aryans, and the nomadic Indo-Iranians around 2500 BCE. These earlier Proto-Indo-European cultures assimilated into their own religions other sacred

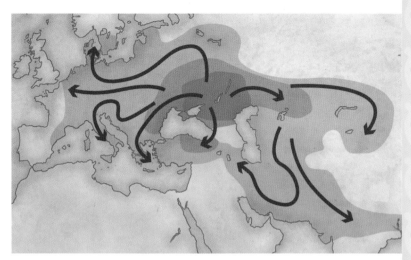

Gimbutas' "Kurgan model" traces the migration of the Kurgan people from their homeland, in the Pontic-Caspian Steppe, across most of Europe, the Middle East, and the Indian subcontinent, thus depicting their influence over many Indo-European cultures.

stories or fused with other cultures and their myths and religions as they spread. The Indo-Aryan mythology and language later developed into the Vedic religion, Hinduism, Buddhism, and Jainism, while Indo-Iranian culture developed into Zorastrianism, Persian, Greek, Roman, Baltic, Slavic, Celtic, Norse, Latvian, and Armenian languages and mythologies. *Aryan* comes from a Sanskrit word meaning "noble" or "honorable." The Aryans brought their own belief system and mythology to the Indian subcontinent around 2000 BCE.

Date discrepancy

However, English archaeologist Colin Renfrew (1937–) hypothesized that the Indo-European culture spread peacefully into Europe from Asia Minor at a much earlier date, around 7000 BCE with the development of farming and animal husbandry, pre-dating the Kurgans by thousands of years.

23

Civilizations and sources

The retelling of myths provides the basis of a traditional belief system for each culture or civilization. This reflects not only its social or economic needs, but also its spiritual or religious ones. There are two different ways of sourcing the myths that have been retold in this book.

In some cultures, ancient writings have been found that provide excellent sources, for example in the myths of India, ancient Greece, and Egypt. Where there are no recorded texts in tablet, hieroglyphic, or written word form, then the sources are usually the historical records of folklorists and anthropologists who have visited, listened, and later written down stories from the oral traditions of other societies. Most Oceanic and African myths have appeared in this way. However, when settlers, missionaries, or invaders infiltrated a culture or society, the stories may have been distorted, developed, or embellished to suit their own ends. Inevitably, some of the original meanings, ideas, or tales may have been lost along the way.

Some myths were passed down via stories being told to the community by the local shaman or tribal leader.

Time gaps

Civilizations are separated not just by continents or culture, but by huge timescales as well. The time chart shown on pages 26–27 will help you to understand which cultures were active and where at any given time around the globe. Obviously, with

In some cultures, such as ancient Egypt, Mesopotamia, and India, mythology was recorded in sacred scripts.

over 4,000 years of history, the times and dates when myths first emerged are often loose and ambiguous, but the chart does help to give some sense of what was going on and when. Feeling our way back in the dark and discovering that time is merely an invention of humankind actually provides us with our own connection to the power of these myths, and, as you will see, certain themes predominate irrelevant of time or place. In fact, many of the concepts, gods, and goddesses discussed in this book are as much a part of life today as they were four or five millennia ago.

Timeline of world mythology

This is an easy visual reference to the important dates and periods which are referred to throughout this book.

Obviously, with thousands of years of history, dates can be quite vague, and often the sacred stories actually date back to even earlier times, before they were recorded. Also, cultures and beliefs are intertwined throughout

3500 BCE	3000 BCE	2500 BCE	2000 BCE	1500 BCE	1000 BCE

◄ Great Goddess 4000 BCE

Kurgan expansion 3500–2500 BCE

Vedic beliefs in Indian subcontinent 1700 BCE

Rig Vedas c. 1000 BCE

First Dynasty of Egypt c. 2600–2200 BCE

Eighteenth Dynasty of Egypt 1550–1070 BCE

◄ Sumer c. 5300–2000 BCE

Babylonia c. 1730–1500 BCE

Old Assyria c. 20th–15th century BCE

Ancient Greece 1500–146 BCE

Polynesia reaches Fiji, Tonga, and Samoa 1300–900 BCE

◄ Hunter-gatherers arrive in Australia 40000 BCE

◄ Original migration from Eurasia to North America, via the Bering Land Bridge 10000 BCE

3500 BCE	3000 BCE	2500 BCE	2000 BCE	1500 BCE	1000 BCE

world history. For example, the Aryan Vedic gods were assimilated into India's Hindu belief system some time between 1000 and 550 BCE. It is, however, fascinating to be able to see both the similarities and the contrasts between the mythologies across the ages in different civilizations.

Belief in the Great Goddess is thought to have prevailed since about 4000 BCE, and dominated most cultures' belief systems for a long time.

500 BCE	0	500 CE	1000 CE	1500 CE	2000 CE

Vedic merge into Hinduism 900–550 BCE

Beginning of Buddhism c. 560 BCE

Beginning of Taoism c. 600 BCE

Beginnning of Confucianism c. 550 BCE

The *Kojiki* 680 CE

The *Nihoshoki* 720 CE

Rise of Shinto c. 6th century CE

Rise of Zoroastrianism c. 450 BCE

Neo-Assyrian Empire 934–609 BCE

Roman conquest of Greece 146 BCE

Ancient Rome 753 BCE–500 CE

Celtic civilization 1100 BCE–400 CE

Kalevala published c. 1835

Norse mythology 200–1030 CE

Slavic mythology 1000 BCE–6th century CE

Basque mythology 1st–4th century CE

Ashanti kingdom founded 1670s

First Yoruba kingdom founded 4th century BCE

First Dogon settlements 1500

Kingdom of Banyarwanda founded 15th century CE

Polynesia reaches the Cook Islands, Tahiti, and the Marquesas Islands 300 BCE

Polynesia settles Rapa Nui and Hawaii 300–500 CE

Western settlers in Australia 1770

Mayan Classic period 250–900 CE

Aztec empire 1300–1521 CE

Incan civilization 1200–1526 CE

Western settlers in the Americas 1500 CE

500 BCE	0	500 CE	1000 CE	1500 CE	2000 CE

Mythology and psychology

Archetypal figures such as the hero, mother, or father display profound psychological truths. Both depth psychology, such as Freud's psychoanalysis, and Jungian analytical psychology have drawn extensively on mythological themes in their work.

However, it was Sigmund Freud at the beginning of the 20th century who was one of the first to latch on to the symbolic use of myth when he introduced his well-known "Oedipus" complex; Jung later tagged the female version of the Oedipus complex with the name Electra. Freud's controversial theory suggests that a girl, like a boy, is originally attached to the mother, but then at the phallic stage of development she discovers she lacks a penis, resents and blames her mother (unconsciously) for castrating her, and turns to her father for love.

Carl Jung took a greater interest than Freud in mythology for its own sake, believing that the function of myth was to reveal the workings of the unconscious. Jung worked with dreams and, with knowledge of people's lives, symbols, mythology, and religion, he concluded that a diversity of energies or archetypes (defined as "original patterns or models") inhabited the unconscious. He described these mythical archetypes as the "great dreams of humanity." Jung also believed that "we have recollected ourselves from the universe" and that our projections happen to us, rather than us making them happen. In a sense, it is the myth dreaming us, rather than us dreaming the myth. Jung called the collective unconscious "a reservoir of the experiences of our species." Joseph Campbell and many others agreed with Jung that myth represented the human search for meaning or what gave significance to our lives. These psychological archetypes are an innate universal blueprint available to us all.

Myth as psychology

The term "narcissism" was derived (originally by Freud) from the well-known myth of Echo and Narcissus. Narcissism is defined as an over-emphasis of self-love, delusions of grandeur, and pathological envy. It is now recognized as a psychological clinical condition known as NPD, Narcissistic Personality Disorder.

The myth of Narcissus tells how he fell in love with his own reflection, spurning the nymph Echo for love of himself.

The Swiss Jungian psychologist, Marie-Louise Von Franz, wrote many notable books based on mythical archetypes in fairy tales. Her book on the liberation of the feminine principle in men is centered around the Roman tale of "The Golden Ass of Apuleius," which includes the first version of the myth of Psyche and Eros. Later, Jungian analyst Dr. Sigmund Hurwitz was influenced by Franz's work to write a book on Lilith and aspects of the dark feminine.

Mythology and the arts

Mythology is a creative expression of the human imagination, and for thousands of years it has not only been written down or told orally, but its imagery has flourished through each culture's art, whether to serve a decorative function or for ritual and religion. Great myths have also inspired artists, writers, and musicians through the ages. Because this subject is worldwide and immensely vast, here are just a few examples.

In Western Europe, Greek mythology has had a powerful influence on the art world. The ancient Greeks depicted their gods and heroes everywhere, whether in sacred temples or in day-to-day ornaments, jars and vases. The battle between the Centaurs and the Lapiths is depicted on the Parthenon frieze, which, according to some sources, later inspired Picasso's frenzied horses in his painting *Guernica*.

Apollo was one of the most popular gods represented in Greek sculpture, while Oceanus, who ruled the great river that encircled the Earth, was a favorite on Roman bronze ornaments.

Enduring images

Images of Medusa were originally used to ward off evil, and during the early 20th century in France, door knockers were forged in the shape of Medusa's head of coiling snakes and Art Nouveau-style elongated features. Tragic tales such as that of Orpheus and Eurydice appealed to late 19th-century Symbolist painters such as Maurice Denis and inspired Stravinsky, Henry Miller, and Cocteau. The story of Narcissus influenced the painters Caravaggio, Poussin, Raphael, and Gustav Moreau, and tragic Cassandra appeared in Euripides' *Women of Troy*. Virgil's *Dido* was again based on Cassandra, who also influenced Shakespeare's Ophelia and the mad but moody heroines in operas by Berlioz and Donizetti. Leda's seduction by Zeus in his guise as a swan inspired poets such as Goethe, Yeats, and Gide.

Crossing continents

Chinese and Indian deities were depicted in lavish paintings, temples, and statues, but were also extensively popularized. The Chinese god Kui is the god of success in examinations, and good wishes are still exchanged in the form of Kui cards or pendants, and his name is an icon on brushes and ink stones. The Incas and Aztecs carved sculptures, created gold masks, and golden temples, while native North American peoples produced carvings and totems of animal ancestors. In Aboriginal art, imagery of the snake was sacred and is still favored by modern Australian artists. It had as many images as it had myths, but was always a vast multi-colored band representing life. The snake either surrounded the inner design of the painting or wove its way through the labyrinth of patterns, coils and swirls. Aboriginal rock art found in the landscape usually has a

The Chinese god Kui is still considered good luck in exams and is often depicted on pens, pendants, and "good luck" cards.

hidden message, its intricate patterns depicting the local myth associated with the Dreaming, sacred sites, and invisible pathways.

In the West, Arthurian and Celtic tales inspired writers such as Sir Thomas Malory in *Le Morte d'Arthur* (1485), and artists such as the 19th-century Pre-Raphaelite painters who created a whole new medieval world of elegance out of the darkest of tales. These paintings later inspired film-makers and playwrights—Robert Bresson's broody film *Lancelot du Lac* and the stage musical *Camelot* are two such examples.

Myths, symbols and you

What is a symbol? The word comes from an ancient Greek word meaning "to throw together." We use this word to denote any thing, idea, or action that is an outward sign or indication of something else by indirect suggestion.

The hero Gilgamesh embodies all that is selfish in the individual, as well as the acceptance that one is only human.

For instance, we use the color red to denote or represent anger, while green is used to suggest jealousy, and so on. Symbols are also "correspondences." So, for example, red can be linked symbolically to the element of fire, the sun, dynamic action, and the heroic quest. The late 19th-century French Symbolist movement rejected realism in literature and art and expressed its ideas through a symbolic world of subtle suggestions, signs, and images. Mythology is a symbolic language too, because it "throws together" ideas that are an outward representation or projection of our inner world. We can use mythology symbolically to learn more about ourselves and our life journey.

There is not enough space in this book to reveal what every myth means on an individual level, but here are some examples of how a specific myth symbolizes a psychological process or experience in life. At some times we identify very strongly with the myth, while at others it may be more relevant to someone else.

Making myth a reality

From the *Mythical Lovers* section (see pages 304–331), the story of Pomona and Vertumnus symbolizes fear of rejection in love and how only by being true to ourselves can we be truly loved. On another level, the tale within a tale reveals how fear of our feelings means that we often lose out on love, too.

Gilgamesh is a fine example of a "bad" hero with a rather selfish quest to become immortal. His mission is never fulfilled and he learns that he is only human. Similarly we, too, must learn to accept our mortality and our flaws, but that doesn't stop us having goals and dreams in life.

Orpheus foolishly went against Hades' command and looked back in the Underworld to make sure Eurydice was behind him, and so he lost her. This echoes our lack of trust in others and in ourselves. It also suggests that if we continue to yearn for what once was, we will never be able to move on and start again.

In the myths of *Sun, Moon, and Sky* (see pages 246–277), the simple tale of Thunder and the Elephant can be used to explain how man is more powerful than either animals or nature. On a psychological level, this myth symbolizes how we must strive never to underestimate anyone, as this usually proves to be the most dangerous kind of arrogance of all.

Vengeance is also a common theme, such as the story of loss and revenge in the Alaskan Inuit myth of the trickster god Qayaq (see page 209). After avenging the death of his brothers and after years of adventures, he returns home to find his parents long dead. In his grief, he transforms himself into a wander-hawk.

The African tale of Thunder and the Elephant exposes the psychological vulnerability of making assumptions.

Deities as archetypes

The archetypal nature of the gods speaks for itself. There are archetypal fathers and mothers, archetypal lovers, villains, and heroes—in fact every sort of human condition and experience is reflected in the range of deities from around the world.

There are father-figure archetypes who can be both nurturing and destructive, such as the Hindu god Shiva or the ruthless Greek god Kronos, who prevents his children from overthrowing him by eating them alive. The mother, too, is a dynamic archetype. Earth Mother, the Great Goddess, or the Mother Goddess was widely worshipped in pre-Hellenic Greece by the most ancient matriarchal cultures, such as the Minoans. She was both fertility goddess and dispenser of nourishment, often associated with the water, sea, and Moon. However, with the change to patriarchal civilizations, the mother archetype was assimilated into the new mythologies.

Earth

We still find the real jewels of the Great Goddess heritage studded in the fabric of male-dominated myths. In an early pre-Hellenic version of the tale of Orpheus, Eurydice was actually the mother of fate, and the snake her companion in the Underworld who merely welcomed Orpheus rather than killing Eurydice. As a source of life, the Great Goddess was also the ever-fruitful womb, and whether she manifested later as Hathor, Cybele, Ishtar, Gaia, Parvati, Tara, Kwan-yin, Sophia, or Mary, she is beneficial, nurturing, and creative. She is everything to do with Earth, as the male or father archetype is all things to do with sky. However, the Great Mother has another darker,

The Earth Mother has been a powerful archetype since Neolithic times.

The Sun god Mithras eventually evolved into a hero with a cult following among the Roman legions.

more terrifying aspect. She is both sorceress and death-dealer, as when she appears as Astarte, Kali, or Durga, or in the worship of Artemis, Hecate, and even Diana. Female goddesses evolved out of each other much as male gods did, and nowhere is this more apparent than in the many goddesses of Hindu mythology, whose primary source was Devi. Similarly, the frightening mother appears in Aztec mythology as the terrifying Earth goddess Coatlicue, the Mayan goddess Ixchel, the Greek Medusa, and later projections of "evil" onto the mythical "femmes fatales" such as Lilith.

Sky

Sky gods and creators eventually became storm or fertility gods and are ubiquitous deities throughout world mythology. With historical changes over many thousands of years, these early sky gods were eventually assimilated into a male/female union to create divine pairs, like Freyr and his sister Freyja in Norse myth and Osiris and his sister Isis in Egyptian myth. As sky gods became less favored, they were transformed into Sun gods in Persia, Peru, Mexico, and Egypt. Mithras, for example, began life as a sky god, was transformed into a Sun god and later became a hero. Thus the Sun god turned hero fulfils our unconscious longings to escape the cruelty of nature and conquer the "Great Mother."

Sun

On the east coast of India there is a temple at Konarak (Place of the Sun) dedicated to the Vedic Sun god, Surya. The temple is designed in the shape of a huge chariot; like Helios and many other Sun gods, Surya needed a chariot to carry him across the sky on his daily travels. The walls of the temples are decorated with 12 stone wheels, each about 10 ft. (3 m) high and bearing eight spokes. Like the zodiac wheel, originally called the House of the Moon by the Babylonians, the wheel eventually became associated with solar worship. To both the Hindus and the Celts, the wheel was more than just a solar symbol—it was the cosmic center of their world.

Some Sun gods are depicted with rays radiating from their heads, or surrounded by halos. Shiva has a halo of flames, while Apollo and Mithras are often depicted with mystic halos. Gold, the color of the Sun, symbolized eternity and incorruptibility. To the Aztecs, gold was the light of their god, and to the Egyptians, the flesh of the gods.

Huge chariot wheels decorate the temple at Konarak in India, dedicated to the Sun god, Surya.

Moon deities like the Roman goddess Diana are prolific throughout world mythology.

Moon

The Moon had profound implications on the cycles of birth, life, and death, affecting the tides of the sea, associated with women's menstrual cycles, the fertility of the land, and the timing for crop-gathering and initiation ceremonies. In fact, the ancients believed that the Moon controlled these events, and it became associated with goddesses such as the Greek Artemis and Hecate, the Roman Diana, Nantu, the beautiful Moon goddess of the Jivaros of Ecuador, and Heng-O in Chinese myth, who went to live a lonely existence on the Moon.

Other archetypal deities are the lover/harlot goddesses such as Aphrodite, Ishtar, and Inanna. The eternal youth appears as Narcissus, Hyacinth, and Eros, and the trickster appears globally as Enki, Coniraya, Bluejay, and Tjinimin.

Interpretations

As myths are symbols of human experience, they have been analyzed in different ways, depending on the perspectives of the culture, era, or individual. Over 100 years ago, myths were thought to have been created as a way to observe and give reason to the forces of nature. Heroes were considered literal symbols of the Sun; monsters represented clouds, storms, or night and were the enemies of the Sun. Thus, hero stories became associated with good and evil, night and day, and so on.

The Greek mythical figure of Oedipus was used extensively in Freud's psychoanalytical studies and theories.

However, in the early 20th century, with the development of psychology, and the profound interest in the unconscious expressed and examined by two of its most radical theorists at the time, Sigmund Freud and Carl Jung, all this changed.

Freud

The father of modern psychoanalysis, Austrian Sigmund Freud (1856–1939) and his followers viewed myth as the expression of an individual's unconscious wishes, desires, drives, and fears. Freud disciple Otto Rank, for example, suggested that the myth of the traditional hero was likened to infantile hostility and rebellion against one's father. Freud, of course, created whole complexes out of the Greek myths of Oedipus and Electra;

both complexes describe the rivalry between child and either father or mother, due to our innate sexual and instinctive drives.

Jung

However, it was the Swiss psychologist Carl Jung (1875–1961) who made the biggest breakthrough, or at least change of perception, with regard to mythology. Jung viewed myth as an expression of a universal, collective unconscious. He believed that innate psychological qualities were common to all human beings and these determined how people experienced their lives. This collective pool of unconsciousness was made up of archetypes, such as the hero, the

Carl Jung founded the school of analytical psychology and was renowned for his theory of the collective unconscious.

trickster, the fool, and the wise woman. These were images embedded in the unconscious, but depending on the individual's personal life journey, the shape and form of these archetypal images would be expressed differently. Sometimes only one archetype would dominate, then another at different periods of one's life. At other times they would be acted out simultaneously.

The fact that myths throughout the world contain many similar themes and archetypes reflects the existence of a collective or universal unconscious.

Eliade

A Romanian historian of religion, Mircea Eliade (1907–1986), interpreted myths in a different way. He saw myth as the essence of religion, and believed that it was the sacredness of the myth that gave it structure and usefulness. We can experience the religious moment—a reconnection to the "source" or the place from which we have come—through mythic images and stories. The ancient

Diverse religions are connected through the similar themes that are found in mythology worldwide.

world contained many different religious ideas and structures, both polytheistic and monotheistic, as well as the worship of nature or of ancestral spirits. Eliade believed that mythology connects all these very different types of religion through the similar themes that are found across the globe.

Lévi-Strauss

The eminent French anthropologist Claude Lévi-Strauss (1908–) sees myths as abstract constructions rather than symbolic of experience. The structure of the human mind is the same, whatever place, timescale or culture you were or are in. So the mind solves problems and explains things the same way. Similarly, myths are identical creations from identical minds the world over, and their purpose is to reveal the conflicts between opposing forces in human nature. It is the underlying structure of the myth, not the symbolism or narration, that provides the answer. Myths prove that the earliest primitive peoples had the intellectual capacity to understand or make sense of the world.

Radin

American anthropologist Paul Radin (1883–1959) saw myth as arising out of economic problems and political and religious manipulation of the people. Faced with the struggle for survival, and the uncertainty or climate of a particular culture, people became fearful. Thus mythological systems gave them something to believe in and live by; similarly, a mythological belief system gave both political and religious leaders power over the community.

Some say that myth arises from the religious manipulation of people by institutions such as the Church.

41

Campbell

American professor of mythology Joseph Campbell (1904–1987) is highly regarded for his work as a writer and student of mythology. Although he drew on Jung's interpretative techniques, he followed Heinrich Zimmer's theory that mythology in itself was a roadmap to self-discovery. Campbell relied more on the symbolism, meaning, and imagery of myth. He saw religious symbols as metaphors for bigger philosophical ideas. He agreed with Jung on the impact of mythic archetypes, but believed that spirituality (in whatever form) was a search for the source from which everything has come, is part of and will return to. It is "unknowable" because it existed before words. This universal force is expressed through metaphors—in other words, through the myths, stories, art, and imagery that we create in the world.

Campbell was particularly concerned with the hero and devised the word "monomyth" after being influenced by the work of James Joyce. Heroes were important because they conveyed universal truths about oneself or one's role in society. A line translated from the Rig Vedas sums up his belief system: "Truth is one, the sages speak of it by many names."

A line from the Rig Vedas, still used today in Brahmin processions, sums up Campbell's belief system.

Hillman believes Greek mythology, such as the tale of Theseus, is a form of psychology.

Hillman

In the late 20th century, American psychologist James Hillman (1926–) made a radical break from Jungian thought with his advocacy of the belief that mythology was psychology, and vice versa. His "archetypal" psychology focuses on the soul rather than the ego and on the deepest patterns of psychic functioning. This "soul" attempts to recognize the myths that shape our individual psychology, and the ego is just another fantasy among a myriad of fantasies or myths. Hillman has attempted to restore the "soul" or "psyche" to its proper place in psychology and to value our dreams not just for evaluating the state of an individual and its underlying symbolism, but as a pure experience of that archetype.

Hillman noted that the Greeks had no depth psychology, but they had myths; his theory is that polytheistic mythology (mythology with many gods and goddesses) is the same as psychology. He also believes that we should get to know these sacred forces and energies as represented by the gods. The power of myth is that it asks us to know ourselves better.

Part 1

WORLD
MYTHOLOGIES

ASIA

Asian mythology, with its huge range of gods and goddesses, is as vast as the continent itself. This section covers the main countries of India, China, and Japan and includes deities such as the Chinese Jade Emperor, the Japanese Seven Gods of Luck, and major, yet multi-tasking Indian deities such as Ganesha, Agni, and Tara.

History and background

A vast continent with diverse cultures, the one common denominator in Asian mythology is the infinite number of gods and goddesses, spirits and divine essences that seem to permeate each different culture and civilization.

The myths of India, China, and Japan stand out from all the others in that they have ancient roots and writing traditions spanning many centuries, which provide valuable evidence of the earliest myths. However, their cultural mythology is highly complex, and similar deities with multi-tasking roles and many aliases mean that there is a lack of structure and consistency.

From the Himalayas to Tokyo, the geography of Asia is not only vast, but encompasses extremes of temperature, climate, and landscape. With the snow-capped peaks of the Himalayas, heavy monsoons in India, extreme drought in

The mythology of the Asian continent is as varied and extreme as its climate and landscape.

some of the wastelands of China and tropical conditions in Indonesia, the mythology of the continent was originally formulated from belief systems that centered around the landscape as well as how the universe began and how it might end.

Indian mythology

Perhaps the Hindu belief system is so distinct from all other belief systems simply because, according to its beliefs, "anything or anyone goes." Hindu myth developed from the earlier Vedic beliefs of the invading Aryans, a warrior people who spread from the

One of the oldest living cities in southern India is Madurai, whose cultural heritage goes back 2,500 years.

west into the steppes of central Asia and easily conquered the agricultural and peace-loving pastoral Dravidians. The Aryans brought with them their own mythology and beliefs that merged with the earliest surviving myths of around 4000 BCE. But the Aryans had never been settlers and their gods were connected not with the Earth, but with the abstract forces of the universe itself. The Rig Vedas were a collection of hymns or poems that were completed around 1000 BCE, and are the main source for most of the Vedic mythology that was prominent until the emergence of Hinduism.

By the end of the Vedic period—around 900–550 BCE—early Hinduism was evolving and the search for a supreme deity began. This Brahmanic age evolved out of the confusing hierarchy of the Vedic gods and reflected the desire for a simpler, more structured pantheon—there was a feeling that the new deity Brahma would be a suitable candidate. When he was joined by Vishnu and Shiva (creative energy and destructive energy respectively), a more structured doctrine evolved as a never-ending cycle of creation and destruction. Later, sacred texts such as the Puranas, the Mahabharata, and the Ramayana are often different versions to replace the preceding ones.

49

The mythical Chinese dragon is a potent symbol of auspicious energy and power.

Chinese mythology

Chinese mythology is as diverse and colorful as that of India, and is composed of tales and concepts from three very different belief systems. Its vast collection of deities is derived from Taoism, Confucianism, and the introduction of Buddhism from India, where elements from all these teachings were incorporated into Chinese myth, and vice versa. Confucianism absorbed the rulers of ancient mythology and also embraced the Taoist belief of a spiritual paradise. Chinese myth was originally passed down orally and was later written down in texts and often appeared in the form of theater, dance, and song.

Myth and reality merge together throughout the history of China, where gods become mortals and historical characters join in the mythic pantheon. Reality and fantasy are confused, and the most important concept— immortality—means that many "real-life" heroes or dynastic rulers were immediately promoted to immortal status once dead.

Japanese mythology

The *Kojiki*, or *Record of Ancient Things*, is the oldest surviving book of the history of Japan. An amalgam of folk legend, Shinto, and Buddhist traditions, Japanese myth consists of innumerable deities and spirits known as *kami* and their equally numerous aliases. Many of the gods and their stories had originally been imported from Chinese and Indian mythology around the 4th century CE when the Japanese conquered mainland Korea. But this triggered a need to establish and re-examine Japan's own "folk" mythology, resulting in the *Kojiki*, and later in the 7th century CE, in the *Chronicle of Japan,* known as *Nihoshoki.* Both collections of stories allowed the ruling emperors to be traced back to the gods themselves and to establish the link between the supernatural and the mortal. The Shinto belief that the supernatural was in everything, whether man or beast, meant that emperors could also claim god-like status. This continued right through Japanese history until the end of the Second World War when Emperor Hirohito (1901–1989) relinquished his right to divine status and was officially declared a mere mortal. Shinto shrine practice is still followed throughout Japan.

The goddess Amaterasu is worshipped at the Ise Jingu,
a Shinto shrine in the Japanese town of Ise.

India's Rig Vedic deities

Both Indra and Agni play major roles in the early pantheon of Indian gods—Indra was the Aryan god of thunder, while Agni was the god of fire.

Indra

In the Rig Vedas, Indra is by the far the most talked-about god. In a thousand hymns, he appears about 250 times. Originally the Aryan's chief god, Indra formed a duality with Varuna (encompasser), god of the sky, embodying morality and amorality. He banished Vritra, the god of drought and death, and brought rain to India. His life-giving qualities made him a star, and he was renowned as the god of water, rain, and thunder.

Indra was known to carry a thunderbolt, which he used to defeat enemies, but also to split open mountains to release life-giving floods. His first appearance in the world was preceded by the rumble of a gathering storm as his chariot lurched across the sky pulled by a pair of golden horses. Some sources say he arrived in the world on his war-elephant Airavata, and his companions were the Ahvins, or healers. Indra has a thousand eyes and a thousand testicles which no one has ever seen, and his nature is made up of human strengths and weaknesses. He was a glutton, seducer, and heavy drinker of the ritual drink Soma, which often made him drunk and crotchety.

Indra with his thousand eyes and thousand testicles, descended to earth on his warrior elephant, Airavata.

In art he is often depicted riding his warrior elephant or in his chariot as the chief god. His huge appetite for sex and food made him a rather bawdy deity and he was popularized in many later stories and anecdotes.

Agni

First appearing in the 17th century BCE, Agni's powers were as important as Indra's and Varuna's. He had thousands of aliases and was the supreme god of fire—this covered everything from the flames of desire to the lightning in the sky. Agni would appear as a glistening prince riding a sacred ram or wild chariot; he had red flesh and cloaks of smoke, his hair consisted of licking flames, and he had many faces, gold teeth, and fourteen tongues which spouted flames.

He was thrice-born from Water, then Air, then on Earth. He was born full-grown like Indra and was so hungry that he ate his parents Privithi (Mother Earth) and Dyaus (Father Sky) and then began lapping sacred butter from the gods' altars. He finally devoured a whole forest, which he still does throughout the world when there is a forest fire. He was known as the god of immortality and also as a mediator between gods and mortals. He hung the stars in the sky and created the Sun, and warred with demons and monsters.

Agni was the god of fire. Responsible for creating the stars in the sky, he also devoured whole forests with his flames.

Progression to Hindu deities

As Vedic myths were absorbed into Hindu belief systems, the deities' roles often changed, even though many of the names were carried over.

Brahma, Vishnu, and Shiva

All three of these deities were originally creator gods in Vedic myth when the Aryans invaded India in the 17th century BCE. However, in Hindu myth, the gods formed a triad of preservation (Vishnu), destruction (Shiva), and mediation between the other two (Brahma). The triad maintained both universal order and justice.

Brahma

The lord of all time, one of Brahma's days last 4,320 million mortal years. His life is a cycle of 157,680 million years and is an eternally revolving wheel of time. He sees and hears all that happens for he is all that happens, everywhere and at the same time. This very abstract concept of Brahma developed after he initiated creation with little thought for what he would establish. In some accounts he first made a river that flowed out of his hip. This became his consort Sarasvati, a beautiful goddess. Together they made everything in the universe. In other accounts, he created mystics who were able to use their knowledge

The Hindu triad of Brahma, Vishnu, and Shiva: they were originally the creator gods in Vedic myth.

to create the universe, but they were more interested in wisdom than action. Brahma was furious, and Rudra (storm and lightning) burst from his forehead and completed creation on Brahma's behalf.

Brahma lives on Mount Meru, the tip of the Heavens thousands of miles above the mortal world. Because he is all that is, he doesn't need to leave Heaven, and spends most of his time in meditation, which keeps the universe alive. As an intellectual concept, it is difficult for artists to depict Brahma, but he usually appears holding the Vedas, riding a swan or peacock, or reclining on a lotus.

Vishnu

Vishnu was the first force in the universe, also known as Ananta (infinite) and Keseva (hairy). His all-pervading light was the source of the universe itself. From his navel, Brahma was born, and when demons and gods argued about who should rule the universe, Vishnu turned himself into a dwarf and offered to give the demons as much of the universe as was left after he took three strides. They agreed and Vishnu covered the whole of the Earth, Middle Air, and Heaven in three huge strides and there was nothing left for the demons.

In Hindu mythology, Vishnu is the god of preservation and personifies sacrifice. Lakshmi was his wife and they lived in Heaven among the lotuses. Vishnu had hundreds of avatars (the earthly forms he took when visiting the mortal world to save it in some way), but his most important forms were Matsya the fish, Kurma the tortoise, Varaha the boar, and Rama, Krishna, and Buddha.

Shiva

Shiva was originally the storm god Rudra in the Vedic prayers, until he became a god in his own right in the 2nd century BCE. As Vishnu was the preserver, so Shiva was the destroyer, yet he was also a merciful judge, a unifier as well as a shatterer. The god of opposites, Shiva led a wild frenzied dance and sided with demons and outcasts. His non-stop meditation and dance gave him great power and strength. He had invincible weapons, such as his terrible third eye, trident, sword, and thunderbolts. At each cycle of the universe, Shiva opens his eye and dances, destroying everything in his sight, including the universe itself, until creation begins again.

Lakshmi

The goddess of luck and good fortune, Lakshmi was popular among women and was originally the goddess of prosperity in Vedic myth. As Vishnu's consort, beautiful, faithful, and smiling, she never left his side. Whenever Vishnu was angry, she was calm, and whenever he went to the mortal world as Rama she would accompany him as Sita. When he went as Krishna she became Radha, the most beautiful woman in the world. Lakshmi could become anything or put herself wherever she wanted to be in the mortal world, and would appear on doorsteps to bring good luck or would nestle in people's bodies. This brought luck to whatever part of life corresponded to the body area: in the heart, the granting of your heart's desire; in your reproductive organs, good luck in finding a partner; in your bosom, good fortune for children. She was a favorite subject in art, and is often depicted on a lotus flower, with Vishnu riding Garuda, or surrounded by beautiful objects.

Lakshmi would nestle in someone's heart to bring luck and happiness to their love life.

Devi

Sometimes known as the Great Goddess embodying all the other goddesses, Devi was also Shiva's consort. She may well have predated the heavenly triad of Brahma, Shiva, and Vishnu. In fact, in some accounts, the Hindu triad was a personification of Devi's divine energy. Devi means "goddess" and she had many roles, as the peaceful creator Jaganmatri (all-mother); as Mahadeva (great goddess), and Uma (peaceful). As Shiva's consort she was both Sati (virtue) and later Sati's reincarnation as Parvati (sweetness). Her other roles were as dark as her light ones, both as the war goddess Durga (unapproachable) and as Kali, another aspect of Durga as the personification of horror and death.

Durga

As Durga, Devi has the power of the cosmos on her side, and is the embodiment of warlike energy and thus more frightening than any other god. She came into being as a gathering of all the gods into a powerful army to rid the universe of demons. Not only did she destroy the demon king Durga (after whom she named herself) in her role as Devi, but she then went on to destroy the gigantic demon Mahisha with Agni's lightning, the thunderbolt of Indra, Shiva's trident, and Vishnu's discus. The shape-changer Mahisha eventually turned into a giant and Durga stabbed him to death.

There are many demon-killing tales of Durga, and she is usually depicted in art as a smiling warrior with hundreds of arms, riding a tiger to symbolize her power. She is often portrayed as the conqueror of the universal fight against evil, as a warrior-queen on a lotus throne, reposing with her sacred snake. However, in her emanation as Kali she is considered the personification of evil itself and is depicted with black flesh, fangs, and a necklace of skulls.

Durga was one aspect of Devi. In her role as Durga she was the terrifying demon-killing war goddess riding a tiger.

57

Ganesha

The son of Shiva and Parvati, Ganesha is the god of problem-solving and good luck. With the head of an elephant, a pot belly, stumpy legs, and only one tusk, Ganesha is a popular domestic deity and his statues are still found in shrines, at crossroads, and in the home.

Ganesha rode a demon king who was reincarnated as a rat, and there are several stories explaining the strange appearance of this rather benign but jovial character. In one tale, Ganesha was so handsome at birth that, to save him from Shiva's jealousy, Parvati cursed him with ugliness. Another story tells how he was decapitated to punish Shiva for killing the Sun, but Shiva brought him back to life and gave him the head of the first animal that came along.

The most popular tale tells how Parvati created Ganesha from all the scraps and flakes of her own skin. Shiva was intent on having sex with Parvati when she was bathing, so Parvati told Ganesha to stand guard to warn her of Shiva's approach. But Ganesha foolishly challenged Shiva, not realizing who he was, and Shiva cut off his head in a rage. Parvati was so upset that Shiva restored Ganesha to life and gave him the head of an elephant, the first animal to show itself.

Ganesha was also known as the god of literature. When the sage Vyasa was writing the epic poem the *Mahabharata*, he employed Ganesha to help him and even used one of his tusks as a pen to write down every word.

A popular domestic deity, Ganesha was unlucky to have the head of an elephant and a pot belly.

Krishna

The eighth incarnation, or avatar, of Vishnu, Krishna came into the world solely to destroy the demon king Kansa. However, Krishna's popularity as a deity meant that he became the object of "bhakti" worship (devotion to a supreme god) even though his power, as avatar, was limited. His sensuous, yet lusting nature inspired artists and writers alike, and although he was known for his passion for milkmaids, he was the one god who genuinely fell in love with a mortal, the cowgirl Radha. Krishna became known as "Hari Krishna," the stealer of hearts, and his love for Radha was celebrated in a very beautiful poem called the *Gitagovinda*. Their idyllic relationship continued until Krishna began his epic struggle against the demon king, when marriage and heirs became more important than the passions of true love.

"Hari Krishna," the stealer of hearts, eventually fell passionately in love with the cowgirl Radha.

Krishna was actually more promiscuous in his marriages than during his early love affairs. During the first battles against the demons, he married eight wives and conquered evil through all of them. After the demon armies were vanquished, Krishna married more than 16,000 more wives, all virgin prisoners of the enemy. When he returned from the war, he agreed to marry them all, as each had fallen madly in love with him. He lived with them all at once and managed to pleasure them simultaneously, so that each wife eventually bore him ten sons and one daughter. Even with so many wives, Krishna was able to attend to their every desire, need, and whim—a seemingly perfect husband.

Garuda

Garuda has the body and limbs of a man and the head, wings, talons, and beak of an eagle. His face is white, his wings red, and his body is so golden and dazzling that he was mistaken for Agni (the fire god) when he first hatched from an egg. The bird-king could fly faster than the wind and flew around the world devouring everything that was evil.

He particularly hated snakes, due to the tragedy that had befallen his mother, Vinata, one of Daksha's daughters. Vinata had an argument with the serpent mother Kadru about the color of a horse. Whoever was wrong would be imprisoned in the Underworld; unfortunately, Vinata chose the wrong color. Garuda immediately went to release her, but the serpents demanded a ransom for her release. In one account, the serpents demanded a cup of *amrita*, the god's drink of immortality. Garuda eventually snatched the *amrita* and rushed back down to the Underworld. Indra was angry and hurled his thunderbolt at Garuda, who smashed it to pieces and gave the *amrita* to the serpents. Just as they were about to drink the potion, Indra snatched it back, and as the serpents tried to lap up the last drops, the power of the *amrita* divided their tongues and to this day serpents have forked tongues and must renew their skins each year in honor of their immortality. The gods realized that Garuda was more powerful than they thought, so to keep him on their side they awarded him a place of honor as Vishnu's charioteer.

Tara

Tara appears in Hindu, Buddhist, and Tibetan mythology. She was probably originally Devi, the Great Goddess, or Parvati (another aspect of Devi). Her role in Hindu mythology was as the beautiful consort of Brihaspati, the teacher or guru of the gods. Tara was lusted after and abducted by Soma, the Moon god. This created a war between demons and gods. Finally, Brahma persuaded Soma to return Tara to Brihaspati, but, finding her pregnant, he refused to have her back. When the child was born, it was so beautiful that he claimed it as his own. Soma believed it was his child, too. To settle the dispute Brahma gave Tara to Brihaspati and the child became the father of all the future lunar dynasties, thus creating harmony between the gods and the celestial bodies.

Tara was a multi-tasking deity in Hindu and Buddhist myth. White Tara was specifically compassionate.

In Buddhist myth Tara was originally a sea goddess, but she was adopted in the 6th century CE as the expression of "Mother of Perfected Wisdom," and the first feminine principal to be assimilated into Buddhist belief. Tara has many different aspects: White Tara is associated with compassion and the healing force of the universe; Green Tara as savior and pure enlightenment; Red Tara with goodness and discriminating awareness; Yellow Tara with prosperity and wealth; Blue Tara was the transmutation of anger. Tara was also known as the Mother of the Buddhas and subsequently the mother of all human beings on Earth. She became popular as an object of worship, particularly in Tibet, by the 7th century CE.

Maya and Mara

In Buddhist myth, Maya was Buddha's mother. She died soon after his birth from the sheer joy of his existence and was reborn in Heaven. *Maya* is also the Sanskrit word for "illusion," and the Hindu belief is that the world itself is *maya*. In other words, our perception of reality is an illusion.

While Buddha was meditating under the *bho* tree in order to achieve enlightenment to try to see the distinction between self and the universe as a false duality, Mara, as king of the demons, became worried that his power was under threat by the Buddha's growing enlightenment. He first sent *maya* to create an illusion in Buddha's mind that a rival prince called Devadatta had stolen his throne, but Buddha wasn't deceived.

Maya *is the Sanskrit word for "illusion." Hindus believe that the world itself is an illusion.*

Mara threw rocks at him, flailed him with burning coals and tempestuous storms, but Buddha felt nothing. Mara sent all kinds of earthly temptations—beautiful seductresses, delights and delicacies—but he ignored them. Mara even sent the Buddha's own mother, Maya, to try to seduce him from his meditation, but even the army of demons and his mother's visit from Heaven could not stop him from meditating. Mara then hurled his own thunderbolts at Buddha, but they changed into garlands of flowers around the Buddha's head. Mara then began whispering in Buddha's ear, telling him to abandon the world and enter nirvana while he could, but Buddha again ignored him. In Buddhist cosmology, Mara is considered to be the personification of those things in life, such as materialism, power, and lust, that lead the individual away from their true spiritual path.

Nanda

In Buddhist myth, Nanda is the Buddha's half-brother. Buddha was much older than Nanda and had already begun preaching and converting the people. On Buddha's journey, he passed by Nanda's house one day, but Nanda didn't recognize him and tried to send him away by offering him alms. Although Nanda had just married a beautiful young woman, he was hypnotized by the enlightened words of Buddha and found himself following him to a monastery where he became a monk. But the joys of the secular world remained in his mind. One day he decided it was time to return to his beautiful wife. Buddha stopped him by showing him a blind old monkey and asked "Is your wife as beautiful?" Nanda indignantly replied, "Much more." Buddha took him to Heaven and showed him that, compared to the gods, his wife was no more beautiful than the monkey. Nanda decided to devote himself to his austere life so that he could go to Heaven and be as radiant as the gods. So Buddha took him to Hell and showed him a cauldron of boiling water. This was what awaited him if he could not let go of his attachment to the world of desire. From then on, Nanda devoted himself to the Buddhist Way, and his story became a lesson to all Buddhists—self-denial is the pathway to enlightenment.

Nanda was enthralled by Buddha's teachings and devoted himself to the Buddhist Way.

Japanese mythology

The deities within Japanese mythology are derived from a number of cultural influences, including Shinto, Hindu, and Buddhist sources. The Sun as a symbol has particular resonance in Japanese culture.

Amaterasu

There are very few Sun goddesses in world mythology, particularly after the dissipation of the female goddess cults by most of central Asian, European, and eastern patriarchal civilizations. Yet Amaterasu is a highly respected and powerful mythical deity in her own right and she is still important in Shinto religion in Japan. In secular Japanese life, women achieved status as female warriors or prophetesses thanks to worship of Amaterasu.

The powerful interplay between the Sun and Moon was essential to the fertility of the world in early Japanese mythology. Amaterasu was the daughter of Izanami and Izanagi, the last two deities to grow on the cosmic reed at the beginning of the universe. Her important myth concerning Susano (see opposite) lies at the heart of Shinto worship and the political and social dynastic rule of Japan. The imperial family of Japan believed themselves to be direct-line descendants of the Sun goddess herself.

Amaterasu's symbols of power as the Sun goddess were a necklace made of light, the Milky Way, and the first clothes ever made, sewn with fabulous jewels, precious stones, and the golden light of the Sun itself. She has been worshipped from ancient times as the Great Heaven Shining Deity, and every twenty years her simple thatched shrine at Ise on Honshu is renewed in her honor.

Susano

Susano was Amaterasu's brother and was given dominion over the sea and Earth, but refused to accept it. The storm god in Japanese myth, he was born from the drops of water that fell from Izanagi's nose as he washed away all the pollution of the Underworld that had tainted his body. (In some accounts when Izanagi blew his nose, Susano was born.) In his refusal to be the god of the sea, he raged around the universe, causing destruction wherever he went, not only causing the death of his sister Wakahirume, the dawn, but forcing Amaterasu to retreat and hide in a cave, taking the sunlight with her.

Transformations

Later, punishment by the gods softened his temper and he saved a beautiful girl called Kushinada from the jaws of a terrifying water monster. He turned the girl into an ornamental comb and stuck it in his hair, then told her parents to fill eight barrels with saki (rice-wine) and offer one each to the eight heads of the monster. The beast fell over drunk and Susano chopped off all its heads. He turned Kushinada back into a woman and then married her. Later Shinto priests embellished this myth by adding that Susano also discovered a magic sword in the monster's belly and gave it to his sister Amaterasu, who later gave it to her grandson Ninigi when she sent him to rule the Earth. This sword was handed down from generation to generation and became one of the most sacred objects in the imperial family, proof that they were descended from the gods.

The storm god, Susano, defeated many demons and monsters with his thunderbolts and lightning.

65

The Seven Gods of Luck

Drawing on Hindu, Shinto, and Buddhist origins, the Seven Gods of Luck have always been extremely popular in Japan. Each god was responsible for a certain aspect of luck and could be called on for help as appropriate.

- **Benzaiten**, the goddess of all that flows, looks after rivers, music, knowledge, and words. She is often referred to as the goddess of happiness, love, and the sea in her aspect as Benten, and carries a stringed instrument called a *biwa*. Originally, Benzaiten was a protective deity, but eventually became known as a goddess of good fortune. She is derived from Sarasvati, an earlier Hindu river goddess. The other gods of luck include:

- **Daikoku**, the Shinto god of wealth, good harvest, and care of the household. He was often depicted seated on a bale of rice, wearing a flat black hat and carrying a hammer.

- **Bishamon**, the god of fortunate warriors and punisher of criminals; his symbols were a lance and a pagoda.

- **Ebisu**, said to have been one of the children of Izanagi and Izanami; born without bones, he was the god of work and was often known as the laughing god.

- **Hotei**, best known as the laughing Buddha and highly popular in Japanese temples and restaurants. He is often worn as an amulet and depicted as a great fat Buddhist monk accompanied by children; Hotei was beneficial for families.

- **Jurojin** favored long life and his symbols included the tortoise and the turtle, both signs of longevity.

- **Fukurokuju**, god of wisdom and long life, is often shown with a walking stick and accompanied by a stork.

Jurojin would bring you long life if you carried his talismanic tortoise or turtle.

Hachiman

The Shinto god of war, Hachiman was also the divine protector of Japan. Originally he was a god of fertility as well as agriculture and fishing. In the 4th century CE, it was believed that Hachiman was a real figure known as Emperor Ojinm, a renowned military leader with the power to change the tides and prevent invaders from landing. With the arrival of Buddhism in the 8th century CE, Hachiman became associated with the Bodhisattva Diabosatsu and was later worshipped by the Samurai in the medieval period. Many Shinto shrines are devoted to Hachiman, whose main cult following is the temple at Kamakura. Young men still celebrate their rite of passage into adulthood at Hachiman temples.

Hachiman shrines are still used by young Shinto followers to celebrate their rite of passage into adulthood.

Uzume

It is not exactly clear whether Uzume was the original goddess of dawn herself or the sister of Wakahirume (see page 65), whose death made Amaterasu retreat into a cave and leave the world in darkness. Some accounts also suggest she was the consort or sister of Ninigi, the founder of the imperial dynasty, but originally she was known as the goddess of both magic and dance. She was instrumental in enticing the fearful Amaterasu out of her cave to bring light back to the world, by seducing the other gods into revelry. Uzume was rewarded by being given the Milky Way. Her priestesses brewed imitation potions in her shrines and her knowledge of herbal remedies led to Uzume being worshipped as the goddess of well-being.

Chinese mythology

As an exceedingly ancient culture, China's mythology draws on many cultural and religious belief systems, including Taoism, Confucianism, and Buddhism.

According to Taoist myth, the Jade Emperor was responsible for creating the twelve animal signs of the Chinese zodiac.

The Jade Emperor

The Jade Emperor of Taoist belief was originally the supreme being Shang Di, the power that initiated creation and the universe, and the force that generated the continuation of all life.

Shang Di was considered a sort of heavenly equivalent to an emperor on Earth and presided over vast arrays of deities and servants. By Confucian times he became a more abstract concept, and it wasn't until about the 11th century CE that he merged with Yu Huang, the Jade Emperor and head of the Taoist pantheon. From then on the Jade Emperor was the only supreme being, known as Yu Huang Shang Di. With his smiling face, long beard, and benevolent face, the Jade Emperor had attained enlightenment by following "the Tao" (the Way), the central philosophical belief of the Taoists. He was also popularized as the ruler of all Heaven, a little aloof, but with a vast court of deities and courtiers.

Animal signs of the zodiac

One Taoist story tells of how the twelve animal signs of the zodiac were chosen. The Jade Emperor wanted to make the Earth more harmonious. So he asked all the animals to visit him in Heaven so that he could divide up the years between them, with each animal ruling a certain lunar year. The cat needed her beauty sleep, but she worried that she'd miss the trip, so asked the rat to wake her in time. But the rat, sure the Emperor would prefer the cat's beauty to the rat's ugliness, didn't wake her and let the pig take her place. That's why cats and rats hate each other, and the pig has a whole year to itself, unlike the cat, and doesn't mind rats hanging about in the sty.

Fu Xi

After a terrible flood sent by demons to drown the world, Fu Xi and his sister or consort, Nu Gua, escaped by floating in a gourd. Once the waters had receded they returned to Earth and recreated civilization. Nu Gua made mortals from clay and Fu Xi showed them how to farm and fish, chart the seasons, hunt, farm, and forge metal. In very early myth, once the Earth was repopulated, he retired to Heaven with Nu Gua. But it was later claimed that he reigned on Earth from 2852 BCE to 2737 BCE. He invented writing and how to calculate time.

Eight Trigrams

Fu Xi is also credited with inventing the divinatory symbols of the "Pa Gua," or Eight Trigrams. Each of these was formed of three lines, either broken (yin) or unbroken (yang), representing the eight elements of the Earth. Fu Xi's successor combined the trigrams to create 64 hexagrams. He also discovered the magic square or "Lo Shu," apparently found on the back of a tortoise shell, whose square of nine numbers represents universal harmony and always adds up to the number 15, an auspicious Taoist number. The Pa Gua and the Lo Shu together form the symbolic "Ba Gua," still used today in feng shui.

The Ba Gua or Pa Gua compass is used in feng shui to discover the most harmonious living positions.

A fertility goddess in Taoist myth, Guan Yin was worshipped by women to ensure successful childbirth.

Guan Yin

Merciful and compassionate, Guan Yin is a popular and important deity in Chinese Buddhism, with her flowing gowns and beautiful benign face. In Taoist myth she was a fertility goddess; it was she who made it possible for humans to eat rice for the first time. Every year she squeezed milk from her breasts into grains of rice so that they were edible.

In Buddhist myth, she helped carry the sacred text of Buddhism from India to China, cured ill children, and comforted the distressed or imprisoned. She helped the poor and the oppressed and was the protector of travelers and seafarers. Revered by women, Guan Yin was the goddess who was able to bring fertility to childless couples.

Shen Nong

Fu Xi's successor, Shen Nong, was the second of the Three Sovereigns. He was a cultural hero and mythical emperor who was the son of a mortal princess and a sky dragon. A shape-shifter, he usually took the form of a human with an ox head, but could change into a scorching wind and create huge forest fires to teach mortals how to lay waste the land for agricultural purposes. He taught many secrets of successful agriculture as well as being credited with inventing Chinese medicine. Some accounts say he ruled from 2737 BCE to 2697 BCE, and many scholars now think he is the same emperor as Yen Ti, the apparent third successor of the Three Sovereigns. In one story, he ruled for seventeen generations of humans, and used his transparent stomach as a testing center for medicinal plants. But one herb poisoned him to death and he was immortalized as one of the gods in the realms of the sky.

Yao

One of the Five Emperors, Yao's rule marked the time when the world changed from a place of barbarism to that of civilization, but he continued to inhabit the imperial family's

Herbs are an integral part of Chinese medicine, their medicinal value being credited to Shen Nong, more than three thousand years ago.

thatched hut, eat porridge, and live a very austere life. He had many battles with storm gods and water monsters, and was famous for employing Yi, the archer, to destroy the demon Fei Lian and Ho Po, the water god. Yao's 70-year rule was soured by corruption due to the growing strength of the barbaric people and he trusted no one, not even his own sons. In his search for a successor, he chose a humble man called Shun, who was always kind, generous, and patient. After a series of tests, Shun married one of Yao's daughters and was appointed Yao's heir. Once Shun took over as the Fifth Emperor on Yao's abdication, the universe fell into chaos, and Yi was sent to shoot down the rebellious ten suns until only one was left (see page 256). He then sent Yu, the Dragon Lord, to control the floods and once order was restored, he ruled in peace and harmony.

ANCIENT EGYPT AND MESOPOTAMIA

Both ancient Egypt and Mesopotamia were not only great civilizations, but sophisticated and highly mystical cultures. From the pyramids of Egypt to the ziggurats of Mesopotamia, much written evidence documents the detailed and extraordinary range of beliefs and mythology. In hieroglyphics on stone tablets as well as Egyptian writings on papyrus, these two very ancient worlds truly sparkle with epic stories and magnificent deities.

History and background

Ancient Egyptian and Mesopotamian mythology was largely influenced by the harsh geographical landscapes in which these civilizations emerged.

However, their vastly different cultural development meant that Egypt's mythology was highly complex, insular, and identifiable, while Mesopotamia's earliest mythology became assimilated into the monotheistic religions that arose in this part of the world—Islam in the south, Judaism and Christianity in the west, and Zoroastrianism in the east. In all cases, these later religious systems took what they wanted from the original mythology and reinvented the myth according to their own dogma. Mesopotamian mythology was an amalgamation of Sumerian, Babylonian and Assyrian traditions, the last two drawing largely on Sumerian myth and its polytheistic religion.

Egypt

The mythology of ancient Egypt was influenced not only by the geography of the region, but also the extraordinary timescale of its conservative belief system. Around 5,000 years before the Christian era and right up until the Roman conquest in the 1st century BCE, the culture and religious attitude were dominated by the royal dynasties, which stretched from the First Dynasty marked by Great Pyramid in around 2600 BCE to the Eighteenth Dynasty 2,500 years later. Myth, religion, and culture walked side by side, and even though the country was not isolated, it was still inward-looking.

Mesopotamia

Mesopotamia contained some of the most ancient farming and city settlements in the world, dating back to 3000 BCE. With the vastness of the area and the harshness of its land, Mesopotamian mythology was reliant on the great cultural centers of civilization, such as Babylon and Ur in the south. The Great Flood story is typically found amongst people whose lives and work depended on the annual inundations. The same story would be told throughout

*An aspect of Ra, Aton the solar disc was worshipped by the
pharaoh and his family.*

Mesopotamia, but with local variations. The cultural protagonist of the Flood
story was known as Noah in Ur, Utnapishtum in Babylon, and Atrahis in
Shurupak. If Egyptian civilization was insular, Mesopotamian culture was
outward-looking, and the Mesopotamian influence eventually spread to the
mountainous area now known as Kurdistan, the coastal area east of the
Aegean Sea and also into Persia and as far as Egypt.

Egyptian beliefs

With the Nile at its center, Egypt is surrounded by desert, mountains, and sea. The earliest gods were associated with floods (Khnum) and the relentless Sun (Ra). Creation wasn't considered to be a great cosmic merger of Chaos and Matter, but instead was woven on a loom by Neith and Ptah, the metal-worker who forged living beings.

The earliest beliefs created a popular pantheon of gods and anything from a dwarf (Bes) to a dung-beetle (Khepri) could be deified. There were thousands of deities, all of whom had useful personifications in daily life. Many of the local gods eventually crossed over into the more formal religious mythology. There was very little exclusivity in Egyptian religion, and variety, diversity, and a richness of belief meant that there were hundreds of stories and many more myth cycles than can be discussed here.

The Ennead

The most dominant surviving religious mythology was the cycle known as the Ennead, concerning nine gods. It centered around Ra, in his aspect as the Sun, and the major theme of light (Osiris) versus dark (Set). It was also concerned with the story of Ra as he sailed through the sky by day and disappeared into the Underworld by night. This was to be the primary source for the first cult of reincarnation.

The Ogdoad

Another major myth cycle, concerning eight gods known as the Ogdoad, arose in Upper Egypt, but these weren't so much beings as personifications of abstract ideas. Each would have a male and female form. So the gods of darkness were Kek and Keket, those of invisibility were Amun and Amaunet. Amun later became the supreme god of all gods and merged with the Sun and was worshipped as Amun-Ra.

EGYPTIAN FAMILY TREE

Neith

Ptah	Ra	Atum*	Apep
	aspect of Atum	aspect of Ra	Ra's enemy, the serpent

Mankind   Khnum — Satet   Shu* — Tefnut*

Anuket
guardian of
the Nile

Nut* — Geb*
sky goddess   Earth god

Bastet	Sekhmet	Thoth	Ma'at	Isis* — Osiris* — Nephthys* — Set*	Blind Horus
goddess of fertility	war goddess	god of knowledge	goddess of truth		

Seshat   Hathor — Horus   Anubis
            goddess of   reincarnation   guide to the
            childbirth   of Blind Horus   dead, possibly
                                            illegitimate
                                            offspring of
Ra, in his aspect as Atum, created the eight gods of the   Osiris' affair
Ennead cycle as well as himself, all marked above with an *   with Nephthys

Mystery cults

There were many mystery cults, such as the mysteries of Isis favored later on by upper-class Greek and Roman women. Even the Roman emperor Caligula took part in the cult of Isis, and she became one of the major deities throughout the Mediterranean in the Hellenistic period. Still later, temples to Isis were found in Europe, Africa, and Asia, and she was considered to be the "Queen of Heaven" by cult followers. There was also the cult that blended Osiris with Hap the Bull to create the single deity Serapis. One of the earliest gods, Thoth, inspired yet another mystery cult based on secret writings that were supposedly said to contain all the secrets of the universe. This cult began in prehistoric times, became important around 2000 BCE, and is still a prominent cult today, expressed as the writings of Hermes Trismegistus.

Egyptian deities

All three of these gods were part of the very earliest mythology in Egypt—Neith and Atum as creation gods and Ra as symbol of the Sun, the source of all life on Earth.

Neith

Neith, or Neit, was already considered an ancient deity in Egypt by the time of the First Dynasty (c.3100–2890 BCE). The tomb of Tutankhamun (c.1325 BCE) has a golden statue of Neith in her aspect as a golden cobra, wearing the shuttle on her breast as a sign of a goddess who rules destiny. As the early goddess of weaving and the loom, she was also the goddess of creation and no mortal could look upon her face. Neith was also considered to be the goddess of war and hunting.

Originally Neith was one of the aspects of the Great Goddess of the Nile Delta region. From the primeval waters of nothingness, she arose spontaneously and created childbirth by bringing forth the great god Ra. But Neith was not satisfied with only the primordial ocean and one god as her creation, so she took up her shuttle and, by stringing the sky across her loom, she wove the universe. She dipped her net into the primordial waters, gathered all living things, and placed them on the world she had created.

When the gods Set and Horus were battling for power, the gods asked Neith who should be allowed to win. She said they both had the right to reign supreme and, if they didn't follow her advice, she would unpick the tapestry of the universe and destroy all that she had created.

Neith has been linked with the goddess Astarte (also known as Ishtar).

Atum and Ra

Atum was worshipped in Heliopolis long before Ra, who took over as the supreme power of the universe. Atum was the originator, the primordial ocean itself from which Ra created himself. Eventually Atum became an aspect of Ra, as Atum-Ra, the god of the evening Sun. There are many versions of these intertwining myths, but they are still pre-dated by those of Neith, her loom, and her fragile threads of creation.

Atum, as the primordial ocean, created himself. Some say that he spat into the void, others that he masturbated into it, to make Shu and Tefnut, the air and the moisture. Some Egyptian priests changed the story so that Atum used his male part (penis) and his female part (hand) to

Atum-Ra was a dual-aspect god: Atum created Ra and Ra created Atum. As one deity, he was the god of the evening sun.

mate together. The "Hand of Atum" was, in fact, worshipped as a separate deity. As the cult of Atum declined, Ra began to be regarded as the creator of Shu and Tefnut, who in turn became the parents of Geb the Earth and Nut the sky. Geb and Nut then mated to create the universe and the other gods Osiris, Set, Isis, and Nephthys.

Ra would sail across the sky every day in his golden boat, traveling along the pathway of the Milky Way, which some say was the arched body of Nut (see page 80). At night he would travel through the Underworld, avoiding the jaws of the great serpent Aapep. Aapep was Ra's greatest enemy and a personification of all that was dark and evil, as opposed to the light and goodness of Ra. Aapep was responsible for solar eclipses, but the worship of Ra ensured his return to the sky.

Sekhmet

The daughter of Ra, Sekhmet carried a fire-spitting cobra and was lion-headed. When she was angered, she transformed herself into the Eye of Ra and became a fierce war goddess from whom even the snake Aapep hid. She breathed flames, fire darted from her eyes, and the parching winds of her desert fumes seared holes in the ground and killed people wherever she went. She charred her enemies and burnt them to the ground, then gulped up their blood.

Ra, even though a god, could take human form as the pharaoh so that people could worship him. Although he was immortal, his human shape deteriorated, and people started to turn away from the Sun and worshipped Aapep instead. In fury, Ra sent Sekhmet to punish the mortals and destroy the world. Sekhmet filled the Nile with human blood and the world seemed doomed. At the last minute Ra changed his mind and tricked Sekhmet. He concocted a mixture of pomegranate juice (some sources say red ochre) and beer, which he spilled across the land. When she swooped down to lap up what she thought was blood, she fell asleep like a cat and Ra saved the world from destruction.

Nut and Geb

Nut and Geb were the sky and the Earth respectively. Born locked in a tight sexual embrace, their grandfather Ra ordered Shu (air) to separate them and, as she forced them apart, Nut was pushed upward to form the sky and Geb downward to form the Earth. Nut's body was the huge vault of the sky and her hands and feet were the four cardinal points of Egyptian astrology. The eastern horizon marks where the Sun rises, the west where it sets, the zenith is the highest point of the horoscope when the Sun is at its apex in the sky, and the nadir marks the lowest point of the horoscope and the darkest moment of night. If Nut was ever to fall back onto the Earth (Geb), chaos and disaster would reign.

Nut was also the mother of Osiris, Blind Horus, Set, Isis, and Nephyths. In Egyptian art she was often depicted as standing on all fours above the Earth or holding it aloft. Occasionally, she was associated with the cow goddess Hathor, holding a cow above her head with milk streaming from its udders to fertilize the world.

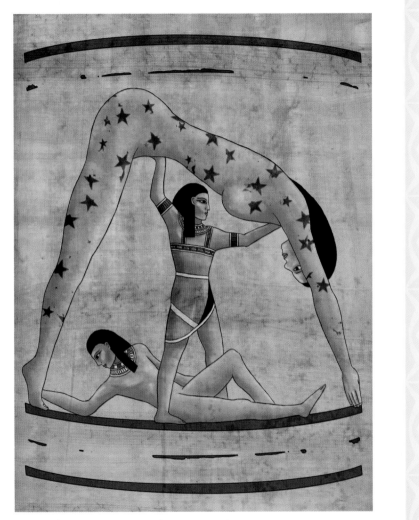

Nut and Geb pushed apart by Shu (the air) to create the sky and Earth.

The sacred island temple of Philae, in Egypt, was the focus of worship of the goddess Isis.

Isis

Originally known as Aset, Isis was the daughter of Nut and Geb (see page 80) and sister of Osiris, Set, and Nephthys. With Osiris as her husband/brother, she ruled Egypt. After Osiris was killed by Set (see page 369), Isis impregnated herself with his penis and became pregnant with Horus. Osiris, however, could not return to the world and was sent to rule the Underworld, so Isis set out to wreak vengeance on Set.

Horus and Set were eternally in conflict, which was to Isis' advantage. One tale tells of how Horus went to Isis complaining he'd been raped by Set. Isis asked Horus to masturbate over a lettuce bed, a leaf from which she then took to Set, who hungrily ate it. Isis took him to the court of the gods claiming that Set had stolen something from Horus. Set said he hadn't stolen anything, but as he spoke, Horus' semen flowed out of his mouth straight back to Horus, to prove that Set had been lying.

Tricky Isis

In the Delta myth cycle, Isis tricked Ra into giving her some of his powers. Ra's power depended on guarding his secret name so that no other being in the universe could know it. Isis gathered some of Ra's spittle and molded it into a snake that bit him. In terrible pain he begged Isis to heal him, and she agreed only if he would tell her his secret name. Each time he told her a false name the pain became worse, so finally Ra spoke the true secret name and was cured.

The Mysteries of Isis was a popular cult in Greek, Egypt, and Rome from about the 1st century BCE to the 4th century CE. The followers of Isis believed that knowledge of this secret name made Isis more powerful than any other god or goddess. In initiation ceremonies devotees would be told the secret name and would acquire some of Isis' magical healing powers.

Ma'at

The goddess of truth, justice, and morality, Ma'at was the daughter of Ra. The word *ma'at* means "that which is true." Ma'at was often depicted as a small figurine sitting or standing in the pharaoh's hand as he held it out to the gods to maintain justice. In Heaven her laws guaranteed the stability of the whole universe, and gods would swear in her name if they had to make any promises or take oaths. Ma'at wore a single ostrich plume in her crown, a measure of weight against which people were judged. If you lied, it

In the Egyptian Underworld, souls of the dead were weighed by Anubis against a feather from Ma'at's headdress.

would weigh heavier until you were condemned. Souls were also judged in the Underworld—Ma'at's feather was put in one pan of a set of scales and the soul in the other pan.

Thoth

Often depicted with the head of an ibis, Thoth was the god of knowledge, writing, magic, and the phases of the Moon. In some accounts, he was born from Set's forehead and in others he was the son or tongue of Ra. He was also depicted as a baboon holding up a crescent moon. Thoth was the scribe to the gods and invented writing and hieroglyphs. He prepared the calculations for the position of the Heaven, stars, and Earth, directed the motions of the heavenly bodies and had mediating power to restore the balance between right and wrong. He knew all there was to know and gave the power of words to the gods. They treated him with respect, for without words, the gods would not exist.

The god of all knowledge, writing and magic, Thoth was a deity respected by the other gods.

The origin of Hermes

The ancient Greeks considered Thoth to be the inventor of astronomy, astrology, mathematics, medicine, and the true author of every work of every branch of knowledge, human and divine. He thus became known as Hermes Trismegistus ("Thrice-Great Hermes"), because of his similarity to the Greek god Hermes. Cult members believed that Thoth's magic books were hidden by his priests and that if you learnt to decipher the secrets you would know all there is to know in the universe.

In the Ogdoad cosmogony (theory of creation), Thoth gave birth to Ra, Atum, and Khepri by laying an egg while he was in the form of an ibis. He was the deification of the Moon and was said to be Ra's advisor, traveling across the sky beside him during the night, accompanied on the other side of the sky-boat by Ma'at. Later on in Egyptian history, millions of ibis birds would be ritually killed and mummified in his honor and the Greeks renamed his cult center Hermopolis, "city of Hermes."

Horus

Two gods, in fact, were called Horus: Blind Horus was killed by Set, the god of chaos, and later reincarnated as the son of Isis and Osiris, named Horus. At one point in the ongoing struggle with Set for the throne, Set tore out Horus' eye, which was healed by Hathor. The *udjat* eye subsequently became the most common Egyptian amulet, symbolizing protection, strength, and perfection.

Horus was also a hawk-headed warrior and was Osiris' representative in the Upper World after Osiris became ruler of the Underworld. Horus was rather like Hermes (see page 84), able to mediate between the two worlds, guiding the souls of the dead to be judged by Osiris. He was also known as the protector of pharaohs and their households, and pharaohs would often call themselves "loving Horus."

The udjat, *the eye of Horus, is one of the most well-known Egyptian hieroglyphs, and was used extensively as a symbol of protection.*

Bastet

Originally a solar goddess, Bastet was the daughter of Ra and was associated with the roaring lioness Sekhmet. Around 2800 BCE she was portrayed as a lioness or wild desert cat, and by 1000 BCE she began to be depicted as the goddess of domesticated cats. By this time she had also taken on a gentler role as the kind and compassionate goddess of fertility, childbirth, and laughter. Cats were sacred to her, and she was often portrayed as a woman with a cat's head, sometimes just as a cat or as a woman with kittens playing at her feet. Her main temple and cult were in Bast (now known as Tell-Basta). Worshippers would sail to Bast for the annual festival where dead cats were embalmed, mummified, and then buried in sacred graveyards.

Benu Bird

The Benu Bird was originally depicted as a giant heron, and in some accounts it was the first-ever living being who flew across the dark waters of Nun and landed on a rock called the Benben Stone. Here its flight brought creative energy and sunlight and its cry heralded the beginning of the world. Later, the Greeks reworked the myth, calling the Benu Bird a phoenix as one form or aspect of the Sun god Ra. Amulets and carvings of Benu were often buried with bodies to help them on their way to a second life.

Anubis

Anubis was known as the canine god of the dead, and was usually depicted as a dog or jackal-headed man. Originally he was the god of putrefaction and it was only in later myth that he became the protector of the dead against robbers and the patron god of embalmers. He supervised the weighing of souls of the newly deceased before Osiris' judgement throne. Anubis was the first god to create a mummy when he wrapped up the dismembered corpse of Osiris. In the necropolis, priests would wear a jackal mask when bodies were being embalmed to show that Anubis was present.

Anubis, canine god of the dead.

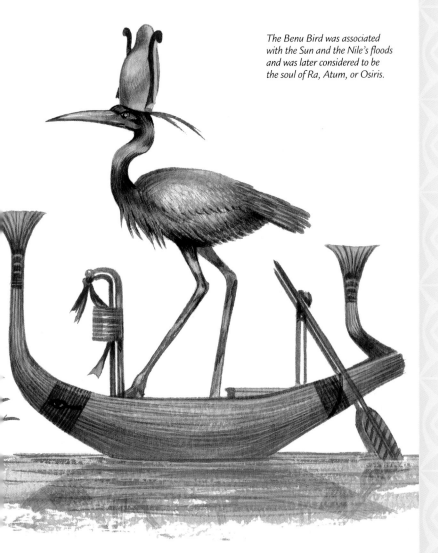

The Benu Bird was associated with the Sun and the Nile's floods and was later considered to be the soul of Ra, Atum, or Osiris.

Mesopotamian beliefs

The civilization of ancient Mesopotamia in what is now known as Iraq was a mélange of powerful kings, huge temples in the shape of ziggurats (stepped pyramids), and city settlements.

Core myths developed in their own individualistic way, depending on the local city or cult. For example, the eighth inner gate to the city of Babylon was devoted to Ishtar, who was also known as Inanna in other areas. Due to the much later dogmatic interpretation of the ancient sacred texts by the monotheistic religions, some of the earliest tales vanished completely. Some remain only as individual stories, such as the epic tale of Gilgamesh, but most were separated and split off from the cultures in which they flourished.

Mesopotamian mythology had a hierarchical pantheon of gods at its core. There were abstract forces of pre-creation such as An or El, triads of conflicting powers such as Space, Water, and Storm. There were pairs of gods, for example

The eighth Inner Gate to Babylon was constructed, mainly of blue tiles, around 575 BCE by King Nebuchadnezzar II.

About 30,000 stone tablets were recovered from the ruins of Hattusa, once the capital of the Hittite civilization.

Chaos (Tiamat) and Order (Marduk), and Light (Inanna) and Dark (Ereshkigal). The latter pairing was eventually assimilated into religious thinking and given a moral twist, as in Yahweh and Satan.

Written evidence

The creation epic of Babylon was known as the *Enuma Elish*. Recited every spring equinox, it celebrated the victory of Marduk over Tiamat and his role in keeping the universe orderly. Gods like Enki, Enlil, and Lilith in Hebrew myth were either given a bad name or became less important and were pushed very much to the sidelines. Most of Ugaritic, Hittite, and Hurrian mythology is fragmented. However, around 10,000 clay tablets were found in the ruins of Hattusa at the beginning of the 20th century, inscribed with Hurrian and Hittite myths that included fertility myths and stories of the battle between gods.

Zoroastrianism (founded by the prophet Zoroaster) flourished in the 6th century BCE in pre-Islamic Persia. Its mythology is documented in the texts of the *Avesta* and *Gatha*.

Mesopotamian deities

While Marduk was the chief god of the Babylonian deities, Ishtar had widespread influence throughout the region in her many guises. As a goddess of fertility and sexuality, she is perhaps a precursor to Aphrodite.

Marduk

During the first Babylonian dynasty (c. 2057–1758 BCE), Marduk was the chief god and most important of the Babylonian deities. He was the son of the water lord Ea and it was he who created the universe and everything in it. The story of creation and his struggle with Tiamat (see page 92) was found among the ruins of King Ashurbanipal's library at Nineveh, which dates from around 650 BCE. However, fragments of earlier texts suggested that the end of the story is based on the belief that gods created humans to be their slaves. The later story was probably a piece of propaganda to uphold Marduk's power and his high-ranking status in Babylon. The Babylonians maintained that the city was created by the gods especially for him. As the supreme god, Marduk could assume the role of any god, and he became identified with the Sun, the planet Jupiter and with powers equivalent to those of the Moon god Sin.

Some people believed that Marduk supported the universe as he sat on his throne; if he ever stood up, the stars would start to move backward and Tiamat would return to Earth and destroy all living things.

A fragment of the seven clay tablets that recount the Enuma Elish *and the story of Marduk.*

Ishtar

Ishtar had many aliases in Mesopotamia, including Ashtart, Astarte, Ashtoreth, Inanna, and Isis. She was worshipped from Nineveh to Thebes and from Babylon to Cyprus. She was not only the courtesan of the gods, but her cult involved sacred prostitution—her city Erech was known as the city of the sacred courtesans. It is highly likely that the cult of Aphrodite originated from Ishtar, because Ishtar was also identified with the planet Venus. She was both a fertility and sex goddess and was the Evening Star itself (as Venus). She bathed in a sacred lake every evening to restore her virginity after mating with as many gods or mortals, animals, or abstract concepts as she could. One of her best-known stories is that of her love for the mortal Tammuz and how when he died, she descended to the Underworld to retrieve him. She was also a war goddess in Assyria, where her war-cries froze the enemy's blood, and her priests would make offerings to her of the dismembered hands of their prisoners. Both cruel and fickle, terrifying yet loving, she has similar attributes not only to Aphrodite, but also to the Hindu goddess Kali.

On her descent to rescue Tammuz she cried, "I will smash the doorposts, I will force the doors. I will bring up the dead to eat the living. And the dead will outnumber the living."

Ishtar was associated with Venus as the Evening Star and with sacred sexuality.

The terrifying monster Tiamat gave birth to thousands of offspring in the form of serpents and dragons.

Tiamat

Before creation, there was only chaos and one half of this was Tiamat (salt water) and the other half was Apsu (fresh water). They were also accompanied by the mist, Mummu. When the waters merged, generations of gods were created. At first they lived in harmony, but Ea (see below) challenged Apsu and killed him and Mummu. Tiamat, in revenge, turned herself into a dragon and led an army of monsters against Ea and his son Marduk (see page 90).

An

An or Anu was the supreme god of Heaven and in some accounts was the offspring of Ansar and Kisar (light and horizon), and in others the child of Apsu (fresh water) and Tiamat (salt water). With his sons Ea and Enlil, he threw dice to see which kingdoms they would win. Ea got the sea, Enlil dry land, and An the sky. (There is a similar division of the kingdoms in Greek mythology.)

An was a fairly benevolent but aloof god and, after he had been attacked by Marduk, he withdrew from the universe to became formless and invisible. An's shrines were oracular centers and in some accounts the seven judges of the Underworld were called Annunaki (An's children).

Lilith

In early Sumerian texts Lilith was handmaiden to Inanna. She guided people to Inanna's temple to enjoy her sacred sexual rituals. However, there is much controversy over Lilith's roles—she has been labeled seductress, handmaiden, prostitute, and demon in Hebrew mythology, succubus and child-killer. Her association with the Garden of Eden is also much discussed. She was possibly the first wife of Adam, but when God decreed that she must take a submissive sexual position, she took off like the "storm wind" or "screech-owl," a form that she is believed to have been able to assume.

Lilith was originally one of Inanna's handmaidens or sacred temple harlots, later debased by patriarchal religions.

The myth of Lilith has been debased over the centuries and distorted by patriarchal myth-makers as a danger and evil to men. She became a popular "femme fatale" figure in the 19th century. Lilith seems to represent that part of feminine sexuality which has been misunderstood by patriarchal religions—the ability to freely abandon oneself in the sexual act as a source of healing and regeneration.

Ahriman was the personification of all that was evil in the world, his twin brother being the force of all goodness.

Ahriman

In pre-Islamic Persian myth, Zurvan Akarana was a primoridal being who existed before existence and inseminated itself to create twins in its womb. Ahriman was the personification of evil, death, and darkness and his twin was Ahura Mazda, lord of light. From the moment they were conceived, Ahriman did everything he could to destroy his opponent. In fact, it was Ahriman who ripped open the womb of Zurvan Akarana and leapt out into the world ahead of Ahura Mazda. He ruled and created all the destructive forces in the universe and used demons, storms, and disease to force the worshippers of Ahura Mazda to worship him instead. Ahriman provided an essential juxtaposition for the continued balance of the universe.

Enki

Associated with many different roles throughout Mesopotamia, Enki is best known as a trickster god who created life on Earth. He was originally a water lord, and lived with his Earth goddess wife Ninhursaga in Dimun. Enki's cult center was Eridu, in what are now the salt marshes of southern Iran. The people of Eridu believed Enki gave them gifts such as happiness, respect, negotiation, and families, and that other cities and their gods would try to steal this precious treasure. He was also the god of wisdom and magic, and the owner of the sacred powers that controlled world order, known as *me*.

Enlil

The wind lord Enlil was the ruler of the Earth, and his city Nippur had existed long before the creation of humankind. He was regarded as a god of agriculture and civilization, and his cult center was at the temple of E-Kur at Nippur in the Zogros Mountains. Enlil fathered the stars, Moon, and a whole family of gods. He sent out his orders via Anzu, his messenger giant, but Anzu betrayed him—one day he waited until Enlil was bathing and stole his thunderbolts, the source of Enlil's power and ability to preserve universal order. However, the giant was stupid and didn't know what to do with the thunderbolts. Luckily, Ninurta the war god seized them from the giant and returned them to Enlil before the universe reverted to chaos.

The light of Ahura Mazda was always at odds with the dark, but he always won through in the end.

Ahura Mazda

The twin brother to the evil Ahriman, god of darkness, Ahura Mazda was all goodness and light. Whereas Ahriman sought to destroy humankind, Ahura Mazda was concerned with creating the perfect universe. The struggle between the Holy Thought of Ahura Mazda and the Evil Thought of Ahriman created the entire history of the world in Persian mythology. It was believed that Ahura Mazda would finally win over Ahriman with the help of Saoshyant, a child born to a virgin mysteriously impregnated with the prophet Zoroaster's sperm. Ahura Mazda created Atar (fire) and defeated the three-headed dragon Azhi Dahaka when Ahriman sent it to destroy all human beings.

Telepinu

Like many other agricultural deities in world mythology, Telepinu was an amusing but rather brainless figure in ancient Syrian myth. Rather like his father, the weather god Taru, Telepinu had a terrible temper and would take offense at the slightest thing. One day he disappeared in a fit of rage and all the plants in the world died. The goddess Hannahanna sent a bee to find him, knowing he was probably asleep in the meadows. But the bee stung him, which made Telepinu even madder and he began raging at the gods. Eventually the goddess of healing, Kamrusepas, offered him some magical herbs and Telepinu finally agreed to carry on keeping the world in order, which was what he did best of all.

Nanna

When Elil raped Nihil, the goddess of the harvest, he was punished with banishment to the Underworld. Nihil followed him so that he could see the birth of his son. Nanna was born in the darkness and, because his light was pale and cold, he became the Moon god. As he traveled through the sky, demons and monsters bit at him and it was only because humans made sacrifices to Nanna that he returned to his complete self every month. His name was written as the number 30, the approximate length of the lunar cycle. His wife was the goddess Ningal and their offspring included Inanna (see page 91) and the Sun god Utu.

The ziggurat at Ur was constructed in the 21st century BCE and was said to be the dwelling place of the god Nanna.

THE CLASSICAL WORLD

The world of classical mythology is filled with sweeping epics, passionate lovers, exaggerated deities, and dramatic irony. Historically, it has been a rich source of archetypal and psychological symbolism in the Western world. Even today it is not only vividly conveyed in literature, art, film, and music, but astronomers and astrophysicists still name cosmic bodies after Greek and Roman deities.

History and background

The classical world is mostly concerned with ancient Greece from around 1500 BCE until the end of the Roman period in about 500 CE. Greek myth was first recorded by Hesiod and Homer around the 8th century BCE, and later became part of Roman culture.

Greece

Ancient Greece was a diverse region divided into several hundred states, separated not just by cultural differences, but also by water, islands, and mountains. There was not only a diversity of geography, but of minds and story-tellers. The region had an extraordinarily lively and vivid mythology, both secular and sacred. Its popularity could be seen in everything the Greeks did, from temple offerings and theatres dedicated to particular gods, to vases, jewelry and household items decorated with famous scenes and symbols from favorite tales.

Gods and goddesses flourished, had feisty characters, and were usually quite irresponsible. By the time Hesiod wrote his *Theogony* (*Origin of the Gods*) the extraordinary "soap-opera" behavior of the gods seemed to reflect the antics of humankind. This developed into a new wave of mythology where mortal heroes and their quests became essential counterpoints to the vanity of the deities. Possibly because the Greeks traded and exchanged ideas as well as their wares, many stories were compared, exaggerated, changed, and imported from wherever they traveled. Fascinated by the power of the mind, the Greeks told, retold, wrote down, expanded, annotated, and embellished their mythology. The written word ruled supreme.

Rome

Roman mythology merged early Italian pastoral gods and their tales from the countryside with the local mythology of places conquered by the Roman empire. As long as the people obeyed Roman law, they were free to follow

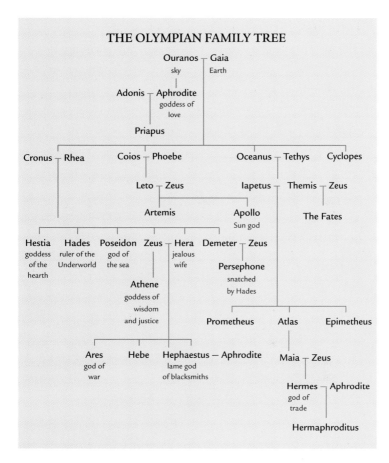

THE OLYMPIAN FAMILY TREE

Ouranos — Gaia
sky   Earth

Adonis — Aphrodite
        goddess of
        love

Priapus

Cronus — Rhea   Coios — Phoebe   Oceanus — Tethys   Cyclopes

Leto — Zeus   Iapetus — Themis — Zeus

Artemis   Apollo   The Fates
                  Sun god

Hestia   Hades   Poseidon   Zeus — Hera   Demeter — Zeus
goddess   ruler of the god of   jealous
of the   Underworld   the sea   wife
hearth   Persephone
                        Athene   snatched
                        goddess of   by Hades
                        wisdom
                        and justice   Prometheus   Atlas   Epimetheus

Ares   Hebe   Hephaestus — Aphrodite   Maia — Zeus
god of   lame god
war   of blacksmiths   Hermes — Aphrodite
                                          god of
                                          trade

                                          Hermaphroditus

whatever religion they liked. The Romans also assimilated the entire Olympic pantheon into their own religious and political system after they conquered Greece. Virgil built a whole historical dynasty out of the saga of Aeneas and his settlement in Italy, linking this story with Romulus and Remus as the founders of Rome.

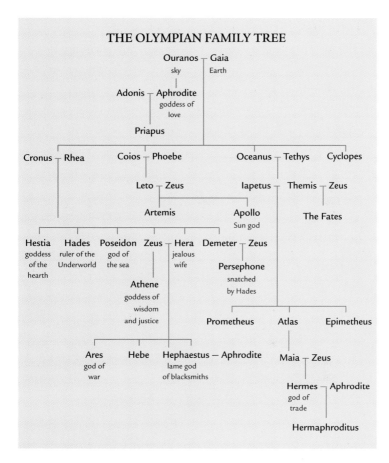

Greek mythology

Hesiod's *Theogony*, recorded at the end of the 8th century BCE, describes the creation of the first gods and the act of creation itself. James Lovelock, a modern-day scientist and environmentalist, has developed a philosophy known as "the Gaia hypothesis" based on this myth, which states that all things must be in balance to ensure the survival of the whole.

Creation according to Hesiod

Spontaneously out of Chaos appeared Gaia (Earth), Tartarus (Underworld) and Eros (Love). Then Nyx (Night) and Erebus (primeval Darkness) also arose out of Chaos. Gaia gave birth to her equal Ouranos (the Heavens), whom she allowed to cover her like a cloak. Gaia also gave birth to the mountains and sea by herself, then embraced Ouranos, who shrouded her again with a great canopy of dark rainclouds. His life-giving rain filled Gaia's river beds and streams, until all living things came into being.

POLIDORO DA CARAVAGGIO INVENTORE

Gio. Bat. Galestruzzi fece   1

Gaia and her son Cronus castrated Ouranus so that the Titans could safely rule the Earth.

Children of Gaia and Ouranos

The children of Gaia and Ouranos were numerous. There were the Cyclopes, the Hundred-Handed Giants and twelve of the many Titans who ruled until overthrown by the gods of Olympus. Ouranos could not bear to look at the ugly Cyclopes and, as they were born, he hid them in the Underworld so that they could never see the light. Gaia feared for the Titans, so with her son Cronus she hatched a cunning plot. They lay in wait for Ouranos when he came to make love to her one night. Cronus leapt from his hiding place and, with the jagged sickle given to him by Gaia, castrated Ouranos. Droplets of blood became the Erinyes (angry ones), who became the Furies in Roman myth;

The Erinyes were the personification of horrifying vengeance, usually driving their victims insane.

Cronus flung the genitals down from Heaven and they fell into the ocean, causing the sea to foam. Out of this foam arose the goddess of love, Aphrodite.

Nyx

In later Greek texts attributed to Orpheus, lesser-known Nyx (Night) was considered to be the first principal of creation rather than Chaos. With Erebus she had many children including Hemera (Day), Nemesis (Retribution), Hypnos (Sleep), Eris (Strife), Apate (Deceit), Moros (Doom), and Momos (Blame). With Ouranos she had one offspring, Lyssa (Madness). Hemera (Day) leaves Tartarus (Underworld) just as Nyx enters. When Hemera returns, Nyx leaves. This echoes the story of Ratri (Night) and Ushas (Dawn) in the Sanskrit Rig Vedas (see page 250).

103

Greek deities

Leader of the gods and ruler of Olympus, Zeus also had a huge sexual appetite. Promiscuous, judicious, and omnipotent, he embodied the archetypes of passion, power, and judgment. Equally promiscuous (and some sources believe the original lord of the universe), Poseidon, as god of the sea, was as dangerous with his trident as Zeus was with his thunderbolts.

The Greek god of the heavens, Zeus, is well known for his promiscuous escapades and irresponsible behavior.

Zeus

Cronus, leader of the Titans, had been told that his children would one day overthrow him, as he had overthrown his father Ouranos. He therefore devoured all of his children as soon as they were born. However, when Zeus was born, Cronus's wife Rhea, in fear for her new son's life, sent Zeus away to Crete so that Cronus couldn't eat him, too. Rhea substituted a stone wrapped up in baby clothes and Cronus gulped it down, believing it to be Zeus and that the prophecy could now never come true. Zeus then grew up in Crete with mountain nymphs, and, when he was old enough, Metis, the goddess of wisdom, explained to Zeus how to rescue his other siblings from Cronus' belly. Disguised as a cup-bearer, Zeus gave his father a drink of deadly nectar and Cronus vomited up all the other fully grown gods. This resulted in the battle between the gods and the Titans. Cronus was eventually exiled to Tartarus when the gods won.

Once the Titans were banished, Zeus met with the other gods to decide how to divide the rule of the universe. His sisters Hestia and Demeter were happy to remain on Earth, so the three brothers cast lots for their kingdoms. Zeus won the sky, Poseidon the sea, while Hades got the Underworld. His third sister, Hera, however, was resentful from then on because she had not been consulted and neither was she given any kingdom of her own.

Quarrelsome Poseidon ruled the oceans and it was only the sea nymph, Amphitrite, who calmed him down.

Poseidon

Brother to Zeus and ruler of the sea, Poseidon was given his trident by the Cyclopes for his battle against the Titans. It could fork up mountain ridges, underwater shelves, islands, and even continents. After the war the trident became his most powerful instrument. He would hurl it at cliffs when humanity annoyed him. He would stomp around in his watery kingdom causing earthquakes and tidal waves, and stirred the sea into whirlpools or churning foam to capsize vessels and destroy islands. He could also calm the sea with a single glance. Poseidon was never truly satisfied with his watery kingdom and had many quarrels with Zeus, Athene, Dionysus, and Hera. Sexually rampant, he fell for nymphs, mermaids, and mortals, but finally settled down and married Amphitrite, a sea goddess who seemed to calm him down unless he was challenged or enraged, as when Odysseus blinded his son Polyphemus, one of the Cyclopes (see page 345).

Seductive, yet jealous, Aphrodite had many lovers and was responsible for the onset of the Trojan War.

Aphrodite

By no means pure, Aphrodite's role as goddess of sexual love was consistent with her appetite for men and gods alike. Aphrodite was both beauty and love personified, and would restore youth and beauty to those who honored her. When she later became assimilated into Roman religion, she was identified with temple prostitution and sacred sexual rituals. The origin of her name is usually given as meaning "foam-born" after the method of her birth.

Aphrodite emerged from the billowing foam that was created when Cronus castrated his father Ouranos and threw his severed genitalia into the sea. She was blown across the ocean by the west winds to Paphos, where she was washed up on a beach; other traditions suggest that she was the daughter of Zeus and the relatively unknown Dione. Aphrodite was married off to Hephaestus, the crippled smithy god, and was eternally unfaithful to him. Seductive and vain, she had no hesitation in stealing lovers and was jealous of anyone who challenged her beauty, as in the tale of Eros and Psyche.

She had affairs with Ares, Dionysus, and Anchises, and one of her greatest loves was Adonis, with whom she had three children—two mortal and beautiful and the third, an ugly immortal called Priapus (although some sources claim he was fathered by Dionysus). Priapus was so promiscuous that the gods refused to have him in Olympus. With Hermes, she gave birth to Hemaphroditus.

Best known for bribing Paris of Troy in a beauty competition, she was instrumental in causing the Trojan War. Aphrodite's girdle of desire (which no man or god could resist) created havoc wherever she went.

Apollo

Many shrines were dedicated to Apollo, the most famous of which is at Delphi. Here, Apollo slew the Python, a serpent-like monster who had been sent by Hera to hound Leto, his mother, for her affair with Zeus. At Delphi the priestess was known as the Pythia, who sat above the snake pit. From the ominous depths the rising hallucinogens would send her into a trance, through which she transmitted Apollo's riddles for the priests to decode.

Apollo had numerous lovers, both male and female. He even fell in love with Hermes' lyre, which he exchanged for the caduceus, and chased poor Daphne, who was eventually turned into a laurel tree. Apollo promised the gift of prophecy to Cassandra if she allowed him to seduce her. But after their first encounter she rejected him. In revenge he gave her the gift of prophecy anyway, but this turned out to be a curse: she could only ever predict tragedy and whatever she said would never be believed.

Athene

Also known as Pallas Athene, she was sometimes warlike and definitely on the side of heroes. Some sources suggest Athene was originally the Libyan goddess of wisdom and became assimilated into the Greek Olympian pantheon as the daughter of Zeus, born from his own head. However, Zeus could only lay claim to intellectual and judicial knowledge by devouring Athene's mother Metis (another aspect of wisdom), when she was pregnant. Thus when Athene was born, she sprang from Zeus's head, and subsequently proved to be the strongest and most loyal supporter of Zeus in Olympus. As a virgin goddess, she sublimated her sexuality into intellectual and creative skills. She became known first for her patriotic warrior spirit and was later worshipped for her protection of the state. She was admired for possessing right-brain intellect, but never valued for her female wisdom. She was not only formidable, but just, and the inspiration behind the Trojan horse.

Demeter

Demeter was usually known for her benevolence as bringer of fertility and the goddess of agriculture and the harvest. She was part of a long ancient tradition of Earth goddesses of the Mediterranean area, and was best known for her part in the story of the abduction of her daughter Persephone by Hades to the Underworld. The relationship between Demeter and Persephone holds the key to the whole Hellenic philosophy of death and rebirth and the changing cycle of life and the seasons. Demeter, in her grief for the loss of her daughter, ensured that all fertility was withheld on Earth and that all must suffer with her. It was only when the gods stepped in and decided that Persephone could stay six months with Hades and return to Earth for six months that Demeter relented. In this sense she embodies the power of passive aggression.

Hera

Hera was the sister of Zeus, who in his usual lustful way wanted to ravish her, but she refused. One day he turned himself into a bedraggled cuckoo and, feeling sorry for it, she held it to her breast. As soon as she did so, the cuckoo changed back into Zeus—who raped her. She married him out of shame and her children included Ares, Hephaestus, and Hebe.

Hera's role became one of the ideal wife, and her marriage to Zeus became the prototype for monogamy. She became the protector of wives and had the power of prophecy. She later became symbolic of pathological jealousy—not only fueled by her resentment at being left out of the initial division of the universe, but also due to her endless revenge on Zeus' many lovers. Her constant emotional conflict with Zeus was highly suggestive of the difficult assimilation between the invasion of the followers of Zeus and her own indigenous goddess cult. She became known as the shrewd, yet subtle manipulator as well as the perfect and totally faithful wife. Majestic, but sullen, her sacred emblems were the cuckoo, the cow, and, in later Greek times, the peacock.

Hera was the epitome of the good wife, but sought vengeance on many of Zeus' lovers.

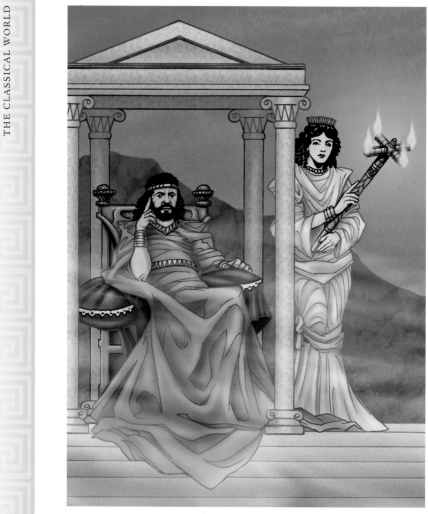

The Underworld was known by many names, including Tartarus and Hades, after its invisible ruler.

Hades

Hades means "unseen"—and, during the war with the Titans, the Cyclopes gave Hades a helmet of darkness. Invisible, he slipped across to the Titans' camp and destroyed all their weapons. Hades became the ruler of the Underworld after the Titans were overthrown, and was often known as "Plouton," relating to "wealth" in his other role as ruler of precious stones, metals, and the hidden wealth buried in the Earth. Hades only visited the Upperworld when searching for a consort or when overcome by lust. He abducted Persephone, then later fell for a Cocythian nymph called Minthe. Several sources suggest that either a jealous Demeter or Persephone trampled Minthe to dust in their rage and that Hades changed her into the mint plant, or that Hades transformed her into the plant to protect her from the green-eyed Persephone.

Prometheus

The myth of Prometheus, originally told in Hesiod's *Theogony*, was embellished later on by many writers, such as Sappho, Plato, Ovid, and Aeschylus. The Titan Prometheus was favored by the gods and, to bring a smile to their faces, he made little replicas of them out of mud. Athene was so charmed that she breathed life into them. Prometheus wanted these little mortal dolls to have all knowledge, but Zeus was adamant that they could live only on Earth, have no access to his heavenly kingdom, and were to be denied knowledge or immortality.

To get his own back, Prometheus stole fire from the gods, hid it in a fennel stalk, and gave it to humanity. Zeus was enraged and, as punishment, Prometheus was chained to a rock, where his liver was eaten every day by a bird of prey, only to be renewed again every night. Eventually Prometheus changed places with the ill-fated centaur, Chiron (see page 252). Prometheus usually means "foresight," but the Indo-European Vedic *pramathyu-s* means "thief."

An eagle or vulture was destined to gorge on Prometheus' liver every day; each night it would be renewed.

111

Eros

One of the earliest Greek gods of chaos, pre-dating Zeus and arising from the time before creation, Eros (desire) became identified with the Roman god Cupid. A much-maligned and misrepresented god, he was an ancient symbol of potent life force and was a primal, phallic deity in pre-Hellenic Greece. He was later manifested in the Olympic pantheon as the offspring of Aphrodite and Zeus, Ares, or Hermes. He was depicted as a winged cherub who flew around causing gods and mortals to fall in love with each other with one arrow from his bow of desire.

Dionysus

The son of Zeus and the mortal Semele, Dionysus was brought up by mountain nymphs in safety far away from the jealous wrath of Hera (see page 105). He spent most of his time wandering around the world with satyrs, mountain nymphs, and wild dancing women known as the Maenads. On one of his trips around the world he was captured by pirates hoping to sell him at a slave market.

But far out to sea the ship suddenly changed to vines, the sea to wine and Dionysus to a lion. The pirates threw themselves into the ocean and became porpoises. Dionysus invented the orgasm, ecstasy, revelry, and wine for mortals. He was also known as the god of "the moment of choice" and of the moment before surrendering to the irrational or resisting it.

Dionysus was best known for introducing wine and revelry to humans. He was also known as Bacchus in Roman mythology.

Adonis

Adonis was born in very strange circumstances. The king of Assyria unwisely boasted that his daughter Smyrna was more beautiful than Aphrodite, so in revenge Aphrodite filled him with lust and he raped his own daughter. Realizing that Smyrna was pregnant, the king tried to kill her, but Aphrodite changed her into a myrrh tree. In the spring, the trunk split in half and Adonis emerged. Aphrodite fell madly in love with Adonis and hid him in a box. She gave him to Persephone to guard, but she too fell in love with him. Persephone, wanting Adonis all to herself in the Underworld, went to see Aphrodite's consort, Ares, and told him about his mortal rival. Ares disguised himself as a boar and, while Adonis was out hunting, the boar killed him. Persephone was overjoyed to see Adonis in the Underworld, but Zeus stepped in and decided that half the year he would live with Aphrodite and the other half of the year with Persephone.

A central cult figure in many mystery religions, Adonis is an eternally youthful god of the cycles of nature.

Hermes

The winged messenger of the Olympian gods, Hermes ran errands between Heaven, Earth, and the Underworld. Hermes was the son of Zeus and Maia, the daughter of Atlas. From the moment he was born he was a prankster, and within hours he'd stolen Apollo's cattle and traded his lyre for Apollo's friendship and knowledge. As a trickster god of cunning, thieves, boundaries, writing, travelers, and commerce, Hermes appears in many myths, and made important appearances in the *Iliad*, the *Odyssey*, and the myths of Perseus and Prometheus.

He had many consorts, including Dryope, Aphrodite (with whom he fathered Hermaphroditus and Tyche), Penelope, and Crocus. With his winged sandals and helmet, Hermes also escorted souls safely to the Underworld and transmitted messages from the gods to mortals.

Muses

The mountain spirits, water nymphs, or a sisterhood of goddesses called the Muses or *Mousai* were the daughters of Zeus and Titan Mnemosyne (Memory). They lived all over the world and sang, danced, played, and laughed to the joy of any mortal who happened to be passing by. The most well known were the nine muses who danced on the slopes of Parnassus at Delphi with Apollo. They included Urania, Calliope, Erato, and Terpsichore, but all Muses were inspirational for poets, writers, artists, and musicians in later history.

Sibyls

The Sibyls were prophetesses who guarded entrances between the Earth, Heaven, and the Underworld in their shrines. The Sibyl of Cumae was the most respected and was believed by the later Romans to have been a real person.

In Greek mythology she was known as Deiphobe, and Apollo fell in love with her beauty. He gave her the gift of prophesy, but also promised her immortality if she would have sex with him. But each time he granted her wishes, she rejected him, until finally he punished her because she had not asked to keep her beauty, and as the years passed she grew more and more wizened.

By the time she was assimilated into Roman culture she was about 700 years old. She visited King Tarquin with nine books of prophecies, saying they contained the secrets of all Rome's future. She tried to sell them to him, but he refused, so she burnt them one by one until only three books were left. Tarquin finally bought the remaining three and the Sybilline verses were consulted by priests in troubled times.

Fates

The three Fates or *Moerae* ("apportioners") were, in some traditions, the daughters of Zeus and Themis, in others of Zeus and Nyx. For Homer, they were the individual and inescapable destiny that followed every mortal being. Their names were Atropos (unbending), Clotho (spinner), and Lachesis (allotter). Clotho would spin the thread of life, Lachesis would unwind and measure it, and Atropos would cut it. No other deities had so much power as the *Moerae* since they were the goddesses who controlled both mortal and divine fate.

Three nights after a child's birth, the Moerae *or* Fates *would determine the destiny of his or her future life.*

Helios was the personification of the Sun. His chariot careered across the sky each day drawn by fiery steeds.

Helios

The Greek Sun god Helios was never given the importance or cult following assigned to Apollo, who was the god of life-giving light. Helios was the son of Hyperion, a Titan, and brother to Eos (Dawn) and Selene (the Moon). He epitomized the Sun as a body in its own right as it rose in the morning and set in the evening. In his golden chariot he galloped his horses across the sky each day, and by night he sailed around the Earth in a golden bowl on the waters of the ocean. When he arrived back in the east just before dawn, Eos would remind him that it was time to leap into his chariot and start again. His son Phaethon was foolhardy and one night he leapt into the fiery chariot and careered around the sky like a madman, but then lost control of the wild stallions. Luckily Zeus grabbed the reins and stopped the chariot before it fell to Earth and set fire to the world. Phaethon himself wasn't so lucky—he fell out of the chariot and drowned in the ocean.

Selene

Aloof and elusive, Selene was the Moon and preferred night to day. She rode bareback or drove a silver chariot pulled by ghostly oxen through the dark night. Sometimes you can see her faintly in the distance, pale and wan, while at other times she is bright and bigger than the Sun itself. Selene loved Endymion, a shepherd she saw sleeping naked on Mount Latmos. She swooped down to Earth in her chariot and had sex with him. But, wanting him all to herself, she kissed his eyes and he then remained in a permanent dreamless sleep except when making love to Selene. They had many children, which are all the stars in the sky.

Eos

Described as a beautiful goddess who opened the gates of the east every morning with "rosy fingers," Eos was the dawn. Sister to Helios and Selene, some sources say she was married to Astraeus and their

The Moon goddess, Selene, had a love affair with Zeus. Their daughter was the light of the full Moon itself.

children were some of the stars. She had many affairs, including one with Ares. This angered Aphrodite, who cursed Eos, so that from then on she was only able to lust after mortals, like Tithonus of Troy. She begged Zeus for immortality for her lover, but forgot to ask for his eternal youth, and so was fated to watch him age, becoming ever more disgusted with him.

The ancient citadel of Mycenae was once ruled by the notorious Atreid Dynasty, including Clytemnestra.

Clytemnestra

Homer's account of the tragic story of Clytemnestra in the *Odyssey* paints her in a rather pathetic light, whereas Aeschylus' (525–456 BCE) better-known version in the *Oresteia* has been used by painters, writers, and playwrights alike because it is a bloody tale of vengeance and murder by one of the first "femmes fatales." In some sources, Clytemnestra was the daughter of Zeus and Leda, a twin of Helen of Troy, but she was possibly fathered by Leda's mortal husband, King Tyndareus of Sparta.

Clytemnestra had four children by her husband King Agamemnon: Iphigenia, Electra, Chrysothemis, and Orestes. While Agamemnon was on his way to retrieve Helen, who had been taken by Paris to Troy, he foolishly sacrificed their own daughter Iphigenia to the gods in exchange for fair winds. This is the most common account of why Clytemnestra would plot to kill her husband. During Agamemnon's ten-year absence she took a lover, Aegisthus, and ruled in Agamemnon's name. Pretending to welcome him back, Aegisthus then murdered Agamemnon, splitting his head open, and then the couple butchered all his supporters. They continued to rule Mycenae for another ten or more years.

Orestes managed to escape after the murder and grew up in exile. As soon as he was old enough, his sister Electra, rabid for vengeance at the death of her father, arranged for Orestes to return and kill Clytemnestra and Aegisthus.

Pandora

The myth surrounding Pandora is well documented, but shrouded in confusion. Pandora means "all-giving" and many scholars believe that her appearance in Hesiod's *Theogony*, as the bringer of all evil to humankind, was perhaps a misogynist retaliation against an earlier fertility goddess. Zeus' retribution for Prometheus' gift of fire to humanity was to order Hephaestus to make the first woman out of clay, but with a twist. She was given beneficial as well as deceitful attributes by the gods and then sent to Epimetheus, the brother of Prometheus, as a wife. She arrived on Earth with her jar of gifts and Epimetheus could not refuse.

If it was Pandora who opened the jar, or whether Epimetheus did, is not clear. But as it opened all the evils, misfortunes, and disasters of the world flew out, except for "hope" or "expectation" (according to the translation of the Greek word *elpis*). But was this a good or a bad thing for humankind? If "hope" or "expectation" is imprisoned in the jar, then the human race is doomed; if hope or expectation, however, is kept safe in the jar, then human beings cannot corrupt it. The interpretation here is entirely dependent on the individual's perception of the myth. Pandora's story is inconclusive. No one seems to be able to recount what happened to her afterward, although the myth has been embellished and analyzed throughout history.

"All-giving" Pandora was probably a pre-Olympian Earth goddess, not just Hesiod's first woman and wrecker of humankind.

Roman mythology

The profusion of Greek deities was slowly assimilated into Roman culture around the 2nd century BCE, but the Romans also drew on the belief system of the Etruscans, a highly cultured and indigenous people of central Italy who were finally overthrown at the sacking of Veii in 396 BCE.

Jupiter was benevolent, yet authoritarian. His temple on the Capitoline Hill in Rome was the center of his worship.

The Etruscans believed in a ruling triad. This was composed of Tinia, ruler of the Heavens, Uni, the goddess of the cosmos, and Menrva, goddess of wisdom. Similar to the Greek goddess Athene (see page 108), Menrva was also born from the head of her father. In Rome the triad developed into Jupiter, Juno, and Minerva. Local gods were soon amalgamated into the Roman pantheon, the best qualities and attributes being lifted from Greek gods, and the odd cultish deity, such as Apollo, being accepted directly into the Roman canon.

Mars

The deity who personified Roman power, majesty, and fair dealing, Mars was venerated throughout the Roman world as a close second favorite to Jupiter (see opposite). He developed from one of the oldest Italian gods, Maris, who was originally a spirit of farming and agriculture and an early Etruscan deity, and who then merged with the warring attributes of the Greek war god, Ares. But the Romans civilized the rough, brainless, berserk nature of Ares to create their imperial Mars. Thoughtful, protective, and self-controlled, he eventually became a well-respected military deity and fathered the twins Romulus and Remus, the founders of Rome.

Jupiter

Jovial and almost too good to be true, Jupiter ruled supreme. Statues of him were everywhere and his noble, yet politically correct qualities and attributes could hardly be more different to the philandering, careless Zeus from which he was adapted. Also known as Optimus Maximus ("best and greatest") his temple on the Capitoline Hill carried a huge statue of this benevolent dictator. The Romans believed Jupiter ruled rather like a boardroom chairman, with his fellow decision-makers Juno and Minerva. As leader of the council of the gods, he was worshipped in temples dedicated to him all over the Roman empire and was famous for wielding three categories of thunderbolts: one to warn; another more serious, on condition the other gods agreed; and the third mighty and awesome, deployed only with permission from the hidden gods who were creators before the Olympian dynasty.

The Saturnalia

Identified with Cronus and the story of his overthrow of Ouranos (see pages 102–103), Saturnus was one of the older Roman gods. However, instead of being exiled to Tartarus, as Cronus was, Jupiter let Saturnus escape to Italy where he reigned with Janus. This was an era of peace and prosperity known as the Golden Age, and the Saturnalia was held in his honor each year around the winter solstice.

The Saturnalia provided brief orgiastic festivity during the more disciplined, but prosperous life of Saturnus' reign.

Identified with lust and self-mutilation, Cybele and her secret cults were revered by the Roman aristocracy.

Cybele

Although Cybele was a goddess with particularly lurid associations in Greek mythology, she was revered and adopted with passion by the Romans. Originally a goddess of Phrygia and protector of wild animals and caverns, chasms, and cliffs, the Greeks discovered her shrine on Mount Ida and "adopted" her during the Trojan War.

According to the Greeks, Cybele lusted after Attis and he was so horrified that he castrated himself. From then on, Cybele was known as the goddess of unrequited lust. Her priests, the Corybantes, worked themselves up into an orgasmic frenzy as they danced, and then performed self-mutilation acts with sickles and, in extreme cases, castrated themselves. This was never popular among the Greeks, but became a curious cultish fascination for young Roman aristocrats—from the 4th century BCE they formed secret sects in Rome and visited the original shrine on Mount Ida to experiment with self-mutilation and erotic dancing. In later Rome, an annual ceremony honoring Cybele re-enacted her complete story.

Bona Dea

An aloof, virginal goddess whose cult following was very different from Cybele's, Bona Dea was revered as the goddess of healing, fertility, and virginity, and it was only women who were allowed in her shrine. Secret rituals and worship were conducted at the home of a prominent Roman magistrate, and women alone were allowed to be present, assisted by the Vestal Virgins. Her devotees included many freed slaves and lower-class citizens. She was the daughter of the god Faunus and sometimes called Fauna, but the words "myrtle" and "wine" were not allowed to be spoken in her presence because Faunus had once beaten her with a myrtle stick when she'd got drunk.

Diana

The origins of the Roman goddess Diana are intertwined with the Greek goddess Artemis. This means that her ancient cults are diverse and highly complex. She was compassionate and nurturing, yet bloody and merciless. Her later emanations included goddess of the moon grove and of childbirth. Diana's pagan associations were viewed as a threat by Christianity, resulting in her being denounced as a devil goddess by the Inquisition. In the medieval period Diana was propitiated as goddess of the wild woods and forests of Europe. Her ancient cults involved human sacrifice, yet in Rome she was also the protector of slaves and children. Preferring solitude, she was unhappy in the company of men, and males were not allowed to enter her temples.

The Temple at Ephesus is devoted to the Greek goddess Artemis, who had close associations with the Roman Diana.

Other Roman myths

Roman mythology evolved rapidly between 2 BCE and 8 CE with the Roman poet, Ovid, and the historian, Livy. Both were influential in the medieval and early Renaissance period.

Ovid and Livy

Ovid wrote a collection of myths called *Metamorphoses* (Changes), in which the gods or mortals involved transformed in some way. *Baucis and Philemon* is one such example. Livy, meanwhile, wrote a version of the legend of Lucretia, which became a source of insipiration for many artists throughout history.

Baucis and Philemon

For 60 years, Baucis ("modest") and her husband Philemon ("hospitable") had lived in an old cottage in a hillside beside a marsh. When Jupiter decided to

Baucis and Philomen's story was well known in medieval Europe through Ovid's influential Metamorphoses.

exterminate the human race, he and Mercury went down to Earth disguised as tramps to see if there was anyone worth rescuing. Wherever they went people slammed doors, refused them entry, gave them nothing, and treated them like dirt. When the gods came to Baucis and Philomen's house they were welcomed immediately and were given everything they wanted. Baucis only realized they were in the presence of the gods when he noticed that the wine jug kept filling itself up of its own accord. Jupiter rewarded their kindness by transforming their cottage into a temple high above the flood that Neptune sent to punish humanity. When they died, the couple were transformed into trees.

Lucretia

Livy retold the myth of Lucretia as if it were real history, perhaps as an excuse for the uprising against Tarquin and the establishment of republican Rome.

During the tyrannical reign of Tarquin the Proud, adultery was common among Romans. But Lucretia was different, famous for her virtue and fidelity to her husband, Collatinus. While Collatinus was taking part in a siege, an hour's ride from Rome, the young nobles argued about whose wife was the most faithful. On returning to Rome, Collatinus found Lucretia alone with her maids, while the other wives were drunk or having sex. But Tarquin's son Sextus was so overcome with lust for Lucretia that he went back to her house, broke in, and raped her. The next morning, Lucretia was so ashamed that she called for her husband and father, told them what had happened, and stabbed herself to death.

Lucretia's rape and suicide formed a favorite subject for artists throughout history, such as Rutilio Manetti.

NORSE, CELTIC, AND OTHER EUROPEAN MYTHOLOGIES

Many epic tales survive of gods, goddesses, and heroes, from the icy wastelands of Norse mythology to the mystical land of Celtic Britain. But early Ice Age cave paintings, Neolithic carvings, and clay figures of the Great Goddess are evidence that ancient Europe had a vast and vividly inspiring mythology in its own right, even before the arrival of the Celts, Greeks, and Romans and their powerful patriarchal deities.

History and background

The primordial mythologies of Europe have mostly been lost to us, although there are still traces in archaeological finds suggesting that our earliest myths were based around animals and an Earth goddess religion.

But with the rise of patriarchal warring civilizations, male gods took over. From Greece to Scandinavia, from the eastern frontiers of India to the western remoteness of Ireland, warring tribes and races—Aryan, Viking, and Celt—created an extraordinary array of deities along with tales of their heroic deeds.

Celtic mythology

The Celts were a huge grouping of peoples spread across Europe. Consisting of many tribes and settlements, and renowned for their guerrilla warfare, they appeared in eastern Europe in the 2nd millennium BCE and moved west and south, dominating cultures in northern Europe. One of the few civilizations to revolt against Roman rule, their mythology is diverse, and fascinating in its obscurity.

The Celts resisted Roman rule until the 4th century CE and were left with a few outposts in Ireland, Scandinavia, the Balearics, and remote parts of Britain. With the arrival of the Christian era, Celtic religion and myth were treated as devil-worship and went underground. From about the 8th century CE, religious writers tried to rework the myths into a kind of Christian dogma, and stories such as the Holy Grail and the Arthurian legends remain powerful to this day.

Norse mythology

During the 4th century BCE, and originating much further south between the Rhine, Danube, and Vistula rivers, invaders moved north and conquered the Scandinavian countries, bringing with them what is now described as Norse mythology. This mythology remained secularized and intact in spite of widespread Christianity throughout Europe.

A considerable amount of Norse literature appeared in Iceland during the 11th to 14th centuries CE and the best-known works are the *Eddas* and the *Sagas*,

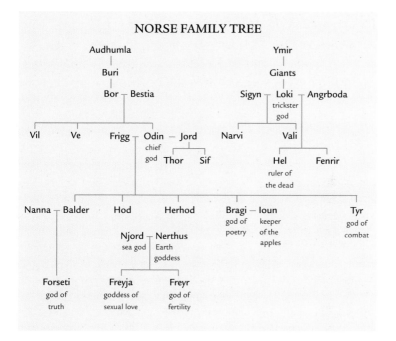

NORSE FAMILY TREE

poetry and prose narratives, some anonymous, others written as riddles or alluding to ideas and wisdom from ancient myths.

Slavic and Basque mythologies

In Slavic mythology, most stories were passed down orally. Slavic myth has many themes and symbols common with other Indo-European belief systems, and various scholars believe its traditions go back more than 3,000 years. With the arrival of Christianity sometime between the 4th and 12th centuries CE, Basque mythology became obscured. Most of what is known is based on local legend or the odd historical reference to pagan rituals. Interestingly, the key goddess, Mari, is the only surviving Mother/Earth Goddess in European mythology since the Indo-European patriarchal cultures took over.

Nordic beliefs

At the heart of Nordic belief is Odin, the god of battle, storm, and the "moment of no return." His role as god of all knowledge led to a widespread mystery cult. It was believed that if anyone was stabbed and hung for nine days on an ash tree like Odin, they would achieve infinite wisdom and conquer death.

Odin

Also known as "Wotan" or "Woden," Odin was the son of Bor, the spontaneous offspring of Buri, the third living being in creation after the primordial cow Audumla had licked some ice to find salt and created Buri's form. As a shapeshifter, Odin could move into any place or change from creature to god when he chose. His greatest gift was the wisdom with which he nourished himself, although he occasionally took sips of the "mead of inspiration."

Odin was the ruler of all the Norse gods and he and his two brothers, Vili and Ve, were responsible for the slaughter of the frost giant Ymir. Ymir's flesh was made into earth, his bones into mountains, and his blood became a fathomless infinite ocean surrounding their creation Midgard ("middle land"), where they built a huge citadel called Asgard. Odin and his descendants fought never-ending battles with the ice giants. Married to Frigg, he had two sons—Balder (beautiful god) and Thor (the god of thunder). In an attempt to understand secret knowledge, Odin hung himself upside down on the great ash tree Yggdrasil, the Tree of Life or World Tree. After nine torrential days and nights of pain, he learned all the mysteries and secrets of the runes, which he then gave as a gift to the Vikings.

Runes

Many runic stones still exist throughout northern Europe, the most famous of which is the Bjorketorp rune stone dating back to the early 6th century CE. This spooky rune stone is carved with a warning that says: "the secret of the runes is hidden here, he who tries to remove the stone will be cursed there."

Odin was accompanied by two wolves, Geri and Freki,
while two ravens gave him his secret knowledge.

Thor thrashed around the heavens on his chariot, hurling his hammer at any passing giants.

Thor

The god of thunder and son of Odin, Thor was one of the most popular Norse deities. With his very fierce demeanor, he would crash and tear around the heavens, creating thunder with the rattling and banging of the pots and pans that hung from his chariot. With his powerful hammer Mjollnir, Thor was known as a giant-slayer and hunted them mercilessly. The hammer was like a boomerang and every time he threw it, it would strike his opponent dead and then return to his hand. It often glowed red-hot and Thor would wear iron gloves to hold it.

Thor's worship survived right into Christian times and in fact he became more popular than Odin. Thor was probably only rivaled in popularity by Christ in the 11th century CE. His hammer, shaped like a "T" and cross-bar, became a common symbol, and hammer amulets, rings, and pendants were worn or buried in graves. His sacred tree was thought to be the oak in Germany and the rowan in Scandinavia. In art, he was always depicted as a gruff, flame-bearded warrior with piercing eyes; his chariot was pulled by two winged goats that he ate when he was hungry and then brought back to life by hammering away at their bones.

Frigg

One of the most powerful of Norse deities, Frigg was not only Odin's consort, but also his daughter, and sister to Thor. She lived alone in a palace called

Fensalir ("marsh hall") and would travel across the sky to visit Odin and vice versa. Although she was known as the goddess of marriage, she was also an adulteress and had affairs with Odin's brothers Vili and Ve. As goddess of the rain and the clouds, she would flounce around the skies in her billowing cloaks, made of light or dark cloud depending on her mood, and was often depicted as a woman riding a broom across the sky, which would sweep away the storms. She could predict the future, but she could not change it.

Tyr

In many accounts, Tyr was the original sky god and preceded Odin; in other accounts, he was the son of Odin and Frigg; while in yet others he was an earlier Germanic war god Tiwaz. But all agree that Tyr was a fearless god of war. He raised Loki's wolf Fenrir, but it never stopped growing and soon all of Asgard feared it. It was then Tyr who selflessly sacrificed his sword hand so that Fenrir could be bound for this cycle of the universe. For his noble deed he is safe until the final battle of Ragnarok. Ragnarok means "destruction of the powers" and marks the end of this cycle of creation, when Loki will wreak his revenge on all the gods he hates and wants to destroy. The huge battle will mean that good will destroy evil, and vice versa. However, after Ragnarok, the World Tree Yggdrasil will survive and a new age of the universe will be born.

Tyr's sacrifice meant that the wolf Fenrir, feared by all the gods, could be bound for another cycle.

Yggdrasil

This vast ash tree was named after Odin's sacrificial "ride" in the tree. Odin was also known as Ygg, and the name means "Ygg's Horse Tree." The tree sprang from three great roots and beneath the huge branches were Asgard, Midgard, and Niflheim. One root grew from the Well of Urd or Wyrd in Asgard, where the three Norns watered it daily (see below). The second grew from the icy spring of Hvergelmir in Niflheim, the home of the dead, where it was slowly gnawed every day by the dragon Nidhogg, who tried to kill the tree. The third grew from Midgard, where it was nourished by the well of Mimir and the source of all knowledge. Beneath this well lay the immortal head of the sage Mimir, which Odin had kept after it was severed by the Vanir, the gods who had been at war for hundreds of years previously with the sky gods Odin, Vili, and Ve.

The inhabitants of the tree included a rooster in the highest branches who was fated to crow out the beginning of Ragnarok (see page 133) and the end of this cycle of the universe. An eagle, meanwhile, tried to distract the dragon from eating the tree, and the squirrel Ratatosk scurried back and forth with insulting messages between the serpent and the eagle to perpetuate the competition between them. Among the branches were four stags that nibbled the leaves and represented the four winds that blew between the worlds.

The Norns and the Well of Wyrd

Every deed that was performed (good or bad) would fall into this well and vanish beneath the water, which was constantly in motion, fed by an underwater spring that brought fresh water and by a stream that took away the contaminated water. Each day the Norns would collect from the well water that contained a random selection of deeds. They would then water the World Tree to nurture it, and so the deeds of the past would nourish the tree to influence the future.

The three Norns were Skuld (being), Urd (fate), and Verdandi (necessity). They were considered to shape human fate, rather like the Greek Fates (see page 114). Verdandi was beautiful and young, Skuld an old hag, and Urd older than time itself. They wove tapestries that determined human destiny, and these were so complex and intricate that they could not be understood, which is why human life is so complicated. Unfortunately, Skuld could get angry and would

The World Tree was known as Yggdrasil in Norse myth.
It drew its nourishment from water sources.

then rip and tear the tapestries to threads, throwing human destiny into confusion. If the Norns ever manage to finish a tapestry, human existence will be eternally peaceful.

Freyr and Freyja

Brother and sister, they were offspring of the sea god Njord and the Earth goddess Nerthus. They lived together in Vanaheim, home of the Vanir, a family of gods who were gentle and creative, unlike the other family of gods, the Aesir, who included Odin, Vili, and Ve, and all their incestuous offspring, such as Balder, Loki, Thor, and Tyr. After the war with the Aesir, Freyja married Od, the god of sunshine, and when he vanished she wept tears of golden corn all over Asgard. Freyr lived in Asgard and married the giantess Gerd, daughter of the giant sea king Aegir. Freyr and Freyja were sexually rampant, and Gerd was the only female who could cope with Freyr's excessive sexual appetite.

Freyja's sexual powers were enhanced when she took possession of the magical necklace known as the Brisingamen. Some sources say she bought this from four dwarves by having sex with each of them, while others say that Loki stole it for her. Whatever the reason, it enabled Freyja to guarantee universal fertility.

Hel

Not far from one the roots of Yggdrasil lived Hel, the goddess of the Underworld condemned by Odin to rule the realm of the dead. She was the daughter of Loki and the

The daughter of trickster god Loki, Hel was condemned by Odin to rule the Underworld.

giantess Angrboda and was not only a dark, terrifying figure, but also a very sad one. Her companions, possessions, and qualities reveal the kind of doomed existence that Hel not only experienced, but offered to those who must pass through her realm. Her body was divided into the beautiful upper part, flesh-colored and living, and the darker lower half which was putrid flesh, so black that it was invisible, but stank in the darkness. Her hall was called Eliudnir ("damp" or "dank") and her bed Kor ("sick-bed" or "disease"). Anyone who died of old age or illness would have to enter her miserable realm and wait until Loki returned to call back his daughter to fight at the battle of Ragnarok.

Balder

Beautiful and radiant, Balder filled Asgard with light and cheerfulness. Gentle and wise, this son of Odin and Frigg lived in a golden palace with Nanna, his wife. But Balder was cursed with a dream that one day he would be killed by a fellow god and that his death would create the end of the universe. Frigg could foresee the future, but she could not change it, so she asked every living being in existence to swear never to harm Balder. However, she forgot to ask the mistletoe. When the gods were fooling around at a banquet one day, Loki gave the blind god Hod a stick of mistletoe; he aimed Hod's hand at Balder so that he stabbed him in the heart and killed him. Hel agreed that if every living being wept one tear, Balder would live again. Unfortunately, one old giantess named Thokk (possibly Loki in disguise) refused to cry and so Balder was condemned to the Underworld until the end of the universe.

Beautiful Balder was mistakenly killed by the blind god, Hod, due to Loki's trickery.

Slavic and Finnish mythology

Fertility and creationist goddesses figure in most mythologies, as do deities from the dark side—Mokosha and Luonnator fall into first group, whereas Tuoni, Tuonetar, and Vodyanoi reflected darker, more malevolent forces.

The early Slavic fertility goddess Mokosha, like many other pagan goddesses, evolved into the Virgin Mary.

Mokosha

In Slavic mythology, Mokosh, or Mokosha (meaning "moist"), was both an Earth and a fertility goddess, worshipped mainly north of the Black Sea. Her functions were to protect women, children, and lambs during birth, and to ensure that semen was rich in sperm. She appeared in Russian folk religion as Mati Syra Zemlya and was later associated with weaving and spinning. She was assimilated into Christianity and evolved into the Virgin Mary.

Luonnator

The daughter of the air in Finnish myth, Luonnator was a primal goddess who existed before the universe and brought about its creation. Wandering eternally through the cloudless skies, Luonnator finally fell into the primordial ocean. She rested there for 700 years as the sea washed over and around her, making her boundlessly fertile. A duck laid its eggs on her knee, and as it settled down to hatch the eggs, Luonnator twitched and the eggs fell and broke into pieces. The shells made the sky and the Earth, while the yolks and whites made the Sun and Moon. Her son Väinämöinen (see pages

354–355) wandered around inside her womb until he was thirty, then clambered out and dove into the sea. He became the central character in the great epic poem *Kalevala* in Finnish mythology.

Tuoni and Tuonetar

In Finnish myth Tuoni ruled the Underworld alongside his consort Tuonetar. Tuoni was invisibility and darkness personified, he was non-existence, and together with Tuonetar he created an enormous family of plagues, diseases, demons, and monsters. Only their children were allowed out of Tuonela, the name given to the Underworld. Mortals who tried to enter would have to swim through icy rivers in darkness, battle their way through thorny thickets and then finally face the flesh-eating monster Surma, who guarded the Gates of Decay. Anyone who survived would then be given a beer of oblivion to make them forget they existed, while all the monsters cast huge nets around the realm to stop anyone from leaving.

Vodyanoi

In Slavic myth the Vodyanoi is a water spirit. In some accounts, he lived in a crystal palace beneath the whirlpools of racing millponds and decorated his home with the treasures from sunken ships. Sometimes he looked like a large fish with a human face, or a frog or a seal, but he was usually green-skinned and covered in slime, algae, and weeds. He changed form with the phases of the Moon.

The water spirit Vodyanoi drowned humans and pulled them down to his watery world to be his slaves.

Basque mythology

From Bronze and Stone Age figurines and carvings
throughout Europe, there is strong evidence that the Great
Goddess religion existed before patriarchal civilization, with
its own pantheon of deities, took over Europe.

Despite the relentless influence of Indo-European cultures in the West, the
mythology of the Basques (the Euskaldunak) remained isolated, and the Great
Goddess retreated to the mountains, caves, and chasms of the high Pyrenees.
The remoteness of the region enabled the oral traditions to survive.

*In the Aveyron region of the French Pyrenees, isolated
villages still exude an ancient magic.*

Mari and Maju

The Great Goddess was known as Mari to the Basques and took on many different aspects, such as Mari of the Oven and Mari of the Cave. Her consort was known as Maju or Sugaar, which means "snake," and he would appear as a sickle or half-moon of fire. Mari's servants were known as the Laminak—these were either invisible spirits or nymphs with birds' feet, who lived near rivers and streams. Maju visited Mari every Friday to help comb her hair, but there was always a battle raging between them and whenever Maju appeared, a storm was imminent. In his Sugaar role, he was considered to be the personification of thunder and lightning.

The Great Goddess was known as Mari to the Basque people, and personified many aspects of the nature of the mountains.

Mari also had several different manifestations. At times she would appear as a beautiful woman, at others as a bird, crow, or vulture. She manifested as a tree with a woman's face, a gust of wind, a rainbow, a ball of fire, and even a goat. Mari lived in a subterranean realm of chasms, rivers, and caves adorned with gold and precious stones and had the power to give or withhold abundance. Sometimes she spun gold thread and at other times she would drive a chariot with four white horses across the sky.

Mari and Sugaar had a son called Atarrabi, who was similar to his mother—law-abiding, kind, and compassionate. He was connected to the North Star in the sky, and when it shone it created good fortune for the Basque people. Their other child, Mikelats (it's not known if this child was a boy or girl), brought natural disasters such as landslides and rock falls. When Mikelats' star shone, evil and bad fortune would come to the people.

Celtic mythology

A rich vein of myth, fable, and legend is part of the legacy of the Celtic past, and many of its deities have survived in modern art, literature, and film.

Ceridwen

In Celtic myth, Ceridwen was a witch, renowned as the mother of the great Welsh hero Taliesin. She first gave birth to Morfran, who was horrifyingly ugly and, according to the *Mabinogion* (a collection of medieval Welsh tales), she decided to give Morfran the gift of all knowledge to compensate for his ugliness. Ceridwen filled a pot with a magic potion and set it to boil for a year and a day. After a year and a day there would be only three drops left, which would contain all knowledge. A blind man named Morda tended the pot, while the boy Gwion stirred the concoction. But as Gwion stirred, three drops of the potion spat onto his thumb, and in pain he instinctively licked the potion off his hand. At once he was given all the knowledge in the world and realized that Ceridwen would probably kill him.

But Gwion learned to shape-shift and made himself into a hare, then a fish, and then a grain of corn. Ceridwen, too, could shape-shift and she chased him as a greyhound, an otter, a hawk, and finally a hen that ate the grain of corn.

Gwion was born to Ceridwen nine months later, and instead of killing him outright, she tied him up in a leather bag and threw him in the river, where the current carried him downstream to Prince Elphin, who took the child to his palace. The child Gwion grew up to be Taliesin, the prince's prophet and chief entertainer. A real bard named Taliesin who lived in the Welsh court of the 6th century is thought to have been Gwion.

Merlin and Nimue

Merlin was the famous magician of Arthurian legend, who some sources say created the supernatural construction of Stonehenge. He was also responsible for creating the Round Table and the layout of Camelot. His birth was shrouded in mystery, but his mother was a nun and his father a demon. He is said to have inherited his love of the mortal world from his mother and his restless, shape-shifting talent from his father.

In human form he was a prophet and sorcerer and advised Arthur on many occasions, but he also changed into a seductive young man, fell in and out of love, and would then become a cloud, storm, or even a ripple on a pond.

Nimue was the daughter of a siren and, in some accounts, the Lady of the Lake, while other sources put her as Morgan le Fay (see page 146); she was also a witch and shape-shifter. She looked after Merlin when he was young and lusted after him when he became a beautiful youth, but Merlin left her for the mortal world and her unrequited love turned venomous. Nimue tried to outwit him by changing shape and trapping him, but he always managed to win. Then she remembered his weakness—beautiful women. She turned herself into a mortal and, blinded by his own desire, Merlin instantly fell for her. He made passionate love to Nimue and, as he did so, she changed herself into a drop of amber and engulfed him forever.

The Lady of the Lake gave Arthur the sword Excalibur, but she was also known as the witch Nimue.

Gods of the Tuatha De Danann

The first supernatural race of the people of Ireland, the Tuatha De Danann fought many battles against the Formori, or demons, but they were not immortal and so gradually vanished from the world, their mythic status also diminishing to that of fairies, elves, or spirits in nature.

Danu

There is very little recorded about Danu, but her ranking as one of the more important early Celtic goddesses worshipped throughout Europe is based on her association with place names such as the Danube, Driept, and Don. Danu, sometimes known as Dana and Dannan, was the mother goddess of the Tuatha de Danann. In Hindu mythology, a goddess named Danus is associated with water and mothered a race of Asuras ("power-seeking deities") called the Danavas. It seems likely that Danu has very ancient roots indeed.

The Dagda

The original chief of the supernatural inhabitants of Ireland was the Dagda (good god), married to Danu. He was "good" in the sense of being all-powerful

The Gods of the Tuatha De Danann were some of the first inhabitants of Ireland.

and the provider of plenty. He was rough-mannered and had a pot belly, and was infamous for his club and his cauldron, which was bottomless—deep below the bubbling froth of meat, milk, and vegetables was an orchard whose trees were always filled with fruit. Magical pigs fed on the fruit, were roasted and were then reincarnated for the next day's meal.

Famous for his bottomless cauldron, the Dagda was the king of a race of godlike people who invaded Ireland.

The Dagda used his enormous club to kill enemies on the battlefield, but with the other end of the club he could bring people back to life. Highly lustful, he copulated with numerous trees, humans, and other supernatural beings, but his most famous affair was with the Morrigan, the goddess of war (see page 146). After they had made love by the banks of the River Unius, she promised to support the Dagda's people in their next battle and to give them her eternal protection.

Eriu

According to the 11th century CE *Book of Invasions*, the Irish were descended from Mil Espaine, a descendant of Scota, an Egyptian pharaoh's daughter, and a Scythian called Goidel Glas. In the 2nd to 1st century BCE, the sons of Mil led a force to conquer Ireland and defeat the Tuatha De Danann, and the "Milesians" were said to be the final inhabitants of Ireland.

Eriu, one of the patron goddess queens of Ireland at the time of the Milesian invasion, made a deal with the poet Amairgin that her name be given to Ireland rather than that of her two sisters (Eire is a derivation of this name). Eriu was the mother of the second ruler of the Tuatha De Danann, Bres, an unpopular, cruel, and ultimately unsuccessful king. With her sisters Banba and Fodla, Eriu formed a triumvirate of goddesses much like that of the Hindu goddesses Devi, Kali, and Durga.

The Morrigan

An Irish goddess of war who influenced the outcome of conflicts by terrifying one side or the other on the battlefield, depending on her mood, the Morrigan was part of a trinity of goddesses, along with Badb and Macha, who also appear as aspects of the Morrigan herself. The sisters took the form of huge crows and would perch on rooftops, foretelling the future of wars and battles, then swoop down on the battlefield to ravage the corpses.

Morgan le Fay, a seductive but sinister queen, has also been identified as the Morrigan. In the Arthurian legends she is sometimes also known as Nimue (see page 143) or Vivien, but whatever her true role, she was certainly a prolific shape-changer like the Morrigan. Morgan le Fay also had conflicting roles in the various Christian accounts of Arthur. She was the leader of the nine mysterious guardians of Avalon, the guardian of the magic sword Excalibur, and she entrusted the sword to Arthur for his time on Earth in some accounts. In other accounts, however, she is Arthur's half-sister and rival, endlessly plotting the downfall of Camelot.

The Morrigan determined the outcome on the battlefield by terrifying one side or the other with her frightening appearance.

The Morrigan was ambivalent about taking sides and her ferocious qualities were powerfully linked to her sexuality. For example, she took the side of the Tuatha De Danann after being bewitched by the Dagda, and later she supported the men of Connaught. She was thought to live in the cave of Cruachain in County Roscommon in Ireland. She and her sisters subsequently became identified with the Fates of Greek mythology, the Norns of Norse myth, and the three prophetic witches of Shakespeare's *Macbeth*.

Brigit

Another triad of goddesses, Brigit or Brigid was the name given to each of the three daughters of Dagda and Danu (see pages 144). Apart from her emanation as fertility goddess, Brigit later became the patron deity of the Irish province of Leinster. The eldest Brigit was the goddess of crafts, poetry, and the intellect; the middle sister was the goddess of healing; and the youngest was the goddess of metal-working. Brigit is in fact an honorary name, like "highness," and it has been suggested by scholars that her name was so revered and sacred that no one knew her true identity. Initiates to her mystery cults were the only ones who uttered her name. Later on in Christian Ireland, Brigit became identified with St. Brigit, guardian of the holy fire.

Angus

Angus was a love god who, when he grew older, helped those having problems in their love lives. He was the son of the Dagda (see page 144) and Boann, the spirit or water nymph of the River Boyne. Because Boann was

Brigit was part of a triad of goddesses who were able to predict the future.

*The sacred entrance stone at the World Heritage Neolithic
site of Newgrange in Ireland.*

having an affair with the Dagda behind her husband's back, the great sky lord made the Sun stand still for a day and the child was conceived and born in the same twenty-four hours.

Angus glimpsed his first lover in a dream, when she took the form of a swan. Her name was Caer Ibormeith. The only way he could seduce her was by also becoming a swan. In this form Angus swept around the lake in pursuit of her until she finally accepted him and they flew off around the lake three times singing a magical lullaby. With all the world asleep, they eloped to Angus' palace, Brug na Boinne, the Gaelic name for the Neolithic complex of Newgrange.

Cuchulain

Cuchulain, originally known as Setanta, was the warrior son of the mortal Dechtire and the Sun god Lugh. Cuchulain had magical powers, was ferocious in battle, and muscles bulged from every part of his body. His howling, raging voice stopped opponents in their tracks and his strength was legendary. While he was still a young boy he proved himself to be the strongest at the Ulster court of King Conchobar and became leader of the king's band of warriors. He was nicknamed Cuchulain after killing Chulain's (the local smith's) sheepdog. With no dog to guard the animals, he agreed to watch them for a year until a new dog could be found, so from then on he was called Cuchulain, "the hound of Chulain."

Cuchulain and the Giant

One story tells of how Cuchulain and his two friends Conal and Laoghaire were challenged to a bizarre test by a giant. Each was given the chance to behead the giant, provided the giant could behead the warrior afterward. Laoghaire sliced off the giant's head, but ran away. The giant replaced his head and Conal did the same thing. Finally, Cuchulain chopped off the giant's head, but bowed his own head before the giant as promised. The giant was so astonished at his fearlessness that he proclaimed Cuchulain the bravest man in Ireland.

Cuchulain was the leader of the king of Ulster's warriors and was renowned for his terrible temper.

149

Deirdre

The tragic tale of Deirdre is part of the *Ulster Cycle*, a group of stories about the kingdom of Ulster between the 2nd and 4th centuries CE. Conchobar, the king of Ulster, was dismayed when a druid predicted that Deirdre would bring disaster to the Ulster people. Daughter of the king's storyteller, Deirdre was incredibly beautiful, so the king decided to send her away to foster parents to save her life. He also planned to marry her when she was of age. One day, she told her teacher that she wanted to fall in love with a man with skin as white as snow and hair as black as a raven. The teacher told her there was such a

Tragic Deirdre ended up killing herself when forced to live with the two men she hated the most.

man, called Naoise, one of the king's warriors. So the couple met, fell in love, and escaped to Scotland.

Conchobar was furious, as he wanted Deirdre for himself, so he enticed the couple back with the promise of a pardon. On their return he ordered Eoghan to kill Naoise. When asked by Conchobar which two men she hated in the world, Deirdre replied, "Conchobar and Eoghan"; he then ordered her to spend six months with each of them. In despair she threw herself out of her chariot and took her own life.

Cernunnos

The widely worshipped Celtic horned god Cernunnos was associated with stags, fertility animals, and corn—archaeological recordings of his image have been cited from northern Italy to parts of Britain and Jutland. Rather like Pan, the Minotaur, and Pashupati, the Hindu Lord of Animals, he is a horned male associated with the wildness of nature, and all these may have a common origin.

Cernunnos is usually depicted wearing the horns of a ram and a "torc" or ornate neck-ring denoting Celtic nobility, sitting cross-legged and sometimes accompanied by a serpent. In medieval times he became associated with Herne the Hunter, and some sources suggest that he has the same origin. Herne was an "equestrian ghost" who lived in Windsor Forest and Great Park in the 13th century in England. During the Dark Ages, Windsor Forest was settled by pagan Anglo-Saxons who worshipped their own pantheon of gods, including "Woden" (a form of Odin, see pages 130). The story goes that upon saving the life of King Richard II from a wounded stag, Herne himself became fatally wounded. A witch brought him to life by tying the stag's antlers around his head. Herne was, however, framed for stealing the antlers and therefore lost favor with the king. He was found the next day hanging dead from a lone oak tree.

His ghost continued to haunt Windsor Forest. He was considered to be a phantom of ill omen, joined by his demon hounds, wild beasts of the night, and lost souls he had hunted down.

Cernunnos, god of nature and animals, is still worshipped today in many pagan traditions.

Camelot

One of the most well-loved and well-known European myths is that of King Arthur and the Knights of the Round Table. In some sources Arthur was originally Artos, one of the ancient gods of Celtic myth, and the brother of the war goddess, the Morrigan (see page 146). Artos was eventually sentenced to the skies as a constellation known as Arcturus.

The myths of Camelot and the Knights of the Round Table have remained popular tales in Western culture.

The remains of the castle of Tintagel in Cornwall,
considered to be the stronghold of Uther Pendragon.

Arthur then incarnated as the illegitimate son of Uther Pendragon and Queen Igraine of Tintagel. Brought up in secret, he pulled the magical sword Excalibur from a stone (some sources say he was given it by the Lady of the Lake) and could thus claim his right to be king. In his early years he united Britain, defeated the Romans and established a fantastic, magical court at Camelot. He married the beautiful princess Guinevere and created the Round Table, where warriors, mortals, and magicians alike lived in harmony far away from the mortal world.

Mordred (Arthur's son) and other courtiers conspired to take over the throne. Lancelot, Arthur's most loyal knight and friend, had been having an affair with Guinevere. When Arthur found out and banished Lancelot forever, Mordred and his followers took their chance. They fought bitterly and Arthur killed Mordred, but was so severely wounded himself that he traveled to the land of Avalon where the golden apples of immortality grew and was never seen again. Camelot, too, vanished, and to this day it is believed that Arthur and his men are merely sleeping under a hill (sources usually suggest this is Glastonbury Tor in the southwest of England). When the need is great, they will awaken to restore the golden age.

TRIBAL AFRICA AND OCEANIA

The vast landscapes of Africa, and the isolated and scattered islands that make up Oceania, including New Zealand and the huge landmass of Australia, are home to many small tribal groups and communities. The mythology of these indigenous peoples was concerned with a range of gods and goddesses who were responsible for everything from good harvests to fertility and creation. They also often shared a belief in an animating spirit, or life-force, in all things in nature.

History and background

On the surface, it is hard to think of the mythology of the vast continent of Africa in the same breath as that of Oceania, with its scattering of islands strung across the empty expanses of Pacific Ocean and the continent of Australasia. But the tribal roots of their mythologies give them more in common than may at first be imagined.

Africa

Except for Egypt, Africa has a very scattered and fragmented mythological heritage. With thousands of different languages and traditions and with the geographical isolation of its tribal communities, it is understandable that most of these cultures used myth for community purposes, creating a far more insular and ritualistic use of mythology than those codified belief systems of great civilizations. People lived in very small groups or settlements, and so folktales and ritual were used to sustain their own identity and separate them from warring tribes and, later on, from the conquering nations that have invaded

Indigenous African peoples created their own mythology, lore, and ritual depending on the needs of the community.

Africa over the last 2,000 years. When a people or tribe was eradicated, their mythic beliefs were lost, too. Local customs and many folktales, like those of the Anansi, survive today, but only really through oral tradition.

The major question for tribal Africa seemed to be "Who created the world?" Creator gods, like Woyengi and Bumba, or parents such as Kintu and Nambi or even Mwuetsi and Morongo, were the core myths that explained the cosmos and also defined the social order.

Aboriginal art is used to reinforce belief in the spirits in nature and the sacred importance of the Dreamtime.

Oceania

Made up of Melanesia, Polynesia, and Micronesia, as well as the immense continent of Australasia, this Oceanic region has a geography that is as desolate in places as it is sparse in population. Yet oddly enough, the mythology of this area is surprisingly consistent and rich. The small communities that are scattered across Oceania adapted the key elements of an accepted pantheon of gods, depending on their local weather, geographical, or cultural conditions and needs, and the mainstream myths of initial creators and creation have traveled across Oceania via oral tradition.

After the arrival of the Portuguese explorer Magellan in the 16th century, Oceanic tales were recorded by Europeans, with no doubt much distortion or embellishment of the original stories and the cultural identity of their peoples. Lately, however, the peoples of Oceania and the Aboriginal peoples of Australia have recognized a need to assert their culture by recreating and upholding traditional aspects of their mythology through ritual and the written word, as well as in the form of painting and art on rocks, bark, and skin as reinforcement of the Dreamtime, in the case of Australia.

157

African beliefs

The elements figure prominently in African cosmology, as personified by Olorun and Olokun from Nigeria, who represent the sky and water, and in the case of Amma and his offspring in the mythology of Mali.

Olorun

Olorun (Sky) and Olokun (Water) are the two founding gods in the myths of the Edo and Yoruba peoples of Nigeria. The thousand or so lesser gods decided to hold a contest to decide who would be the supreme lord. Whichever of the gods appeared the most radiant and splendid would win. According to one source, Olorun eventually won because every time that Olokun matched him for color, style, or majesty, Olorun made it clear that he was the original and that Olokun was merely a reflection of his greatness. Olokun, when asked how he might account for this, merely repeated Olorun's words, confirming to the thousand lesser gods that he was unworthy of being the supreme leader. With Olorun on the throne, the work of creation began.

Olorun sent one of the lesser gods down to Earth with a pigeon, a hen, and a snail shell of soil to make the land. Olorun also gave him seeds to create trees and plants and showed him how to mold clay to make animals. At first they were all immortal giants, but Olorun decided that it was too dangerous for the gods to have equals, so he imposed age upon them. As the giants aged, they shrank to miserable, shriveled living corpses about the size of human beings. Olorun felt sorry for them and created death, and thus mankind has never been able to equal the gods.

Yoruba head mask

Amma

The Dogon people of Mali have a very complex cosmology. Amma exists as an abstract principle of creation, who made the universe from an infinite

The Dogon funeral dance is said to lead the souls of the dead safely to their ancestors.

particle that grew into the primordial egg. In other accounts, Amma was the male principle as well as creation itself. He attempted to make a female out of clay in two earthenware bowls. Having created Mother Earth, he tossed away the spare bits of clay and they became the sky, while the bowls were the Moon and Sun. He mated with Mother Earth and three children were born—Ogo and the divine race of twins called the Nummo. Ogo was evil, so Amma created a balance by sacrificing the Nummo and then brought them back to life as mortals to create humankind. The Nummo twins gave birth to four couples, which represented the four elements, the four cardinal points, and the four great skills of medicine, farming, magic, and trade.

159

Eshu is one of the important minor gods or spirits known as oshiras, *who play a major part in the Yoruba people's daily life.*

Eshu

Like many trickster gods, Eshu of the Yoruba people is benevolent, but can also cause destruction. He is both a messenger and a mediator between the gods and men and is responsible for the good or bad fortune of humankind, too. The Yoruba people of Nigeria consider Eshu to be more important to their daily affairs than the creator Olorun.

Offerings must always be made to Eshu before starting any ritual, to ensure that the ceremony itself will be beneficial. Eshu could speak every language created, whether it was the language of elephants or that of plants. He was a shape-shifter, and was also known for his knack of teaching humanity a lesson, whether in order to increase their awareness or, depending on his mood, to cause conflict and malice, or even to misdirect people or divert them from their actions.

Eshu's symbolic colors are red and black. In one account, he was particularly peeved because two good friends were more interested in each other than in worshipping Eshu. To get his own back, he decided to trick them. The friends worked in neighboring fields, so Eshu put on his red-and-black hat and walked between the two fields so that one friend saw only the red side and the other only the black side. Afterward they began to describe how fabulous he was in his "red" or "black" hat and started squabbling. Eshu turned, to show them that the hat was both colors and told them that he had caused them to fight so they would pay him more respect in the future. From then on, the pair respected each other's opinions, too.

The eclipse of the Sun was a powerful symbol of creation to some people, and of disaster to others.

Mawu-Lisa

To the Fon peoples of Benin, Mawu, the female principle, is associated with the Moon, fertility, and compassion, while Lisa, the male principle, is associated with the Sun, power, war, and light. During the first-ever eclipse they fused to create one androgynous being, symbolizing the whole of the universe. Each time there was an eclipse, this led to a new act of creation, and has done so ever since. This abstract supreme principle of male-female guaranteed the stability and continuity of the universe. Mawu-Lisa eventually created offspring, who did have form and required worship from mortals; they included the universal snake Da, who supported the universe in its coils and then carried Mawu everywhere in its mouth. When they stopped for the night, Da made dung heaps everywhere and these turned into mountains. The smith god Gu resembled a trowel and was responsible for making human beings out of droppings from Da's dung heap.

161

Imana

The Banyarwanda people of Rwanda worshipped Imana, who was for them the sole creator of the universe. In his role as lord of all things, he promised immortality to humankind by keeping Death at bay.

Imana spent all his time hunting Death, warning everything in creation to hide away so that Death couldn't find a place to rest. But Death managed to cheat Imana when an old woman crept out of hiding to tend her garden and Death hid beneath her skirt. Imana thought he could manage to fool Death when the old woman was buried, and told the relatives to leave large holes in the earth, so that Imana could bring her back to life. But one of her relatives hated the old woman, and filled all the holes with stones and flattened the ground so hard that Death was trapped, and there was no more immortality.

So Imana decided to help humankind again by building three different but rather rickety kingdoms. These were like dishes propped up with sticks between each layer. The highest land was his own, then the middle land was Mother Earth, home to the mortals, and the lowest was for spirits and Death. Death

According to the Rwandan peoples, the sole creator, Imana,
is responsible for creating their dramatic landscapes.

Village communities in Rwanda believed Death would conquer the world if they didn't worship Imana.

climbed up the sticks and tried to get into the Earthly kingdom. He grabbed at people's ankles and took them down to his own land and gave them to the spirits to eat. The spirits and demons began to outnumber the Earth people, and they too started making holes in the Earth and climbing through cracks in an attempt to take over the middle land. Imana was the only one with the power to keep them at bay. For eternity Imana has had to force the demons back into their own land and simultaneously repair the tottering structure of the universe. It was so rickety, it became more and more fragile and ramshackle. The Banyarwanda people believed that one day, if Imana's concentration lapses for a single second, the entire structure will collapse like a house of cards and Death will conquer the universe. In modern-day Rwanda, Imana refers to the Christian God.

Anansi

The god Anansi was the spider-trickster of the Ashanti people of West Africa. He was first worshipped as an original creator god, spinning the universe into being at the request of the Great Sky spirit. He was a shape-changer and eventually became known as a messenger god who told mortals how to use fire and tell stories. There are hundreds of Anansi tales, and many sources suggest that these replaced stories of earlier ancient gods, their purpose being merely to entertain as they developed into folktales. Anansi usually sets up a situation to trick someone for the sake of trickery, but on occasion he helps out or confuses, depending on his mood. For example, he hides in an antelope's ear to escape a fire and reward her by weaving a web around her to hide her from a pack of lions. In the Caribbean, Anansi is known as Nancy or Annency.

Juok

In the myths of the Shilluk peoples of southern Sudan, Juok was a formless creator who was present in everything. The word *Juok*, along with the aliases Jok, Jwok, and Joagh, was also used to signify the divine spirit itself in all Nilotic (pertaining to the Nile) languages. This divine spark was both good and evil and accordingly determined the fate of humans and animals. To the ancient Shilluk, Juok created people out of sand and river-water. The first people were like lumps of mud and lay on the ground in a messy pile. Eventually, Juok made them arms to plant crops with, eyes to see their way, and legs to move around on. When he got bored with making people, he gave them reproductive organs so that humankind could create itself.

Mwuetsi

According to the Makoni people of Zimbabwe, Mwuetsi was the first human being on Earth. He was created by the god Maori and was carefully placed at the bottom of a lake with a horn of highly fertile *ngona* oil. The lake soon filled with new life, but Mwuetsi didn't much care for fish and slithery things and decided to clamber onto the shore. Unfortunately, there was nothing on the Earth except rocks, so he made a fuss and Maori sent him the woman Massassi to keep him entertained. With the aphrodisiacal *ngona* oil and the union of

In Zimbabwe, lizards and other reptiles were associated with the rape of Morongo.

Mwuetsi and Massassi, the world became filled with plants and trees. Next, Maori sent another woman, Morongo, and their offspring were animals and people. Maori decided that the world was complete and warned Mwuetsi against any more procreation. But because of the powerful lusting agent in the oil, Mwuetsi raped Morongo, and this time she gave birth to poisonous insects, snakes, and lizards. In some accounts the last snake-child bit Mwuetsi and killed him, and his other children refused to throw his body into the primordial lake in case it became polluted, so they buried him. Other accounts say that Maori was so furious at Mwuetsi's disobedience that he cursed the world with drought and famine so that his children strangled him, then buried him with the horn of *ngona* oil, and fertility was once more returned to Earth.

Mwindo

A hero with supernatural powers, Mwindo was a favorite epic tale for the Nyanga people of the Congo River area of central Africa. The son of Shenwindo, a powerful chief with seven wives, Mwindo was born from the middle finger of

The Congo River was a rich source of inspiration for the mythology of the Nyanga people.

one of the wives and could walk and talk immediately. However, Shenwindo had decreed that only daughters were allowed to live. On discovering Mwindo, his father attempted to kill him, but Mwindo used magic to protect himself. Shenwindo then sealed Mwindo in a drum and threw it into the river, hoping that he'd drown or be eaten by crocodiles, but Mwindo again used his magical powers to escape. Shenwindo fled to the Underworld for safety, but Mwindo followed him and met Master Muisa, the Underworld's ruler, who agreed to reveal where Shenwindo was. Finally, Mwindo found his father, who agreed to share his kingdom, and Mwindo restored and rebuilt the village.

Not long after, Mwindo was trying to be a little too clever with his magic and killed a dragon, which was a friend of Master Lightning. Master Lightning punished Mwindo by sending him to the sky for a year, where the searing heat and celestial storms battered him every day. Eventually the sky spirits said that he could return to Earth if he promised never to kill another living thing. Mwindo agreed to be less frivolous with his powers and ruled his kingdom in peace and harmony ever after.

Holawaka

In the myths of the Galla people of Ethiopia, Holawaka delivered divine messages from Heaven to Earth.

One day the Heavenly Sky Spirit told Holawaka to go down to Earth and reveal to humankind the secret of immortality: simply to remove their old skin when it was worn out and take up a new skin, rather like changing clothes. Holawaka traveled as a bird, but he found the journey exhausting. Tired and hungry, he became desperate for food. From his bird's-eye-view of Earth he spotted a snake eating a mouse. He swooped down, landed by the snake and offered to give the snake the secret of immortality if the snake gave him some of the mouse. The snake agreed, and that's why snakes shed their skins whenever they start to grow old and Holawaka birds are condemned to live on Earth among mortals as punishment for their ancestors' foolishness.

Snakes: powerful symbols

167

The Bambini people of the Congo were also known as Pygmies.

Bambini mythology

Khonvoum is the chief god of the Bambini people (Pygmies of the Congo) and is responsible for hunting. He carries a bow made from two intertwining snakes, which appear as a rainbow to humans.

After sunset, Khonvuom gathers stardust and throws it into the Sun to regenerate it for the next day. He sometimes sends his messenger Or (a thunder god and also an elephant) or a chameleon to help humankind. He made people from clay—black clay made very black people, white made white people, and red clay made the Pygmies.

Tore is a forest lord who supplies animals for the hunters. He hides in rainbows and is also a thunder god, and when he comes to Earth he appears as a leopard in initiation rites. The first Pygmies stole fire from Tore, who wasn't very pleased and chased after them, but he could not catch them; when he returned to the sky, his mother had died. In revenge he decided that humans would die too and he became the god of death.

Zulu mythology

The supreme creator god in Zulu mythology was Unkulunkulu, originally believed to have grown on a reed in a formless swamp before he created the Earth.

Other important deities included Mamma, the goddess of rivers (who became associated with the drowning of people and was more like a siren than a beneficial goddess), and Unwabi, a chameleon messenger god who was sent down to Earth to give humans immortality, but was too slow and people began to die. When the chameleon now changes his color from green to brown, he is remembering the terrible misfortune of Unwabi's slothfulness.

When the Earth began, it was covered in a thick dense fog so that people couldn't see the Sun or Moon, and there were no storms or wind. Humans spoke to each other in their minds because there were no words. If you wanted to eat some meat, you had only to think it and an animal that was old or too injured to keep up with the herd would be sent to you; if you needed some fruit, you only had to think of the fruit and a tree would drop some onto the ground before you. But one day a terrible race of gods called the Chattily arrived in great bowls of fire from the sky. They had three yellow eyes and lizard skin. They created languages and the ability to speak, and they invented so many different tongues that they divided the people, who then split into different groups with different ideas and forever after were in conflict with each other rather than in harmony.

In Zulu mythology, the "Amadlozi" are also still an important part of the traditional animistic worship. They are the spirits of the ancestor.

Polynesian beliefs

Polynesia consists of hundreds of small islands throughout the Pacific. In Polynesian culture all things on Earth, whether rocks or people, are believed to be descended from the gods.

Haumea

In Hawaiian mythology, Haumea was the goddess of childbirth and fertility. Before the Earth was created, Haumea lived in an orchard whose trees grew every animal and plant on their boughs, as if they were leaves—there were goat trees and pig trees, fish trees and fruit trees. Haumea also grew leaves as if she were a tree, and one day one of her leaves fell to the ground and changed into a beautiful young man. Haumea fell in love with him and wanted to mate with him, so she grew a vagina out of leaves. But the young man eventually withered and died like an autumn leaf and was trodden into the earth by the passing

animals. Humea was heartbroken and died very soon after, but she was reborn again as a tree and soon grew new leaves; her cycle of birth and rebirth revealed that all that is born must die, but will be born again in another life.

Makemake and Haua

Makemake was the supreme god of the peoples of Easter Island (also known as Rapa Nui), who was responsible for providing all his creations with food. The first Polynesian settlers chose Makemake's representative on Earth every year. In elaborate ceremonies devoted to the "Birdman," as he was known, the

In the rock caves of Orongo, there are many sacred carvings of the gods, especially of Makemake and the Birdman.

Polynesia is made up of tiny atolls and larger islands and covers vast areas of the Pacific Ocean.

island chief would hang a sacred egg in his hut and initiate worship of Makemake. This meant that seabirds would come to the island to nest and provide valuable eggs for the people to eat. In Orongo, there are many carvings in the rock caves of Makemake's skull mask and his wife Haua's vulva (signifying fertility), as well as ones of the Birdman and the frigate-bird god Vie-Kana.

Tane

The son of Rangi and Papa (Father Sky and Mother Earth), Tane was the god of forests. Tane studded the sky with jewels and clothed Earth with trees and plants. He taught the people on Earth everything they needed to know, and because he loved humankind so much he decided to live with them. But no human being could live or mate with a god, so he had sex with rocks and pools and his offspring were dragons and snakes. He asked Papa (Mother Earth) how he could get a wife, and she told him to carve one from sandstone, but warned him that the union would be disastrous. But Tane was so desperate for a wife that he made himself Hine Ahu One, the Earth girl, and breathed life into her. First they produced an egg, which became the ancestor of all the birds on Earth. When they mated again, Hine Ahu One was transformed into her own daughter, Hine Titama. Tane married her when she was old enough and they conceived another daughter. Hine Titama wanted to know who her father was, and when she found out it was Tane, she was so ashamed at her incest that she disappeared to the Underworld, where she became the goddess of death, Hine Nui Te Po. Tane became so dejected, he returned to the sky.

171

A wood carving of Tangaroa, god of the sea and ancestor of all fish.

Tangaroa

In Polynesian myth, Tangaroa was the god of the sea and Papa's eldest son. He had many aliases throughout Oceania, such as Tagaro and Tagaroa, but should not be confused with Tangaloa, creator god in Samoan mythology.

In one story, Tangaroa had a twin called Rongo. Although Tangaroa was the eldest, he allowed Rongo to be born first, then he arrived from a boil on his mother's arm. Rongo was less intelligent, so Tangaroa taught him the secrets of the universe. Vatea, his father, told Tangaroa he was so salty he would destroy everything living, so rule of the land was given to Rongo. Tangaroa accepted on condition that he could rule everything red—red birds, animals, fish, plants, and flowers. Rongo agreed, forgetting that although there are fewer red things in the world, they are usually special.

Tangaloa

In Samoan myth, Tangaloa was the first god in existence—he arrived in a shell, broke through it, and created the universe simultaneously. It was he who made the Polynesian islands by dropping stones in the ocean. His daughter Tuli, who was also a bird, flew down to the islands with a huge vine and after she had planted it, the vine spread across the islands and provided shade and food for her. Tangaloa also created the "Peopling Vine," which divided into plants and vegetation, and then when maggots and grubs started to eat the roots he turned them into all the animals, fish, and humans to finish creation.

The celestial twins

Twins To Kabinana and To Karvuvu were the first beings at the beginning of time according to the Tolai people of Vanuatu. To Karvuvu was the Moon and an idiot, To Kabinana was the Sun and sensible. The Sun made the first woman by breathing into a coconut; the Moon tried to do the same, but it didn't work because To Karvuvu had picked a bad coconut, so the woman was dead. To Kabinana made fish out of wood to feed his children, but when the Moon tried, he ended up making sharks. As the first woman grew old and could no longer bear children, To Kabinana thought it would be a good idea if the brothers took turns looking after her. But when To Karvuvu tried to play nursemaid the only way he could think of protecting her was to kill and then eat her, the origin of cannibalism.

Polynesian islands were dropped into the ocean like stones, according to Samoan mythology.

Tales of the trickster god Maui reached Hawaii, where Maui island is said to be named after him.

Maui

The hero and trickster demi-god of Polynesian myth, Maui has traveled across to New Zealand, Samoa, and Hawaii. The myths telling of his exploits are well known, and many versions appear throughout Polynesia. Like all tricksters, he is ingenious and usually a friend to humankind, but can sometimes be cruel.

He deliberately challenged the authority of the gods, for example when he tried to tame and capture the Sun. Maui decided the Sun was moving too quickly across the sky, so he lassoed it with a coconut-fiber rope, but the Sun burned through the rope. He finally managed to catch the Sun as it rose at dawn, and refused to let it go until the Sun agreed to take longer to move through the sky in the day and less time at night.

His father was a god and his mother was a mortal, and Maui was often involved in escapades to make the world a better place for humankind. Initially, he was given a magic hook by his mother, Hina, and fished the Polynesian islands into being. When he tried to conquer Death herself and bring immortality to humankind, it was his last great heroic act; he failed and was crushed to death between the thighs of Hine-nui-te-po, who had woken up, startled by the sound of the birds twittering at Maui's antics. In one Hawaiian story, the people became so fed up with Maui that they killed him and threw him into the sea. The shrimps fed on his blood and that's why they are pink.

Jari and Kamarong

In Melanesian myth, Jari was the daughter of the primordial snake goddess Gogo. Married to a snake man, she escaped his horrible clutches after he killed and ate her mother. She went around the world looking for a mortal husband, but all she came across was Kamarong, a lizard man whose sperm oozed from his skin and who expelled feces from his mouth. Jari was not very impressed and decided to try to "change" him. First, she created an anus as far away from his mouth as possible, making a hole between his legs, and then she molded a penis from crushed betel nuts. She showed Kamarong how to fish, cook, and grow plants and tobacco. According to the Wogeo people of Melanesia, these were the ancestors of all living people in the world.

In Melanesian myth, Jari and Kamarong, a lizard man, were the first people.

Areop-enap

At the beginning of creation, Areop-enap ("old spider") was shuffling around looking for food in the darkness. According to the islanders of Nauru, she came across a clam that swallowed her and she was firmly trapped inside. The clam refused to open its shell, but luckily Areop-Enap encountered a caterpillar called Rigi. The spider put a spell on Rigi to make him super-strong, and for some time he pushed his head against the upper shell and his legs against the bottom shell, but still the clam resisted. Rigi was so hot that sweat poured into the bottom shell to make the sea, but because it was salty the clam got thirsty and had no choice but to open up and die. From the upper shell Areop-Enap made the sky, from the lower shell the Earth. A snail that had been trapped inside the shell was set high in the sky to become the Moon. Areop-Enap made islands from the clam's flesh and wove silk over the islands to create plants and trees. Rigi had drowned in the sea, exhausted by his battle with the clam, so Areop-Enap wove a cocoon of silk around him and hung him up in the sky as the Milky Way.

Shells are important symbols of creation to many Oceanic peoples.

Hina

In Polynesian myth, Hina was one aspect of the Great Goddess and the personification of the feminine principle itself. There are many different stories about her throughout the Oceanic region, and just as many different aspects of her. In Tahitian myth, she lived with her brother Ru. Together they explored the universe until they found the Moon and Hina decided to stay there forever. Other stories say that she was the wife of Tangaroa, the sea god, but left him for the Moon when he lost his temper. Hina was Hine-Ahu One in Maori myth, the sand woman who married Tane. Some sources identify her as the wife of Te Tuna, the eel-monster, but she became so bored with him that she mated with Maui. Hina has also been identified as the princess of darkness and death herself, Hine Nui Te Po.

Na Kaa

Western missionaries arrived long after this myth was first recorded, but it has interesting similarities with the Garden of Eden story. Na Kaa and his brother Tabakea were the first two beings in creation. Na Kaa lived in a garden so beautiful that when the gods created humans they were only allowed to live beneath two trees—one for men and one for women—but the sexes were unaware of each other. Then one day Na Kaa had to leave paradise and called all the men and women to him to tell them to wait for him under their trees. But as soon as they saw the opposite sex, they lusted after each other and all went back to the same tree to have sex. When Na Kaa returned he told them they had chosen the Tree of Death, not Life, and from then on all humans were mortal. The Tree of Life was kept exclusively for the gods.

Hina, one aspect of the Great Goddess, was identified with the Moon in Tahitian mythology.

Gods were known to disguise themselves as all kinds of animals, such as porpoises.

Dudegera

One day a god disguised himself as a porpoise and played in the sea with a mortal woman, and where her leg rubbed against the dolphin's scales she gave birth to a child called Dudugera (leg child). He was bullied and teased as a boy, and the Massim people of Papua New Guinea believed that he set about seeking vengeance on the world by wanting to destroy it. He rose up into the sky and became the Sun, shooting arrows down on the world so that fires started everywhere and the world was in danger. His mother hid away for a while, but soon realized she had to do something, so threw mud at him to try and blind him. She missed and the mud turned into clouds, which covered the Sun and stopped the arrows. That is how the world continues to survive.

Sido

The parents of Sido, the creator god of the Kiwai and Toaripi peoples of Melanesia, were a pair of Siamese twins, both goddesses, who taught him the secret of immortality after he separated them at his birth. As Sido traveled the heavens, creative power gushed from his penis and fell on the Earth, bringing to life plants, animals, and humans. Each night he removed his skin like a snake and metamorphosed into another version of himself to ensure that he remained immortal. But one night some prying children spotted him halfway through his transformation and the spell was broken. His body eventually died, but his spirit continued to wander the world in the hope of finding a wife.

His twin mothers used his skull as a cup for the water of immortality, but it was only a gift for the other gods and Sido remained a restless spirit on Earth. He eventually married a mortal, but when she died Sido was transformed into a huge pig, which the mourners ate. He then changed into the Realm of Death itself, to guard the dead forever.

Wigan

The Ifugao peoples of the Philippines had a very important deity known as Wigan. He was a cultural hero who made a deal with the sky gods, gave them fire, and was rewarded with rice. The Ifugao culture is based around rice-growing and Wigan is one of a type of god known as the Matungulun (the Paybackables). He and his sister Bugan were the offspring of the sky gods Kabigat and Bugan, and were washed down to Earth in heavy rain. In fact, all 1,500 Ifugao gods have a wife called Bugan. To create more people, the son and daughter married and then their four daughters married four of their sons, and so on. But the fifth son married a pig and gave birth to a whole army of demons with names such as "Restlessness," "Hopelessness," and "Recklessness," which would disturb humankind forever.

Rice production is central to the culture of the Ifugao peoples of the Philippines and so features in their myths.

Aboriginal myth and the Dreamtime

Hunter-gatherers have, according to archaeologists, inhabited Australia since the Ice Age of 50,000 years ago. These peoples lived in small groups and when Western settlers arrived in the late 18th century, it was thought that there were more than 300 groups, all with their own languages.

These Aboriginal peoples lived both on the level of day-to-day existence, but also in the Dreamtime. The Dreamtime was considered to be a mystical dimension of the everyday and the beginning of creation—a time when spirits gave form to the land and stocked it with animals and plants, including everything that was to be born in the future. Dreamtime was intimately connected to the land and everything in it was infused with its own spirit. Even

Aboriginal hunters would set off along sacred trails known only to their own community.

a rock or hollow was invested with its own spirit, as was the apparently empty desert, whose features were assigned spirits known as *djang*. The most well-known and sacred *djang* location is Uluru/Ayers Rock.

Throughout Australia there is a web of mystical trails, sacred sites, and pathways, known as songlines, which connect the entire continent.

This network meant that the Dreamtime was kept alive through story-telling, dance, art, and ritual. If a group of people followed the exact rituals accorded to the sacred place or site, they would be able to directly

The Aboriginal peoples believed in the spirituality of both landscape and nature.

commune with the spirits. By reciting the myths associated with these sacred places, the people entered the Dreamtime themselves.

Marindi

Not far from the huge outcrop of rock, known originally as Uluru, but also famous as Ayers Rock, the Marindi and Adnoartina rivalry in the Dreamtime was played out. According to the Pitjandjara people of west central Australia, they hunted the same prey and constantly fought each other, but because they were equal in strength, neither ever won. One day, Adnoartina changed into a lizard and Marindi into a wild dog. They began to fight on the desert floor just beneath Uluru/Ayers Rock. All day long they fought, to no one's advantage, and Marindi suggested that they wait until dawn to continue their fight, as neither of them could see in the dark. Adnoartina laughed at Marindi and the fight continued all through the night. Finally Adnoartina's lizard jaws clamped around Marindi's neck and he was suffocated. Adnoartina dragged Marindi's body to the top of the rock and ate the carcass. As he ate, the blood ran down the whole rock, which even today glows red in the evening sun.

Rainbow Snake

An important image in Aboriginal mythology, the Rainbow Snake appeared in many different mythologies with many different names, such as Julunggul, Kunmanggur, Ungar, and Yurlunggar.

Creator

The snake emerged from a waterhole during the Dreamtime, and in some accounts it came down from the sky. But in most accounts, as it slithered across the continent, its movement created the valleys, mountains, and waterways of the sacred ancestral landscape. In some stories the snake was the creator and preserver of life, as well as water and fertility. Rainbow Snakes have been both male and female, according to tribal variations, and in most stories, if you treated the Snake with respect, it would carry on sleeping, but it was always dangerous when angered or irritated.

Julunggul

The story from the peoples of Arnhem Land in northern Australia recounts how Julunggul, as the Rainbow Snake was known to them, was basking in its waterhole in the Dreamtime. One day two sisters, Waimariwi and Boaliri, accompanied by their two sons and dogs stopped at the waterhole to rest. While Boaliri made a fire, Waimariwi went to fetch water for cooking, but a drop of her menstrual blood fell into the water. Julunggul happened to be yawning and swallowed it. Disgusted, he surged out of the waterhole to Heaven, creating an enormous tidal wave across the Earth while simultaneously swallowing the sisters, the dogs, and everything they had gathered for food. As Julunggul reached Heaven, an insect spirit bit him and he regurgitated everything back on to the Earth. He repeated this many times until, exhausted, he left all the animals, plants, and people where they fell and vanished into Heaven, leaving the world populated with plants and creatures.

In many stories, the Rainbow Snake hated the sight of blood and refused any such offerings. Instead, the worshippers danced, swayed, and sang repetitive songs to honor the snake. You can sometimes see the Rainbow Snake as a rainbow in the sky.

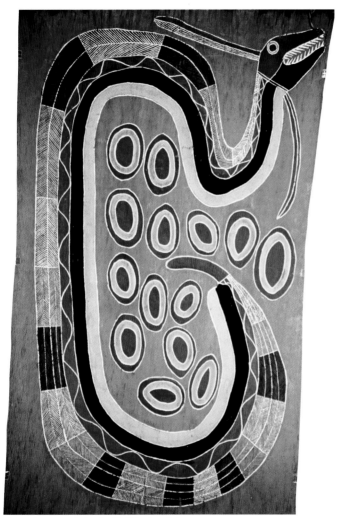

A very important image in Aboriginal mythology was the Rainbow Snake.

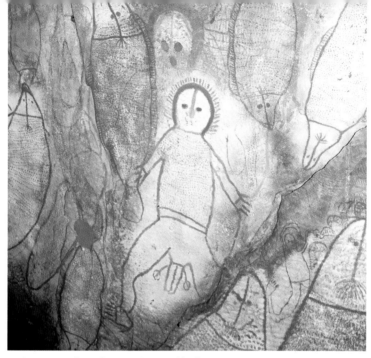

*Ancient images of Wondjina spirits, painted by the Worora
peoples up to 20,000 years ago.*

Wondjina

In the Dreamtime, the Worora and Ungarinjin peoples of northern and north-western Australia believed the Wondjina were rain spirits who helped make the Earth and everything in it. But they became sickened by how cruel human beings had become, so they decided to cause terrible floods on Earth. They opened their mouths and torrential rain poured out, destroying everything. Afterward they recreated the world and flitted around the place, basking on rocks in the form of humans and feeling pleased with what they had done. They remembered never to open their mouths again and eventually, because they had no use for them, their mouths vanished. In time, the Wondjina became formless and they went to live in waterholes and riverbeds as spirits. The Worora peoples painted images of their bodies on rocks where they used to bask in the sun. This was performed at a ceremony every year at the end of the dry season, so that the Wondjina would remember to send rain and make the earth fertile again.

Widjingara

Another myth of the Worora people recounts the first human ever to die in the Dreamtime. Widjingara protected a woman, his wife, against the Wondjina, but they took revenge and killed him. His wife began to cry, the first human being to mourn: she smeared her face with lines of mud and ashes, shaved her head, and wrapped the body in strips of bark. After three days, Widjingara returned from the dead as was expected. But Widjingara was so furious that his wife had changed her appearance that he went back to the Place of the Dead. Ever since then, mourning and death have been part of human experience.

Mudungkala

The Tiwi people of Melville Island believed that Mudungkala lived beneath the Earth in the Dreamtime. This was a dark, dank, miserable place not much better than the Overearth above. But Mudungkala was worried for her three children, who were always cold and unhappy. Even though the Overearth was a swampy sea, she knew it was time for her children to find a better place to live. So she stood up and pushed against the roof of the Underearth until it split open. Burrowing her way up with her children, she then crawled out into the muddy swamps and her belly created waterways, her shoulders the mountains, and her knees the straits between Melville Island and the mainland. She placed her children on the island and filled it with plants and creatures.

For the people of Melville Island, the straits between the island and the mainland were formed by Mudungkala.

THE AMERICAS

The spiritual diversity of the Americas ranges from the animist traditions of both North and South, the belief in spirit, and ancestor worship, to a range of god and goddess worship as practiced by the Aztecs and Incas. Most of these indigenous peoples survived throughout the age's harsh local conditions and European invasion, and it is mainly through oral tradition that their mythology and spiritual beliefs have survived.

History and background

No one is exactly sure when, but between 26,000 and 12,000 years ago, peoples from Asia crossed the Bering Strait and spread across and down the entire American continent.

From the small fishing communities of Patagonia in the south to the Inuit peoples of the Arctic Circle, the mythologies of the Americas are as diverse as the cultural and language differences. Yet there are common threads. For example, peoples from the Great Lakes to Argentina believed that the world was created from primordial mud. Lesser gods were usually the personification of the Rain, Sun, Thunder, and Lightning. The Earth was part of a triad of worlds, the other two being the home of the gods above and the home of demons and the dead below. Animals were adopted as guiding spirits or trickster gods who could work magic for the local community.

The Inuit peoples of the North American Arctic region may originally have spread from Asia.

For the codified civilizations of the Aztecs, Incas, and Mayans further south, the Sun, Moon, light, and dark were the original gods and creators. There was often an eternal conflict between warring gods, and lesser gods were worshipped to perpetuate good crops, weather, to ensure fertility, or to deal with the dead. Civilizations such as the Aztecs appeared to develop a whole ritualistic and bloodthirsty

Chichen Itza, an 11th-century CE Mayan Temple of the Warriors, and its two stone "feathered serpents."

element to their mythology, although there may be considerable influence from the retelling of the stories by later Spanish conquistadors. However sophisticated the geometrical observations and calculations of the Inca and their emphasis on the regular appearance of the Sun and Moon, they were illiterate and it was only the Maya, after retreating to the mountains, who survived the conquering Europeans' decision of what and what not to record.

In North America, from the 16th century onward, the local mythologies were also disrupted by the influence of European settlement and subsequent wars that helped disperse most of the tribal identity and the mythic lore that pervaded their natural world. It was only through story-telling that the spirituality of these communities survived.

Aztec mythology

The bloody rituals and dark cult-following of Tezcatlipoca gave the invading Spaniards a rather handy excuse for exterminating the Aztecs in the name of their own god. But the Aztecs venerated a number of other deities whose functions and attributes were much more life-enhancing.

Tezcatlipoca

In many accounts Tezcatlipoca was responsible for the evil and cruelty that were humankind's lot after he destroyed the Golden Age. Tezcatlipoca ("Smoking Mirror") was the original Aztec Sun god, but in his battle with Quetzalcoatl (see page 192), he became the god of darkness and sorcery. Before creation, he had wrestled with Coatlicue in her emanation as the primordial crocodile in his attempt to make the Earth, and when Coatlicue bit off his foot, he replaced it with a mirror of polished flint that reflected the past, present, and future. After he had been hurled from the sky, Tezcatlipoca became a jaguar on Earth and the Great Bear constellation in the sky.

He was always invisible and could gaze in all four directions of the compass points from four invisible faces simultaneously. He could appear in other forms, too: a naked man who was lusted after by young women; or a warrior with a diagonal stripe across his face and his mirror foot. Sometimes he would appear as a skeleton with a throbbing heart behind his ribs. The ribs opened and closed like a cage and, to win him to your side, you had to thrust your arm through the ribs and tear out his heart. He would then offer you great riches if you would put it back, but that was just a trick to fool you. Once a year a bloody ritual was performed at his altar, where the heart of a living man was torn out and sacrificed to appease him.

Tezcatlipoca's mirror read the future of all his worshippers and also told them his secrets. Eventually, he began to reward the good and punish the wicked, even though he had a thirst for human blood. His later trickery toward his rival and brother Quetzalcoatl meant that he was again the supreme ruler.

The original Aztec Sun god, Tezcatlipoca became associated with death, bloody rites, and prophecy.

Xochipili and Xochiquetzal

In Aztec myth, Xochipili was the god of flowers, music, and dancing, and Xochiquetzal was his female equivalent. Xochipili was a formless spirit, and was often portrayed as red and skinless, while Xochiquetzal was pure body and was often depicted as very beautiful and sensuous. While Xochipili guarded the hummingbird spirits of dead soldiers, Xochiquetzal ruled a kingdom reserved for warriors who had died in battle, or women who had died giving birth to boys who would have been soldiers.

Quetzalcoatl

There are several different stories about Quetzalcoatl, the god of the wind and spirit of life in Aztec myth. Brother to Tezcatlipoca in some accounts and twin to Xolotl in others, he was the son of Mother Earth. He was transformed into a serpent and ripped the Earth to pieces and then recreated it after the human race had died out. This began the "fifth Sun" or fifth cycle of creation. The gods had forgotten to give humans the power of reproduction in the previous cycle, so Quetzalcoatl went down to the Underworld to collect all the bones of the dead. He ground them to dust, although some accounts say that the fertility goddess Cihucoatl did it for him, and then he mixed the dust with his own blood, as well as that of Tezcatlicopa, and breathed life into the molded forms.

As a god who gave humankind protection, Quetzalcoatl taught writing, music, farming, and the measurement of time. He was permanently at war with Tezcatlipoca, who eventually tricked Quetzalcoatl into getting drunk by showing him his evil reflection in the smoking mirror. Quetzalcoatl, believing it was his own reflection, thought himself vile, lecherous, and a drunkard and, thoroughly ashamed, went into self-imposed exile. Some say that he built a fire and, dressed in his finest plumage, walked into the flames. He soared into the sky as a quetzal bird, or some say he became the Morning Star. It was believed that one day he would return.

Aztec ritual and sacrifice

Because the gods had freely given their blood to create humankind, the Aztecs believed that they were indebted to them, so humans were readily sacrificed for their blood. Still-beating hearts were cut from living bodies with sacrificial blades made of obsidian. These were then offered to the gods. Blood-letting and human sacrifice were very much part of their culture, but not all ritual sacrifice involved such gory scenes. To nourish the gods, food, smoke, and tobacco could be offered, and Quetzalcoatl was said to be particularly fond of hummingbirds and butterflies.

The conquistadors played heavily on the more barbaric rituals of Aztec belief for their own ends.

Inca mythology

The Inca belief system was based on many earlier gods who were assimiliated. Their mythology and empire grew and expanded into Ecuador, Chile, and parts of Argentina and Bolivia from 1200 CE until the mid-16th century. The creator god, Viracocha, had molded humans from stone, but it was Inti, the Sun god, who was primarily worshipped in the Temple of the Sun. He was depicted with a golden face surrounded by sunbeams.

Cusco, in Peru, was the founding city of the Inca empire and many excavations are still ongoing in this area.

The last Incan emperor, Atahuallpa, believed that the invading Spaniard Francisco Pizarro (1476–1541) was actually the returning Viracocha who had walked away across the ocean after creating the world. Unfortunately, this case of mistaken identity proved costly and the Inca empire was stripped of its treasures under the hands of the Spanish conquistadors.

Viracocha

As a creator god, Viracocha was also known as the god of the Sun, storms, and light. Creating the Earth, Moon, stars, and sky, he appeared from the depths of Lake Titicaca at the creation of the universe and then set about making humankind by breathing life into stones. But his first race of people were stupid, blundering giants, and he sent a great flood to destroy them all. For his next attempt, he decided to use pebbles and scattered these across the Earth to create the first human race. To make sure they developed knowledge and harmony, he would often disguise himself as a beggar, wandering the world teaching them how to live. In some accounts, each time he returned to the sky he was in tears, saddened by the terrible deeds of human nature. One day it is thought he will return to redeem the human race or drown us.

The Incan creator god, Viracocha, allegedly rose from the depths of Lake Titicaca, on the border of Peru and Bolivia.

Catequil

The god of thunder and lightning, Catequil's role in Inca myth seemed more aligned to that of fertility than mere weather changes. He was often thought responsible for the birth of twins because he would, like Zeus in Greek myth, enter a woman like a lightning bolt just at the moment she made love to her husband, to produce two offspring. He hurled thunderbolts from a sling without much thought about where and why (which is perhaps the origin of his lightning-bolt conception story) and banged at the wind and rain with his mighty clubs to produce thunder.

Chantico

The Inca people believed that Chantico, who was the goddess of the Earth's minerals and precious stones, was made of pure gold. She later became known as the goddess of the hearth and home. However, in her earlier role she was fickle and untrustworthy. Those people who sought out the treasures of the Earth would often face death (in the form of her serpent-tongue of fire or the poisonous cactus around her crown) rather than wealth.

Mayan mythology

Popul Vuh, the sacred texts of the Quiche Maya people of Guatemala, were transcribed in the 16th century and retell the story of creation and Mayan history. *Popul Vuh* (*The Collection of Written Leaves*) begins with the creation of the Earth, followed by several mismanaged attempts to create humankind.

Gucamatz, the sea creator god, and his counterpart Hurakan, Heart of Heaven, created a wide range of humans, but none could speak the names of the gods and simply jabbered, growled, or squeaked, so they became the animal kingdom. At the second attempt the race was made of clay and dissolved in water, so Hurakan tried again. This time he used white and yellow corn, which he crushed into a paste. This made the first four real people, but they were too clever and Hurakan was worried they wouldn't worship the gods. So he breathed a sleeping mist over them, which clouded their judgment and made them less understanding, and when they awoke they found four women who became their wives. From these four couples, the Quiche were descended, as well as all other Central American peoples. After many generations were born, the four couples stood on top of the mountain and watched the sunrise, which turned all the terrible monsters and demons to stone.

Itzamna and Ixchel

In Mayan myth, Ixchel was the goddess of storms and floods. Her name meant "rainbow lady." As Itzamna's wife, she wasn't quite so generous in bestowing her favors as he was. Her palace was filled with huge vats and jars of water, and unless she was constantly pacified, she would pour them down on the world below, causing rain storms and terrible floods. Itzamna, on the other hand, was virtuous—son of the Sun and god of healing, he taught his worshippers how to restore the land with irrigation channels to catch the rain that Ixchel sent down. He also helped women in childbirth, invented the arts to stop humans from getting bored, and revealed the medicinal powers of various herbs

In Honduras, the ruins of Copan are covered with hieroglyphs that reveal a vast Mayan mythology.

and plants. Because he spent so much time looking after the human race, Itzamna became rather shabby, dressed in rags, and lost his teeth. The only red-hot influence he had inherited from his father, the Sun, was his hand that glowed with the heat of his healing power.

Ixtab

Female deities were few in Mayan and Aztec mythology, probably because what was left of their cults by the time the Spanish invaders arrived was quickly destroyed, as were whole civilizations. However, one charming goddess was Ixtab, the goddess of suicide, often depicted with a black ring on her cheek, symbolizing decomposition. The Maya believed that suicide was an honorable way to die and that suicide victims went to paradise and not to the Underworld. Ixtab would drop out of the noose from which she permanently hung in the sky, and she would be welcomed by the relatives of the suicide victims as she claimed their souls.

Other South American deities

Most South American mythology tales are of creator gods, the balance of light and dark, and how the cultivation of plants came about through gods or ancestors. Many people believed they were descended from these gods and that animals and plants were imbued with "spirit."

Ellal

Far south in the vast steppe-like plains of Patagonia, the Tehaelche people believed that Ellal was the first patron of humankind. His father intended to eat Ellal as soon as he was born, but Rat hid him in her burrow in the ground until he was a grown man. This was a time when demons ruled the world and humans ran to the mountains in terror, leaving the remote plains to the evil beings. Ellal decided to kill the leader of the demons. He was swallowed alive, but turned into a gadfly, stinging the demon king in the stomach and poisoning him to death. With the leader gone, Ellal returned to the world and turned trees and reeds into bows and arrows. He gave these to the humans so that they could now destroy all the other demons, and then he flew back up to the sky on a swan that glided effortlessly along the beams of the morning Sun.

Ariconte and Tamendonare

Many modern mythographers have highlighted this story and given it a psychological interpretation. The brothers Ariconte and Tamendonare represent opposing forces in an individual's nature, yet neither can exist without the other.

According to the Tupinamba people of Brazil, Ariconte and Tamendonare were twins, with a mortal mother but with two fathers, one divine and one mortal. After their mother was eaten by cannibals, the twins tracked them to an island in the middle of the river and changed the flow of the river course that engulfed the island. But the cannibals turned into panthers and escaped into the jungle. The twins wanted to find out who their fathers were. They wandered for some time through the jungle until they came to a remote village whose only occupant was a wise old man. They asked him if he knew, but the old man told they would have to perform many tests to prove they had supernatural powers before he would tell them.

Many trials

They leapt between a magic boulder, the Itha-Irapi, which crushed together like the jaws of a crocodile. One twin escaped, the other was crushed to death, but was revived by his brother when he breathed new life into him. They stole bait from the demon Agnen, who fished for food to give to the dead in the Underworld. But one twin was torn to shreds by the demon and the other twin had to piece him together again and bring him back to life. Over and over again each twin would die and then be reborn with the help of his brother.

Eventually, the sorcerer was convinced of who they were and told them he was their divine father, Maira Ata, but he couldn't work out which twin was mortal and which immortal, so they spent the rest of eternity never daring to kill each other.

For the Tehaelche peoples of southern Patagonia, the steppes were ruled by evil demons.

The conflict between light and dark, Sun and Moon, was a key myth for the Mamaiuran people of Brazil.

Kuat and Iae

Another set of twins, but with a different twist, were Kuat and Iae who lived in the eternal darkness of the primeval universe before the world was created. According to the Mamaiuran people of Brazil, Urubutsin the vulture king kept all light to himself, fearing that humans would overthrow his dark kingdom. Kuat and Iae thought of a way to trick the vulture king and sent him a rotting carcass full of maggots. Urbutsin adored maggots and greedily ate them all, asking for more. But this time Kuat and Iae hid inside the carcass and, as Urbutsin soared to pick out the juiciest maggots, Kuat and Iae leapt out and threw a black net over him. They refused to release him until Urbutsin gave them the light. Urbutsin struggled until his head feathers were tattered, his morale low and his belly aching for food, then agreed to give them half the light if they would release him.

As Urbutsin fled, he tossed his store box of light to the brothers, who quickly threw it into the sky. Kuat chose the largest piece of light for his home, which he called the Sun, and Iae chose the smaller piece, which he called the Moon. Between them their power keeps Urbutsin's eternal darkness away for at least half the day. But when the brothers grow tired of watching over the Earth, the darkness begins to nibble chunks out of the light box at the beginning and end of each day. To stop the vulture king stealing the light, the twins wake up quickly and light returns to replace the darkness.

Paraparawa

According to the Trio people of Brazil and Surinam, Paraparawa lived at a time when humankind only ate fish or meat and hadn't learned how to cultivate plants. On one of his fishing trips, Paraparawa caught a waraku fish and was just about to cut off its head when it transformed into a beautiful woman. Paraparawa fell in love with her and asked her to marry him. For the marriage feast the young woman called out to her father to bring some food, and he surged out of the depths of the river in the form of an anaconda, bringing yams, yuccas, sweet potatoes, and bananas. Paraparawa was just about to tuck in when his new bride told him to plant them in the ground instead. As soon as he did so, each fruit or vegetable multiplied a thousand-fold to provide enough food for all the village. At the end of the feast, Paraparawa planted the leftovers and they miraculously sprang up again, as they had the first time. This was how farming and the cultivation of plants was discovered.

Knowledge of the cultivation of bananas is said to be due to one of the Trio people's ancestors, Paraparawa.

North American mythology

The mythologies of North America encompass the Inuit of the Arctic north down to the Navajo in the deserts of the southern United States, and the vast expanse and diversity of cultures between the two coasts.

Sedna

There are many different versions of Sedna, who appears across the Arctic Circle from Greenland to western Canada. The Inuit people of North America consider her to be the mistress of the sea beasts and depend on her good will for a supply of animals to hunt. Some Inuit sources say that she was thrown from her kayak by her father because she was unwanted and unloved. Others say that she deserved to be punished because she was greedy and ate everything in her parents' home.

Her father was the creator god Anguta and she gnawed off one of his arms while he slept. Other stories suggest that Anguta was so angry at her for marrying a dog (or a sea bird), after she had refused to marry his chosen suitor, he decided to kill her. As she clung to the side of the canoe, her father chopped off her fingers until she sank to the depths of the sea. Her fingers became the seals, sea lions, and whales, and she lives there still as a sea spirit and queen of all that inhabit the ocean. When food

Worshipped by Inuit hunters, Sedna was the goddess of all sea creatures.

becomes scarce, a shaman dives down to her underwater home to brush her hair, which gets tangled because she can't unravel it without fingers. Happy again, she drives the seals and whales toward the hunting peoples.

Coyote

For many peoples of the western United States, Coyote was originally a primordial god whose power was reduced when he developed trickster powers. For some he symbolized fire, and for others he was essentially a shape-shifter who preferred the role of Coyote.

Coyote was both a creator god and a trickster. To many indigenous tribal people, the coyote was a sacred animal.

The Maidu people of California told how Coyote was fed up with the perfect world that Earthmaker had created, and introduced suffering to make it more interesting. They also believed he had a shape-changing serpent called Rattlesnake, who took the form of a small dog and whose bite brought death to the human race. The north-western Nez Perce people believe Coyote created their nation from the body of the huge beaver monster Wishpoosh. In Paiute myth he is joint Earth creator with Wolf, while in Mandan myth the Original Creator transforms into Coyote once his work is finished. There are many folk stories about Coyote, based on his ability to wriggle out of corners and the way he tricks and teases humans beings.

Many peoples believed he was a messenger between the real world and the supernatural one. The Sioux said that Coyote made himself a wind horse between the two worlds and then changed dogs into horses so that the people could "ride like the wind" itself. Coyote's good qualities included his morality-lesson fables, but he was also impulsive, unreliable, and the antagonistic brother of the wiser Wolf.

Wakan Tanka

Often referred to as an all-seeing deity, Wakan Tanka means "great mystery." Among the Omaha people, Wakan Tanka is viewed as an unseen mysterious force which pervades everything, rather than as a separate god.

For the Dakota people of the Great Plains, Wakan Tanka existed all alone in the primordial nothingness before creation. Because he was lonely he started to divide himself up. First he channeled his energy into a single force, Rock. From this he made Earth and mated with her to produce Sky. Sky then mated with Rock and Earth to make the Sun. These four High Ones then made four Companions to help them create and people the universe. There were then four Related Ones, followed by four God-like Ones. All sixteen were aspects of Wakan Tanka, who is all of these simultaneously, and they control the universe. All that exists is part of this single organic whole.

Changing Woman

In the southwestern United States, the Navajo people believe Changing Woman is the most important goddess. Talking God brought her to life from a turquoise shape that he found on top of a mountain, and she became the daughter of Long Life Boy and Happiness Girl. She was then looked after by First Man and First Woman. She was given a palace with turquoise doors, clothes, and mirrors. Changing Woman represents the changing cycles of life. She grows old and then young, and like the seasons she alters all the time, rejuvenating herself before growing old again. She can change her age just by walking across the horizon. As she grows old, though, she gets lonely and this is why she created the Navajo peoples from the skin that rubbed off her body when she bathed. She is also known as White Shell Woman and Turquoise Woman: it is believed that as the seasons change, so does the color of her dress.

The Navajo peoples believed they were transformed from a piece of turquoise and given life.

For the Pacific Northwest peoples, the first woman mated with a crab in her lonely tepee on the beach.

Copper Woman

Another lonely soul was Copper Woman in the myth of the Pacific Northwest coastal peoples. The world was as it is today, but there were no human beings. Copper Woman lived by the sea and spent all her time catching fish, spearing seals, and hunting crabs. One day she felt so lonely that she started to cry, and the spirits told her to save her tears because it was a sign that she was human. She put her tears in a crab shell and the next morning discovered it had changed into a strange, wriggling creature with a grain of sand trapped inside it. The watery creature grew every day until it turned into a half-human, half-crab creature. It had pincers for arms, eyes on stalks, and a man's penis and chest hair. The creature never spoke, but played with the other sea creatures by day, and every night visited Copper Woman in her beachside hut to make love to her so that she was never lonely again.

Sky Holder

A creator figure with an evil twin brother Flint, Sky Holder later merged with the cultural hero Hawenniyo in the myth of the Iroquois peoples of northeastern North America.

The twins were born to the daughter of Old Woman who fell from the sky. She was made pregnant by the wind and some sources say that the wind lay two arrows beside her, one plain and the other tipped with flint. Sky Holder created and made life easier for humankind, while Flint tried to undo everything Sky Holder had done. Sky Holder tried to restore order. Once Sky Holder made rivers flow in both directions so that you could paddle a canoe either way, but Flint made them flow only toward the sea. Flint made the first mosquito so big that with one bite it could gobble a horse. Sky Holder made it small again so that it was less dangerous to humankind. Flint put poison in the mosquito's bite just to irritate people.

Tirawa

The Pawnee people of the Great Plains believed that Tirawa (Arch of Heaven) created a bowl that floated in space and this was the world. The Moon and Sun mated to create a son, and the Evening Star and Morning Star mated to create a daughter, the ancestors of humankind. Tirawa sent Lightning to check on the perfection of the finished world. Lightning carried thousands of tiny stars in his knapsack, which he hung one by one in the sky to light his way. But Wolf grabbed the bag and turned it upside down so that all the stars fell out, leaving a trail across the sky: the Milky Way. Fragments of stardust and light fell onto Earth, and they turned into storms, evil demons, and death. Tirawa decided that Earth wasn't paradise after all, and he never went there again, only sending messengers to teach humans about farming and civilization as compensation for their mortality.

Corn Woman

Corn Woman appears in many myths, and her role was to provide the first corn to humankind. In most stories the corn is produced from her blood, nail clippings, or even the lice on her head. In the stories of the Creek people of the

The worship of Corn Woman ensured successful crops and harvests for the Creek peoples of the southeastern U.S.

southeastern United States, Corn Woman lived alongside other men and women before they knew anything about farming. She lived with a big family and produced wonderful meals made of corn every day. Curious to find out where the corn came from, one of the family spied on her when she was in the kitchen and saw her scraping the boils and scabs off her body, then placing the putrid flesh into a pot. They were so disgusted that they refused to eat anything that she cooked, and in her dismay she told them to sow the scrapings in the ground, harvest the corn, and then remove the husk to take out all impurities. This was how mortals learned how to farm. Several myths tell how Corn Woman was also sacrificed and buried in the ground, resulting in new corn each spring.

Kayaks have always been a feature of Inuit life, and the hero Qayaq got his name because he used it for hunting.

Wishpoosh

The Nez Perce people believed that Wishpoosh was a monster beaver who ruled the primeval lake, but he never let any other creature go there. One day, Coyote the trickster decided to go fishing in the lake and Wishpoosh leapt upon him. They struggled for some time and, as they wrestled and fought, they created mountains, gorges, and canyons. Wishpoosh was losing all his strength, so he dove into the lake to gulp as many fish as he could. Coyote floated on the sea as a tree branch to take a rest and, when Wishpoosh realized this, he surged toward the branch and gobbled it up. Now inside Wishpoosh, Coyote turned into a pine needle and stabbed Wishpoosh in the heart. He took Wishpoosh's carcass to the shore and cut it into a thousand pieces to make the first humans.

Qayaq

An important trickster for the Alaskan Inuit peoples of the far north is the cultural hero Qayaq. The son of the Woodman, he was often called "Wander-Hawk," but he was also known as Qayaq because he loved to go hunting in his canoe. All his brothers had been killed while out hunting, so the Woodman made Qayaq magical amulets to protect him from danger. As he grew older, the Woodman tested Qayaq's powers. When he first began to walk, the Woodman tried to trip him, but Qayaq jumped over the trap; the Woodman threw a knife at him, but Qayaq dodged it. Qayaq grew up to be a great hunter and vowed to avenge his brothers' deaths.

Throughout his travels Qayaq met many animals who pretended to be people. He even married a night owl, a beautiful girl who gave birth to a son. Once Qayaq knew the child was destined to be a hunter like himself, he left the night owl in the care of his son. On his travels, he overcame many enemies with his magic amulets and even killed the monsters in the mountains who had eaten his brothers. Qayaq turned himself into a maggot, a fish, and a fox. Sometimes he was caught, but he always changed shape or came alive again thanks to the amulets.

When he returned home, the Woodman and his wife were long since dead, and in despair Qayaq turned himself into a wander-hawk and sat on a tree and cried. Then, spreading his wings, he flew off—never to be seen again.

Some Navajo women still rub spiders' gossamer on their arms to improve their weaving techniques.

Thinking Woman

Among the southwestern Pueblo peoples of North America, the Keres believed that a female creator was at work. Thinking Woman was, in fact, a spider called Sus'sistinako and was said to have created the universe by sending her thoughts out into nothing and weaving the universe with her mind. Similarly, the Hopi thought that Spider Woman made the Moon out of cotton and the first people out of clay, while the Navajo people believed Spider Woman wove a rope ladder to enable the first people to climb into the world. The Navajo also believe that it is unlucky to kill spiders, and Navajo women often rub spiders' gossamer on their arms to make them better weavers.

Thinking Woman first thought the Earth into being. Then she placed Iatiku, the Corn Mother, on the Earth to make all the essential things that were needed—plants, people, and the clown Koshare to make people laugh.

Double-aspect Corn Mother

Iatiku was a double-aspect Corn Mother, both mother of the Underworld and mother of the Upperworld, bringing life, but also taking it away. Her first child was also called Iatiku and her second daughter wasn't given a name. The two girls went first to the Upperworld and decided it needed light, so they created it. They sang a creation song and made the Sun from red sandstone, and then climbed a mountain in the east and hung the Sun in the sky. Their mother had given them baskets filled with colors and seeds and they scattered them all over the Earth and things came alive. The Moon was first, then they made sets of stars and wanted to hang them in circular groups, but someone knocked over one of the baskets and scattered the stars all over the sky.

Iatiku thought her sister had more in her basket than she did, so she called her Nautsiti, which meant "more of everything in the basket." They then held a contest to see who should be more important in the world. Iatiku won because Thinking Woman sat on her shoulder and whispered to her how to win. Iatiku became the mother of all the First Nation peoples and Nautsiti went far away to become the mother of all the white peoples.

Pueblo peoples have had settlements in the southwestern United States for more than one thousand years.

Part 2

THEMES IN
MYTHOLOGY

CREATION
AND COSMOS

Most creation myths focus on the creator god, shaped from himself or arising out of the waters of the primordial ocean or chaos. Usually creation myths are concerned with how humankind and the universe came into being, and for many cultures the "why" does not enter into the myth, perhaps because myth-tellers assumed that creation did not need to be questioned.

This vast range of creation myths demonstrates how our common, collective spiritual quest has many guises. They are often poignant in their simplicity, even though they may understandably be stark in content.

Eurynome

This version of a Greek creation myth is from the ancient cult of the Mother Goddess, which appeared on the Greek peninsula around 3500 BCE when the Pelasgians arrived from Asia Minor. The main theme of Chaos as the beginning of all things is repeated here, as in many other Near Eastern myths, with the essential difference that Chaos was a goddess.

All was chaos in the beginning. The wild emptiness tossed and turned eternally, rolling into spiralling waves that formed a wide, wandering dance of energy. This was Eurynome, who, finding she could neither stop at any moment nor place her feet down to dance, divided chaos into the sea and sky.

As she danced across the lashing waves of the sea, she caused a wind to blow up behind her. The north wind seemed separate from herself, and she thought she could use it to begin her masterpiece of creation. She clutched the north wind between her hands and danced madly with it until it changed into the giant, fertile serpent Ophion. The wilder her dance, the more excited Ophion grew, until he could not resist his lust for her any longer. Once they had mated, Eurynome changed into a dove so that she could lay the first egg on the ocean. Ophion coiled around the egg seven times to incubate it. As the egg hatched, out fell all things that exist—the Earth, the stars, the Moon, and everything that lives.

Eurynome and Ophion ruled Olympus, but Ophion quarreled endlessly with her, claiming that it was he who had created the universe. She fought with him, then banished him to the Underworld, where he swore to be her enemy for eternity. Next, Eurynome created the Titans to rule the seven planets, and finally the first man Pelasgus, the founding ancestor of the Pelasgian people, who taught humans how to live civilized lives. In some accounts she sowed Ophion's teeth in the earth and they sprouted to become Pelasgus and his race of people. Ophion was also later identified with Typhon, the monster who challenged Zeus.

*Eurynome danced the sky and ocean into being, then
mated with Ophion to create the world and everything in it.*

217

Bomong and Bong

The Minyong people of northeastern India were untouched
by the Aryan Vedic mythology and its later resulting
Hinduism. This ancient myth, dating from 2000 BCE, tells
of the overthrow of the originators of the universe by their
offspring and the subsequent need to restore the balance
between light and dark.

First there was only darkness and Sedi the Earth and Melo the Sky. Sedi and
Melo mated and created the first people called the Wiyus, but they were
cramped and crushed between the Earth and Sky, so one of the largest Wiyus
called Sedi-Diyor grabbed his father, the Sky, and kicked him until he fled to
the Heavens.

The birth

Sedi had given birth to two daughters, but because Melo had left her, she could
not bear to look at them. So Sedi-Diyor found them a nurse. By the time they
could walk they shone like stars. They lit up the world with light, but then
died of grief for the death of their old nurse, and the light that had shone from
them died too. All was in darkness again. So the Wiyus were afraid and
wondered if the old nurse had stolen the light from the children. They dug
up her body, but only her eyes were left in the rotted corpse and, as the Wiyus
gazed into her eyes, they saw their own reflections and thought these were the
children. A carpenter was brought to cut open the eyes and remove the
reflections, which then turned into real children.

They called one Bomong and the other Bong. But these children shone so
fiercely that there was too much light and too much heat—the trees began to
wither, the rocks to crumble, and the rivers began to dry up. The heat was
intense and there was never any darkness. The Wiyus agreed that they must
destroy one of the children of light so that the world would have times of rain
and darkness, too.

*The Minyong people of northeast India retained their own
ancient beliefs and mythology.*

Frog

Frog had the terrible task of killing Bong. As she walked past Frog, drying him up in her radiant heat, he shot an arrow into her eyes and she died. Bomong was so scared that she would be killed too that she ran to the forest and placed a huge stone over her head, and the world became dark. Now the Wiyus realized they needed light to keep them alive, so they sent a cockerel and a rat to ask Bomong to come back. But she said, "How can I? You killed my sister; I'll only return if you bring my sister back to life."

The cockerel told the Wiyus, who made a wooden body and the carpenter breathed life into it. When Bomong heard her sister was alive, she took the great stone from her head and light radiated from her once again. But because Bong had been made of wood, her light was gone, and there was balance in the world.

*The heroic Frog nearly shriveled up
in Bong's heat as he killed her with
an arrow.*

Parusha

This myth comes from the Rig Vedas, the earliest sacred books of the pre-Hindu deities, which date from about 2000–1000 BCE. Parusha, primal being, is dismembered and given up to create different principals of the material world. His story is similar to Ymir's (see page 228) in that the essence of the world was created from the greatest kind of sacrifice—self-sacrifice.

In the primordial ocean there floated a golden egg. This egg had floated for 1,576,800,000,000 mortal years in the great churning sea of chaos. Alone inside the golden egg was Parusha, who had had enough of being alone. As the fire heated the dark waters and the ocean churned, the egg cracked open.

Parusha was the universe manifest and he arose from the egg with a thousand heads, a thousand hands, and a thousand eyes. He was lonely, so he divided himself in two. A quarter of him made Earth and Viraj (female universal power); the rest were the gods and the universe. Parusha then dismembered his remaining parts to bring about the rest of creation. His mouth became Brahman, the power of the universe; his eye became the Sun; his mind became the Moon. Nothing was wasted: he became everything and is everything. If he ever changes his mind and creates himself whole again, the universe will end.

Prajapati

Another Vedic god Prajapati is also described as the universal creator. He survived right through to the Hindu period when he merged with Brahma. In some accounts he made the first gods by meditation and fasting. One of his initial creations was his daughter Ushas, the dawn. But he lusted after her, which so terrified her that she turned into a deer. He simply changed himself into a stag and his semen fell all over the Earth and created the first people. In another account, Prajapati made himself out of the primordial sea and cried at the sight of his emptiness. His teardrops made continents and then he unpeeled his body, layer by layer like an onion, and created everything else out of it.

Parusha, in his boredom, cracked open the golden egg that floated on the primordial ocean and became all that is.

African creation myths

In Africa, creation myths vary as widely as the rest of their beliefs. For example, for the Ijaw people of Nigeria, a woman is the initiator of creation, just like Thinking Woman and Eurynome (see pages 210 and 216), while for the Bantu people of the River Congo region, the creator god Bumba dwelt in the primordial waters and vomited up the world.

Woyengi

This myth of the Ijaw peoples of Nigeria was recorded around 1700 CE, but probably dates from around 2700 BCE. In the vast eternity of nothingness, something sparked and time was created. In that split second Heaven and Earth were formed and a lightning storm sent down to Earth the creator woman Woyengi. There was nothing on the Earth—no life, no wind, no movement, nothing. But there was a chair, a huge table, and a flat stone called the Stone of Creation. Woyengi gathered mud in handfuls and sat on the chair because she didn't know what else to do, then put the mud on the table and her feet up on the stone. With the mud she molded and shaped many dolls. After each one was modeled, she placed it on the Stone of Creation between her feet and blew her breath across the doll's face. She asked, "Would you like to be male or female?" Whatever the doll answered, she gave them the right reproductive organs.

The many dolls were placed in rows on the table and then asked what work they would like to do in the world. One by one the dolls chose their task. Woyengi set them down and pointed to two streams that led away from the stone and said, "Now you must follow the right stream and it will carry you to where you must be in the world." Those who had chosen a life of importance or power had to go down the stream filled with rapids, rocks, and dangerous currents. Those who had chosen an easy life had to follow the second stream: clear and calm, but with dangerous quicksand in the shallows. Handfuls and handfuls of dolls stepped into their stream and the waters carried them to where they would fill the world with the first peoples and the lives they had chosen for themselves.

*Creator gods like Bumba were responsible for making
storms, lightning, thunder, and all the elements.*

Bumba

This brief version of Bumba's story is from the Bantu people of the River Congo
region, whose oral history dates back to the 5th century CE.

Bumba was all alone in the dark waters of nothingness. He wanted some
company, but with no light, he couldn't look for it. One day he felt a pain in
his belly and vomited the Sun. Suddenly there was light everywhere. Bumba
then vomited up the stars and the Moon, so the night had soft flickering lights,
too. The next day he vomited nine different creatures including the tortoise,
leopard, eagle, crocodile, beetle, and a fish called Yo. He also created lightning
and then finally vomited men. The creatures recreated themselves and made
other animals, too. Yo created all the fish in the sea, the beetle created every
insect, the crocodile all the animals with cold skin.

Bumba was worried about the lightning. The lightning was a trouble-maker
and he had to chase her back into the sky, although she still found chances to
visit the Earth when he wasn't expecting her. Now that creation was finished,
Bumba disguised himself as a man and traveled around all the villages telling
people how he had created everything in the world except himself.

Ameta and Hainuwele

For the people of West Ceram in Indonesia, creation began with a bunch of wild bananas, which could only be found on Mount Nunusaka. From these bananas were created the Nine Families of humankind, who went to live in the jungle at a place called Nine Dance Grounds.

Ameta planted the first coconut and its leaf became Hainuwele, a major goddess worshipped across Indonesia.

Among these nine families was a man called Ameta. One day Ameta and his dog hunted a wild pig that leapt into a pond and drowned. When Ameta pulled out the pig's corpse, there was a coconut on the end of the pig's tusk, even though there were no coconut palms yet in the world.

Ameta took the coconut home and that night in his dream a man told him to plant the nut in the ground. In three days the tree was as tall as his hut and covered in blossom. As he climbed the tree to cut the flowers, Ameta slipped and gashed his hand on his knife. The blood dripped on one of the leaves below, and a few days later, the leaf changed into a girl. That night the man in his dreams told him to wrap the child in his snake cloth and take her home.

Hainuwele

When Ameta took her back to his hut, he called her Hainuwele ("frond of the coconut palm") and within days she turned into a beautiful young woman. But oddly, whenever she defecated, she produced the most beautiful objects and valuable stones. This made Ameta very wealthy.

At the great Maro dance, Hainuwele was meant to give out betel nuts to the dancers, but instead she gave away coral beads, bush knives, boxes made of gold, and copper gongs. Every night the value of the goods increased, so that people became very jealous of her power and decided to kill her.

Hainuwele's death

At the last night of the Maro dance, some men dug a deep hole and pushed her into the pit. They covered her quickly with earth and trampled it down with their feet. Ameta found her body using his divining rods and dug up her corpse and cut it up into many pieces, then buried them around the dancing ground. All the pieces of Hainuwele grew into many different kinds of plants, and the future source of food for the people.

Ameta gave Satene, the great goddess of West Ceram, Hainuwele's arms. Satene had been created from an unripe banana and was angered at the killing of her sister goddess and vowed that she would leave the Earth. She built a gate and, as she stood in the gateway, she spoke sternly to the people: "You have killed and done wrong. Only those of you who can reach me before I go will remain as people, the rest will be turned to animals and spirits." Those who were strongest pushed past and Satene struck each one with Hainuwele's arm. Some had to jump over five bamboo sticks, others nine. This was the beginning of the first two tribes known as the Fivers and Niners. Satene went to live on the Mountain of the Dead across nine mountain ranges and no one could reach her again.

Nyambi and Kamonu

The Barotse people of the Upper Zambesi in Zambia have a very kindly creator god, who had no choice but to escape from his evil copycat neighbor Kamonu. According to the myth, only when Nyambi returns to the Earth will peace be restored.

Nyambi had created everything in the universe and lived peacefully on Earth with his wife Nasilele. But one of Nyambi's creations was different. He was called Kamonu and he mimicked Nyambi all day long. He was not at all peaceful, so he was sent away to another land, but he simply came back to irritate Nyambi. So Nyambi reluctantly decided to leave the now less-peaceful land he had created and he and Nasilele sailed away to an island in the middle of a lake. But Kamonu made a raft and followed them. Nyambi made a huge mountain and lived on the summit, but Kamonu climbed to the top. In desperation Nyambi asked the Sorcerer how to escape the terrible Kamonu. The magician told him that he must ask Spider to spin silken threads up to the sky, but once they arrived in the sky,

The kindly creator god Nyambi simply wants peace to be restored to the world he made.

he must blind Spider so that she could never find her way back. So Nyambi and Nasilele climbed up the dew-laden web after the spider, and with tears in his eyes Nyambi blinded her with his spear, the only cruel thing he had ever done since creation.

Kamuno built a huge tower to try to reach the sky, but it only got higher and higher and then collapsed. He never found his way to the sky. Every day when the Sun rose, he thought it was Nyambi so he worshipped the Sun, and every full Moon he would worship the Moon, thinking it was Nasilele. And when all the other people saw Kamuno doing this, they copied him and worshipped the Sun and Moon, too.

P'an Ku and the Cosmic Egg

There are many versions of this myth, but they all center around the Cosmic Egg, a symbol of fertility and the coming together of chaos and matter. This was a highly popular myth in southern China from the 3rd to 6th centuries CE. In one version, P'an Ku arose out of "nothing" as a child of chaos.

To begin with, there was nothing. But as time passed, nothing became something and these forces became the Cosmic Egg. Inside the egg was chaos, and P'an Ku floated inside chaos for 18,000 years. Eventually he split the shell and burst out of the egg. He carried a hammer and chisel and two horns grew from his head, a symbol of supernatural power in China. He was covered in thick black hair and two great tusks grew from his jaw. It took another 18,000 years for P'an Ku to chisel apart the Earth and the sky.

In one version, when he cried, his tears became the great Yellow River in China. In another, the sky was shaped from his skull, the fields from his flesh, the rocks from his bones and the thunder from his voice. Yet another story suggests that P'an Ku formed the five sacred mountains of China from different parts of his body.

The lice and fleas that lived in P'an Ku's hair and body, scattered over the Earth by the winds, became humankind.

227

Ymir

This Norse creation myth has much in common with that of the Indian god Parusha (see page 220), in that both Ymir and Parusha were dismembered in order for the world to be created. Many scholars believe these stories originally came from one source.

In the beginning was an abyss called Ginnungagap, filled with frothing, boiling air and liquid, which ran between the endless realms of ice and fire. Long before the world was created there was the universal tree Yggdrasil (see page 134). This ash tree linked the nine other worlds. Under its roots to the south was a hot kingdom of Muspel; to the north Niflheim, a land of ice and darkness. Beneath another root was Hvergelmir, a cauldron of bubbling waters that was the source of twelve huge rivers.

All the water that flowed from Hvergelmir fell into the abyss and became huge glaciers and blocks of ice. When the warm air from the south rose to meet the icy mists, the glaciers melted and spread further and further until they engulfed the flames of the fire kingdom Muspel and then turned to water.

Creation

From the mists a being emerged into creation whose name was Ymir, which means "two-in-one." The primeval cow Audhumla licked the cliffs of ice for nourishment. As she licked, her warm tongue melted two frozen gods who had been trapped in the icy walls. These were Buri and Bor. Unknowingly, while Audhumla licked the ice, Ymir drank from her udders and grew into a terrible frost giant. Ymir created life spontaneously and while he slept he produced more frost giants from the sweat under his arms. These frost giants began to mate with each other, creating a terrible race of giants.

Odin, Vili, and Ve, the three sons of Buri, set out to destroy Ymir. While he slept, the gods attacked him and blood flowed from his wounds like a torrent of icy water. In this great river of blood all the other giants drowned, except

The citadel of Asgard was home to the Æsir, the major Norse gods.

for one couple who escaped. The three brothers threw Ymir's corpse into the icy ocean of Ginnungagap, where it broke apart and made the world. The brothers mixed some of his blood into the swirling ocean and called this creation Midgard. They then built Asgard, which they surrounded with a fortress made from Ymir's eyebrows.

229

Izanami and Izanagi

This Japanese story is based on original Chinese cosmology, which assumed an initial chaos. Izanami means "she who invites," and Izanagi "he who invites." Izanami became a feared goddess of death and Izanagi was believed to be the ancestor of the imperial dynasty.

At first all was chaos. But as this moved and merged, it became like a great porridge in some places and thin brine in others. What was pure and light floated up to become Heaven, and what was heavy and thick settled down to make the bulk of Earth, a semolina-like mass. Heaven and Earth then created eight deities on a reed shoot that grew between them. The twin deities Izanami and Izanagi were invited to be the creators of the world by the great reed shoot, which itself had been transformed into a god.

On the Floating Bridge of Heaven, high above the primordial ocean, Izanagi dipped his jeweled spear into the nothingness and stirred the waters. As he pulled it out, drops fell into the air and created an island. Izanami and Izanagi lived on this island. Their first creation was an ugly blood-sucking leech child and it was so horrible they put it in a boat and left it to drift round the ocean

In Shinto belief, the "Wedded Rocks" off Futami, Japan, represent the union of creator deities Izanami and Izanagi.

230

From the Floating Bridge of Heaven, Izanagi stirred the primeval waters with his jeweled spear.

forever. Their next creations were more successful: the seasons, the eight islands of Japan, trees, animals, and all living things. Next they decided to create a ruler. This was the Sun goddess, who was so beautiful they thought she was too good to stay on Earth and placed her in the sky. The next child was the Moon god and they sent him to the sky to join his sister. But their last creation was the fire spirit, and Izanami died giving birth to him and descended to Yomi, the Underworld.

Izanagi went down to the entrance of Yomi to beg her to return, but Izanami warned him neither to look at her nor speak to her until she had made a deal with the Underworld spirits so that she could leave. But Izanagi was impatient and, with a magic comb, he lit up the Underworld and saw Izanami's rotting corpse. And because Izanagi had brought light into the darkness, Izanami was forevermore the goddess of death. She chased him out of Yomi, vowing to devour a thousand people every day for what he had done.

Marduk and Tiamat

Marduk was the supreme god during the first Babylonian dynasty c. 2057–1758 BCE. The Mesopotamian text on which his story is based was probably a piece of propaganda to uphold his power as chief deity and the status of Babylon itself.

This myth was re-enacted as a new-year ritual, and although the major source was found among the ruins of King Ashurbanipal's library, which dates from 650 CE, fragments of earlier texts suggest the story is based on more ancient beliefs that gods created humans to be their slaves.

In the beginning

Apsu the ocean and Tiamat the primeval waters produced many offspring at the beginning of time when all was chaos. But the younger gods, including Ea, Marduk's father, rebelled and killed Apsu. Tiamat married the monster Kingu, who sent his race of demons and monsters to take revenge on the young gods. Marduk offered to be the gods' champion and to slay Tiamat and Kingu if he was given the role of supreme god. Armed with a bow, the force of lightning, and a net held up by the four winds, Marduk rode on a hurricane to do battle with Tiamat.

Marduk found Tiamat and as she opened her mouth to gobble him up, he hurled the four winds down her throat, then fired arrows into her

The gods built Babylon for Marduk, who became a popular Sun god.

To reinforce her evil associations, Tiamat was usually depicted as a dragon.

distended belly before she could belch them back up. One arrow pierced her heart and she died instantly, letting out one great belch that sent Marduk hurtling backward.

Stealing the Tablets of Destiny from Kingu to make sure he would be the most powerful of all beings, Marduk set about creating the universe. He sliced Tiamat in two and raised half of her to form the Heavens and placed the other half opposite Ea's watery face to make the Earth. Marduk executed Kingu and, under his direction, Ea took the blood to create the human race to be the slaves of the gods.

233

Oceanic creation myths

In Melanesia, the world was created by Qat, who had trouble creating darkness, while the Maori creation myth resembles the Egyptian story of Nut, Geb, and Shu (see page 80).

Qat

For the Banks Islands people of Vanuatu, the center of the world was Vanna Lava where Qat was born. His mother was a great stone that split in two and Qat emerged and named himself. At this time there was only light in the world and no darkness. Qat created fish, pigs, plants, trees, and stones. Then he carved figures out of the wood of the dracaena tree. He placed the figures in a row and sang and danced in front of them. Qat beat his drum and the figures began to dance, too. One of Qat's brothers, Marawa, was stupid and tried to create people too, using the wrong kind of wood—when the people didn't dance, he buried them in a pit and that was how death came to the world.

Qat was worried about people not sleeping because it was always day. He heard that there was something called "night" on another island, so he sailed to Vava. In exchange for a pig, he bought a piece of night from Qong, who lived there. Qat brought back night and showed everyone how to sleep on mats on the floor. As the Sun

Captain Cook's visit to Melanesia in the 18th century prompted the Banks Islands people to believe Qat had finally returned.

moved to the west, he spread night across the sky like a huge cloak of black feathers and told all the things he'd created it was time to sleep. Then he took a knife and cut a hole through the black feathers so that the dawn would break through and the Sun would shine. From then on there was night and day.

The first white man to appear in Melanesia was Captain Cook, and when he arrived, the people mistakenly believed their god Qat had finally returned home.

Rangi and Papa

The story of Rangi and Papa is probably the best known of the Maori creation myths, dating from around 700 CE. Rangi (Sky) and Papa (Earth) had lain together for over a million years locked in an inseparable embrace. From their mating, endless gods were created, who began to get uncomfortable in the cramped dark space. Tu, the father of human beings, suggested killing Rangi and Papa. But Tane, father of the forests, had a better idea. He pushed his branching head on the belly of Papa and, with his roots firmly planted on Rangi's stomach, he grew slowly upward until the Earth and Sky parted and light filled the great space between them. The millions of creatures that Papa had created fell out and became all the animals and people on the Earth.

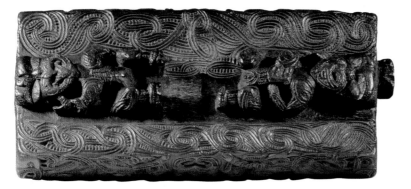

18th-century wooden figurines of Rangi and Papa, the ancestral gods of the Maori people.

Raven

In many myths across northwestern Canada and the United States, and among the Siberian Chukchi and Alaskan Inuit peoples, Raven appears as both creator and trickster, often stealing stones, stars, the moon, or water to create the world.

For the Chukchi people, Raven literally excreted the world into being; then, disguised as a man and with the help of his son Tangen, he made the first people with earth and grass. Tangen wanted the people to talk, but he couldn't teach them, so Raven turned himself back into a bird and cawed at the people and they cawed back. Raven stole the Sun in his beak, but Tangen made Raven laugh and he spat the Sun up into the sky to bring light to the world.

For many, the raven is a sacred bird who embodies the spirit of the creator god.

West coast tales

The Tsimshian people of the Pacific Northwest of North America said that there was no light in the world, and didn't know how to get it back because a great chief had hoarded it for himself in a box. Raven flew up into the hills and changed into a leaf that fell into a cup of water. The chief's daughter drank the water, swallowed the leaf, and eventually became pregnant. The baby was always crying, so he was given a bag of star-rocks that he hurled up through the smoke-hole and they became stars in the sky. But he was still unhappy, so the only thing left to give him was the box of light. As soon as he had it, the child turned back into Raven and flew away to set it in the sky as the Sun.

According to the Kwakiutl people of the Pacific Northwest, Raven carried pebbles in his beak and as he flew over the primordial sea, he dropped them to make the planets and stars. As he passed by, his wings created riverbeds and mountains.

One Unalit Inuit myth from Alaska recalls that Raven made the Earth, but forgot the people. Luckily there was one person hidden in the pod of a beach-pea. He burst through the pod, like breaking out of an egg, and as the man stood up fully grown, Raven pushed his beak up on to his forehead and turned into a man too. He asked the pea-pod man where he came from and the man explained. Raven laughed and said he had made the plant, but had forgotten about people and had never imagined a man would come from it.

A raven rattle, a totemic symbol for the Tsimshian people of British Columbia and Alaska.

South American creation myths

Many of these creation myths involve a female creator, how humans were given fire, unusual matings between deities and indigenous animals, or the struggle between light and dark.

Puana, Kuma and Itcai

The valley of the Rio Capanaparo in Venezuela is home to the Yururo people and their worship of a great goddess Kuma. Only shamans are able to contact Kuma and travel the route to where she lives in the land of the giants to the west. There are many versions of this myth, but this is perhaps the simplest.

Puana the snake created water. Itcai the jaguar made the earth and Kuma created all the people on the land. Kuma wanted to be impregnated in her thumb, but Puana showed her the right way to create children. Her first child was a boy called Hatchawa. Puana made a bow for the boy and taught him how to hunt and fish. Kiberoh was also created at the same time as Kuma and carried fire in her breast. At Kuma's request, she gave it to Hatchawa, but when he wanted to give fire to the people, she wouldn't let him. So the boy threw live fish into the heart of the fire so that the hot coals spread far and wide across the land and people gathered the burning coals and made their own fires.

Kuma taught women everything they know. She also married the Sun and he taught men everything they know. The Sun travels in a boat from east to west and at night visits Kuma's land. The stars are Kuma's children, and they travel only at night. The Moon is the Sun's sister who travels in a canoe across the sky.

Amana

The Calina people of South America believed the floor of Amana's kingdom was the emptiness and darkness of space. Amana was the first being in the universe and she lived in the Milky Way. Amana made beautiful planets but also her greatest rival the Sun. Every time she tried to create new life on Earth the Sun burned it up. The fire serpents destroyed the Moon and left only dust and ashes behind. But she saved the Earth by plunging their fiery tongues into the ocean.

Rio Capanaparo in Venezuela, where boats and canoes are thought to transport the Sun and Moon across the sky.

To stop the Sun's destructiveness, Amana created Tamusi (light) and Tamulu (darkness). They hated each other, but were inseparable, so they agreed that Tamusi would rule the day and Tamulu the night. During the day Tamusi attacked the fire serpents with his sword as they rose out of the Earth's crust like volcanoes. He would slash the serpents into fragments and they turned to comets and shooting stars. In the darkness Tamulu smothered the fire serpents with his black cloak. Amana then ordered Tamusi and Tamulu to people the world now that it was safe. Tamusi created the children of the day—animals, insects, and people; and Tamulu created the children of the night—dreams, monsters, demons, and wild beasts.

239

Water Beetle and the Great Buzzard

The Cherokee were one of the largest native groups in the southeastern United States. When the Spanish explorer Hernando de Soto visited in 1540, he discovered a highly civilized and settled agricultural society. Unfortunately, once gold was discovered, the Cherokee were driven from their lands.

Once all was water. The animals that lived above water had very little room and wondered what was beyond the water. The Water Beetle offered to go and find out. He swam all over the top of the water, but couldn't find anywhere to stop and sleep. So he dove to the bottom and brought to the surface some mud that he spread around until it became the island called the Earth. Someone remembered to fasten this island to the sky with four cords, but no one knows who this was.

To begin with, the Earth was flat, wet, and sticky, so the animals made the Great Buzzard prepare everything for them. By the time he reached the Earth he was very tired, and as he passed over Cherokee country he was exhausted. Where his wings touched the ground he made valleys and where his wings flapped up to the sky he made mountains out of the mud. The animals were so worried that the Earth would be only mountains that they called him back quickly. He turned around just in time, but Cherokee country is mostly mountainous. The animals had done well with the Earth, but

Cherokee artifacts, like this ceremonial stone pipe, are common in the southeastern United States.

Cherokee country is mostly mountains and valleys, shaped by the Great Buzzard's flight.

their one mistake was that they didn't place the Sun far enough away and it scorched the crawfish on his back, which is why he always has a red back. So the conjurors played a trick on the Sun when it wasn't shining, and raised it up seven hands higher until it was just beneath the arch of the sky.

How humankind came to be

Humankind came next—there was a sister and brother, and then the brother hit the girl with a fish and told her to create children. In seven days a child was born, and every seven days after that another child was born, until someone decided that the world wasn't big enough for all these children, so women could only have a child once a year, not once a week.

One day the Earth will grow old and die. The cords that hold the Earth up to the sky will snap apart, and the world will end up sinking into the sea. All will be water again.

Aboriginal creation myths

There is no one Aboriginal creation story. Some believe that the world was created by a group of beings from the Dreamtime, while others believe it was a specific god or spirit.

Djanggawul

For the Walumba people on the northernmost tip of Australia, Djanggawul, the creator brother, and his sisters are celebrated on a regular basis. According to the myth, there was sea, land, and sky in the beginning, but no man. Far out to sea was an island called Bralgu, the Island of Eternal Beings, where the Djanggawul lived and kept sacred objects, drawings, and codes called "dreamings." They left many of their dreamings on the island in the form of paintings and rituals.

Bark canoes have always been a part of daily life for the Walumba people and so feature in their mythology, too.

The Djanggawul were three children of the Sun. The two sisters had the sex organs of both genders, and Djanggawul brother had a gigantic penis, which he hauled after him, making great tracks in the sand.

One day they loaded their bark canoe with their dreamings and sailed across the ocean to the big land they called the Earth. They left their dreamings everywhere, and plants and animals were created wherever they went. When night came, the two sisters fell asleep, but Djanggawul brother went hunting; when he returned he cut off the sisters' genitals leaving them with wounds which became vaginas. They created beings by copulating with their brother—the boys they created were put into the grass to give them whiskers and hair; the girls were hidden under a mat so they would have smooth bodies. The sisters remained eternally pregnant as they traveled, following Djanggawul brother wherever he chose to go, across the deserts and barren mountains.

Wondjina

The Kimberley people of Australia believe in a powerful group of creator gods called the Wondjina. The chief god Wallungunder came down from the Milky Way during the Dreamtime and created the Earth and everything on it. After taking one look at his creation, he realized that he made quite a few mistakes and decided to head back to the Milky Way to get some help. With the aid of the Dreamtime Snake, the rest of the Wondjina spent the Dreamtime teaching and creating people (see page 184).

Dhakan and Eingana

Dhakan was the ancestral creator god of the Kabi people in Queensland. He was half-fish and half-snake and only ever appeared in the form of a rainbow. Eingana was the snake goddess of primordial Dreamtime, and was the mother of all humanity and the water animals.

For the peoples of Queensland, rainbows in the sky were manifestations of the deity Dhakan.

Wuraka and Waramurungundji

In the myths of many coastal peoples of Arnhem Land in the Northern Territory of Australia, Waramurungundji and her partner Wuraka walked out of the sea one day in the Dreamtime. Wuraka had a penis so long that he had to wrap it around his neck. Waramurungundji was extremely fertile, but she had no idea how to get pregnant. When they reached the shore, Wuraka's penis suddenly began to stiffen and he uncoiled it from around his neck just before it suffocated him. The huge penis found its way to Waramurungundji's vagina and impregnated her. She gave birth immediately, filling the Earth and sea with thousands of creatures, and Wuraka gave them the power of language. With creation over, the two deities walked back into the sea again.

Bobbi-Bobbi

According to the Binbinga people of northern Australia, Bobbi-Bobbi was a supernatural snake that was kindly toward the human race in the Dreamtime. When he heard that people were hungry, he sent down flying foxes from Heaven. But because the foxes flew too high for the people to catch by hand, he took out one of his ribs and gave it them and they used it as the first boomerang.

But two greedy men wanted to see what Heaven was like. They managed to trick Bobbi-Bobbi and told him they wanted to thank him for all he had done; instead they threw the rib up into the clouds to tear a great gash in the Heavens. Bobbi-Bobbi was so surprised that the rib bounced off his snakehead and fell back to Earth, killing the two men. So Death became part of human life and Bobbi-Bobbi refused to help people any more.

Wati-Kutjara

In central Australia, the Wati-Kutjara were twins in the Dreamtime. They were also known as Kurukadi (white iguana) and Mumba (black iguana). Long before creation, they slept under the Earth, but suddenly woke up and wandered the Earth, creating animals, rocks, waterholes, and plants wherever they went. Kulu, the Moon spirit, chased a group of women, so the twins killed Kulu and saved the women. Kulu's spirit returned to the Moon, but because he was dead he had no blood and the Moon has always been pale ever since.

In the Dreamtime, Bobbi-Bobbi's rib was the first boomerang, used by indigenous hunters to kill their prey.

SUN, MOON, AND SKY

From solar barges to silver chariots, ancient civilizations had all kinds of explanations of how the Sun and Moon made their way across the sky. As Earth goddesses were gradually deposed by patriarchal sky gods, the Sun usually became a male deity, and the Moon female. Gods and goddesses caused the rain, storms, fire, floods, and personified the natural elements or nature itself. There were probably as many tales of why the stars were in the sky as there were stars themselves.

Sirius

The two most important heavenly bodies to the ancient Egyptians were the Sun and the "dog star" Sirius. Their placement together in the sky marked the beginning of the Egyptian year.

The dog star Sirius was known as *Sothis* to the ancient Egyptians. Plutarch used the name Sirius for the Nile, and the star was an important celestial marker in the Heavens for the summer solstice, the time when the Nile was liable to have just been in flood. This usually coincided with the time when Sirius was lying above the horizon in the east just before sunrise. The Egyptians believed it was the combined strength of the Sun and Sirius that led to the very hot weather that followed.

Isis and Sirius

The universal goddess Isis was linked to the main star, Sirius A. Its companion star, Sirius B, was not known to the Egyptians, but it seems that Osiris was associated with some dark celestial partner, in his title of "black god." The new-year alignment of the Sun and Sirius was a highly important omen for the ancient Egyptians. It was then that Isis and Osiris would appear in the sky to restore eternal life to the gods and to welcome the regeneration of the Nile waters.

Greek interpretations

The ancient Greeks believed that the appearance of Sirius heralded the hot and dry summer. In certain conditions its twinkling effects were considered a bad influence. People suffering from them were said to be "star-struck." The season following the star's appearance came to be known as the "dog days of summer." Coins retrieved from the island of Cos, dating from the 3rd century BC, feature dogs or stars with rays emanating all around the coin.

Some Greeks would offer sacrifices to Sirius to bring cooling breezes and await the reappearance of the star. If it rose clear, it was a sign of good fortune; if it was misty or faint, then it foretold disease and misfortune.

Isis was known as "lady of the star" and was also called Sothis—another name for the star Sirius.

Ushas, Ratri, and Soma

In Vedic mythology, Ushas and Ratri were the sisters of Agni, the fire god. Ushas was the dawn, Ratri the night. Soma, also known as Chandra, was the Moon god.

Ushas and Ratri

Ushas was beautiful and inspired many poems and hymns. Dressed in crimson or carmine-pink robes, each day Ushas would open the doors to Heaven and bring light to the world. She wore a golden veil and was forever young, waking sleepers and giving songs to the birds in their nests. Ushas brought wealth and happiness to those who were good, but left the wicked to sleep for eternity. Her other gift to humankind was time, but also its downside: it brings age and mortality.

Her sister Ratri wore dark robes covered with twinkling stars, and was never afraid to visit the world because then humans would sleep and cattle would rest. Ratri was invoked for protection against robbers and wolves, and people would use her cloak of the night and pray to it. Once her shadow is cast, she wakes her sister Ushas and tells her to return.

Ushas was the goddess of the dawn, and her gifts to humankind included wealth and mortality.

Soma, the Moon god

Soma was the god of the waxing and waning Moon. Surya the Sun nourished Soma with water from the ocean when he was exhausted by the many beings who fed on his light. More than 36,300 deities fed upon Soma to assure their immortality. Animals, insects, and humankind also made use of the fullness of his light until he began to wane.

The Somnath Temple in Gujarat, India, is sacred to the Moon god Soma.

Soma was married to the twenty-seven daughters of Daksha, son of Brahma, but he preferred Rohini to all the others. The other wives were madly jealous and complained to Daksha, who in turn tried to reason with Soma, but it was no use. Like other lesser gods, Soma received a curse for his arrogance. However, thanks to the pleading of the other twenty-six wives, this curse lasted for only a cycle of fifteen days. This was his waning time.

After Soma's abduction and rape of Tara, the beautiful consort of Brihaspati, the gods' guru, Brahma persuaded Soma to return her to Brihaspati; but, finding her pregnant, Brihaspati refused to have her back. When the child was born, it was so beautiful that he claimed it as his own, but Soma believed it was his child, too. To settle the dispute, Brahma gave Tara to Brihaspati and the child became the father of all the future lunar dynasties, thus creating harmony between the gods and the celestial bodies. Meanwhile, Varuna punished Soma by disinheriting him from his place in the Heavens. Shiva came to Soma's aid, however, and wore a crescent moon on his forehead in his honor. But Soma was still sent to the outer reaches and forbidden to return to Heaven. He remained in the cold realms of night, his milky-colored chariot drawn by ten ghostly white horses.

Chiron and the constellation Centaurus

In ancient Greek myth, Chiron was the son of the nymph Philyra and the first Titan, Cronus. In fact, Philyra really wasn't interested in Cronus and changed into a mare to escape his lusting attention. Cronus wasn't fooled and succeeded in mating with her by turning into a stallion.

Chiron was then born a centaur—half-horse, half-human. Philyra was so disgusted with the child that she begged the gods to change her into anything other than a mortal and so she was transformed into a linden tree. The abandoned Chiron was subsequently brought up by Apollo in Olympus. His foster father taught him many arts and skills, including hunting, medicine, music, and prophecy. Chiron became wise and Zeus sent him to govern the unruly centaurs in northern Greece.

One night Heracles was passing and the centaurs invited him to dinner; some wine was opened, but the smell then attracted a group of rogue centaurs who gate-crashed the party. Heracles naturally began to fight with his friends, and the rogue centaurs fled. But as he chased them, firing his arrows, one hit Chiron in the leg. These arrows had already been dipped in the poisonous blood of the Hydra. Chiron was immortal, so he didn't die from the wound, but neither would it heal and he suffered more and more. Although he could not die, neither could he be cured.

Chiron, the last of the centaurs.

*Heracles wounded his mentor Chiron by accident with
a poisonous arrow.*

His pain became unbearable, yet eventually Chiron was released from his
torment by a strange twist of fate.

Chiron's release

Zeus had punished Prometheus for stealing fire from the gods and giving it
to humankind by binding him to a rock between the realms of Earth and
Heaven where every day a great eagle would soar down and eat his liver. His
liver regenerated every night and so the torment went on and on. Zeus
announced the only way Prometheus could be freed was if an immortal took
his place, sacrificing his immortality, and if Prometheus wore a crown of willow
leaves and a ring on his finger forever. Chiron therefore offered to be that
immortal. Zeus eventually agreed and gave Prometheus Chiron's immortality,
then set Chiron in the sky as the constellation Sagittarius to honor him,
although he was later identified with a separate constellation, Centaurus.

The quest for the Sun

The beauty of the West Lake area in Shanghai has always had a certain magic about it. This simple tale, of a mortal quest to find the Sun and thus restore harmony on Earth, is a common theme in many tales in Chinese mythology.

Lui Chun was a farmer who lived on the shore of West Lake beneath the purple canopy of Precious Stone Mountain. The Sun usually rose in the east, but one morning a storm blew up, black clouds gathered across the lake and the Sun dropped back below the horizon. Eventually the clouds lifted, but strangely the Sun had gone. The plants began to wither, the world grew cold and dark and the people didn't know what to do without the Sun. So Lui Chun asked one of the oldest and wisest men in the village where he might find it. The old man told him that the demons from the Eastern Sea had probably stolen it, for they feared its light and heat.

Lui Chun set off on his perilous journey to save the Sun. He was accompanied by a golden phoenix, who would return to his house if he should die. For many weeks there was no sign of the Sun or the phoenix, but then one day it returned to the village and Lui Chun's wife fell down in a faint, realizing that he was dead. But as she lay in a faint, she gave birth to a boy who grew 15 ft. (4.5 m) tall. One day he learned of his father's heroic but tragic deed, and Bao Chu vowed that he too would go to find the Sun.

Bao Chu's quest

For many months he traveled across remote mountains and freezing rivers. Kindly villagers gave him some soil in a bag, which he hung over his shoulder. One day Bao Chu arrived at the Eastern Sea. He emptied the bag of soil into the water and it turned into a chain of islands. He swam from island to island until he reached the last one and, as he put his foot on the land, the island collapsed onto the ocean floor, dragging Bao Chu with it. There he not only encountered demons, but found the Sun inside a huge cave. With the help of the phoenix he fought the demon king, pushed the Sun back up into the sky and, exhausted, fell into

*Since the Tang dynasty of 609 CE, West Lake has been
revered for its tranquility and beauty.*

the ocean and died. The phoenix flew back to Bao Chu's mother and although
she knew he was dead, the Sun now filled the sky with brilliant light.

Every morning the villagers remember the man who gave them back the
Sun, and they call the bright star that shines in the east just before dawn
Bao Chu in homage.

Yi and the ten Suns

The story of Yi and how he shot the ten Suns is well-known in Chinese mythology. Yi lived during the reign of the legendary ruler Yao, in the 3rd millennium BCE. Some sources say that he was banished from the Heavens with his wife Heng-O and exiled to Earth. Less well-known is what happened to them after his heroic victory, when Heng-O flew to the Moon to hide.

Ten Suns mysteriously appeared in the sky, changing the whole course of nature. Disaster was imminent, with too much light and too much heat: the rocks began to melt and nothing could grow. The Suns were the offspring of Di Jun, the god of the east. Normally, each son would take turns crossing the sky, but the sons got bored and rebelled against their father, vowing to remain forever in the sky. King Yao was worried about the fate of the world and prayed for help, so Di Jun sent down to Earth Yi, a lesser god but a skilled archer, along with his beautiful consort, Heng-O. With his ten arrows, Yi began shooting the Suns and each one fell to the Earth like a stone and turned into a golden crow. They still needed one remaining Sun, so King Yao stole the last arrow from Yi's quiver, leaving the last Sun to shine.

Yi and Heng-O

Banished from Heaven by the angry gods, and fearful of mortality, Yi set off to find the howling wolf god, Xi Wang, who held the last two drops of an immortality potion. If two people drank a drop each, they would remain on Earth but be immortal; if one person drank two drops, they would be immortal in Heaven. Heng-O greedily drank both drops and soared into the sky, only to arrive on the Moon. Yi searched everywhere for Heng-O, and then one day Xi Wang took pity on him and he became the Sun god. Yi went to live on the last Sun he hadn't shot down, and he found Heng-O where she ruled from her lonely Moon palace. When the Moon is full, Heng-O is alone, but when it seems there is only half a moon, that is when Yi is visiting her.

Yi and Heng-O eventually found each other in the sky as the Sun and Moon.

Mani and Sol

In Nordic myth, this version of the Sun and Moon story follows on from the creation of the world from Ymir's flesh (see page 228).

After Ymir had been dismembered (see page 130), the gods named two bright fiery embers from the Kingdom of Muspel Mani (Moon) and Sol (Sun). They put them in two special chariots and made them cross the sky. A man then called his son after the Moon (Mani) and his daughter after the Sun (Sol); this so outraged the gods Odin, Vili, and Ve that they snatched the children away from Earth and bound them to the chariots, to drive the Sun and Moon across the sky forever.

Sol was so hot that her two horses, Arvakr and Alsvin, were given protective armor. At the end of the day they turned the horizon red, their silver armor glowing in the reflected fire of Sol. Mani had only one horse, Alsvider. They came so close to the Earth sometimes that one night he snatched two children from the riverbank. He kept them as his companions and they became the waning Moon and the waxing Moon.

Wolves chased after Mani and Sol as they streaked through the Heavens. Mani's chariot was always ahead of Sol, and Sol always tried to catch up with Mani because of the wolves snapping at her chariot wheels. Sometimes the wolves caught one of them and dragged it down to the Earth so that the Sun was blotted out and there was total darkness. When Mani was caught by the wolf, the night became eerily lit with a ghostly haze and people jumped around and made noises to scare the wolves away. But they still fear that the wolves will triumph eventually at Ragnarok (see page 133).

Dag and Nott

Day and night respectively, Dag and Nott were also given chariots by the gods. Nott had a richly carved chariot drawn by a jet-black horse called Hrimfaxi, in which she could encircle the Heavens. When they saw how beautiful and radiant Dag was, the gods gave him a chariot, too. The horse was shimmering white and its mane reflected the fire of Sol and illuminated the world.

*Sol and Mani drive their chariots through the sky, eternally
pursued by wolves.*

Thunder and the Elephant

A simple but striking myth from Kenya, this story tells how thunder appeared in the sky and how humans destroyed the harmony of creation.

There were three beings who lived first on Earth. They were Elephant, Man and Thunder. Although they originally got on, uneasy feelings began to undermine their friendliness when Thunder noticed the difference between them.

One day he boomed loudly to the Elephant: "Man is a strange creation. If he wants to turn over in his sleep, he doesn't have to get up or even wake up. If I turn over, I have to crash through the clouds and bang around in the sky until I come back down to Earth again."

The Elephant agreed: "I can't flick over from one side to another, either. I have to get up on four legs and then lie down again."

Thunder's paranoia about Man grew steadily and he became afraid of his power. "I'm going to leave the Earth, it's safer in the sky." Elephant laughed: "Man is such a tiny creature, how can he ever hurt you?"

But Thunder was already rumbling away in the distance: "Because if he can turn over in his sleep, think what he can do when he is awake."

The Elephant watched as dark clouds rolled through the sky, carrying Thunder with them. Man had also watched the disappearance of Thunder and was actually pleased he had gone. He had always been afraid of Thunder. The Elephant was the least of his problems. Man went into the forest and gathered some poisonous herbs; with the sap he made poison and from the stems he made bows and arrows. Then he dipped the arrows in the sap and shot the Elephant in the back. As the great creature fell dying to the ground he wailed toward the sky: "Take me with you, Thunder, I beg of you!"

But Thunder didn't care. He shouted back: "No, you can't come with me. You said Man was so small he could never do any harm—it's your stupidity that's killed you." So the Elephant died and Man jumped up and down and made more poison, more arrows, and killed many things that had been created. He became the master of nature because he could do more than just roll over in his sleep.

Unlike Thunder, the foolish Elephant didn't realize the power of Man.

Amaterasu and Susano

The interplay between the Sun and the Moon is essential to world fertility in early Japanese mythology. Shinto believers still worship Amaterasu in shrines throughout Japan.

Amaterasu was the goddess of the Sun and her consort Tsukuyomi was the god of the Moon. At first they lived happily in the heavens, but Amaterasu sent Tsukuyomi down to Earth to eat with the goddess of food, Uke Mochi. Not bothering to serve real food to a deity as insignificant as the Moon, Uke Mochi gave Tsukuyomi regurgitated food on the dishes. But the Moon god was highly insulted, picked up his bow, and killed her with an arrow of silver light.

When he returned to the Heavens, Amaterasu was furious and banished him to a different palace in the sky. A cloud spirit gave Amaterasu the seeds, rice, and plants that had sprouted from the dead goddess's face, and she sent the cloud spirit back to Earth to plant them everywhere to ensure the Earth's fertility. But Susano, god of storms, spoiled the first harvest. He caused havoc wherever he went, and in desperation Amaterasu barricaded herself in a dark cave. But her exile meant there was no more light in the world, so the other gods held a council to decide what to do.

The Sun in exile

The god of wisdom, Omoigane, thought of a way to entice her out. The gods danced in front of the cave with the goddess of magic, Utsume. They hung a mirror on a tree with a necklace of stars, and Amaterasu peeped curiously through a crack in the opening and asked, "How can you be so happy in the darkness without me?" Omoigane whispered back, "Because we have found a goddess more beautiful than you."

Furious that she had a rival, Amaterasu then saw her own reflection in the mirror. Believing this to be the most radiant goddess of all, she stepped out of the cave to face her. But the gods grabbed her and asked, "We need you to shine your light, please come back to Heaven." Amaterasu agreed, "I am the most exquisite goddess, and because there is no other I shall return." Susano's fate

Amaterasu was lured out of her cave by the trickery of the other gods.

was to be banished to Earth, but the light of the Sun goddess was always more powerful than his raging storms.

Tsukuyomi could only reflect Amaterasu's light, and became regarded as the god of prophecy. Worshippers could only look at the Moon in a mirror otherwise they would go mad.

Pele

The Hawaiian goddess of volcanic fire, Pele personified the constant eruptions of lava into the sky which are indigenous to the islands. Pele became a highly regarded deity and is an excellent example of the way people create a local deity to suit their particular geographical needs.

Pele had a tempestuous character. She controlled the lava flow, deciding when it would erupt or when it wouldn't, depending on her mood. She fell in love with a young chief, Lohiau, from a nearby island, and decided she would have him and no one else. She sent her sister Hi'iaka to fetch him, promising that no harm would come to the forests or to Hi'iaka's friend Hopoe while she was gone. The young chief had died by the time Hi'iaka found him, so with her magic powers she brought him to life again and they fell in love.

In her fiery jealousy Pele belched out fire and molten lava that flowed across the forests, killing Hopoe. She then set about destroying the whole island, and in her raging ball of fire, burned Lohiau to death. Hi'iaka's magic powers protected her and for many hours she searched for Lohiau's spirit. Then, glimpsing it drifting on the wind, she caught hold of it and returned it to his body. Together they escaped the wrath of Pele and went to live on Lohiau's island.

Pele became a highly significant deity in Hawaiian mythology, and was clearly specific to the local geography.

264

The still-active volcano, Po'o U'u, in Hawaii, as hostile and angry as the goddess Pele.

The Hog man

Pele found different amusement when the Hog man came to court her. He was a shape-shifter and could be anything—a pig, man, or fish. Pele teased and taunted him and their conflict and tests became more dangerous and passionate. Sometimes she would overwhelm him with her flames and lava, but he would throw fog and rain over her mountains, and pigs scuttled across the land making the ground squelchy and sodden. Then, as the rain fell, everything would turn to mud and her fires were put out.

But the gods intervened when they realized that some of their sacred firesticks might be dowsed with water and so they reached a compromise. Pele was given the mountainside, gulleys, and ravines for her lava flow, and the Hog man was given the lush valleys safe from the volcanic path, where he could have mists, rain, and wet places. This therefore ensured the balance between Pele's fiery earth and the Hog man's watery air.

Children of the Sun

The Inca empire began in the Cuzco valley high in the Andes in Peru around 1200 CE. The Incas believed they were the children of the Sun god Inti. There are many different versions of this story, but in this particular myth, Inti is a benevolent and civilized deity who made the creation of the empire possible.

One day the Sun god drew back the clouds and gazed upon the Earth. The lands were untended, the people and animals wild and miserable. Inti decided the world needed some management for its survival and, with a flash of inspiration, decided to send down his daughter Mama and his son Manco to teach people how to improve their life.

As the family reached the gateway of the sky, Inti handed them a golden rod, saying, "As I travel across the sky I watch what the people of the world do, and it brings me great unhappiness to see their ignorance. It is now up to you to rule these people kindly. This golden rod will show you where to build my sacred city. Whenever you stop to camp for the night, push this rod down into the earth. If it sinks right down, this will reveal the place with the most fertile soil for the city of the Sun, Cuzco."

So they set off toward Lake Titicaca (now on the border with Bolivia) and each time that they stopped to eat, drink, or make camp they tried to push the golden rod into the ground, but to no avail. Eventually, reaching a beautiful valley nestled between two hills, they knew that this was the place that would welcome the golden rod. At the crest of the hill they stopped to eat and thrust the rod into the lush grass. The soil was so fertile the rod sunk into the ground and disappeared.

Mama said, "This is where we must build our father's city. This is where we must rule all his people." Manco agreed, "Now we must gather the people and bring them to this hidden valley. We'll teach them how to be civilized and rule them with kindness and justice as our father told us."

*The Temple of the Sun at Machu Picchu, not far from
Cuzco in Peru.*

Manco and Mama set off back to the plains and lakes and found many people who wanted to come to Cuzco. When the miserable people saw the children of the Sun they gladly followed, knowing they were in safe hands. These people became the Inca race and were educated in everything from farming to irrigation. They worshipped the Sun, and in Inti's honor built a fabulous temple on the hill where the golden rod had sunk beneath the soil. The Inca empire was born and the Sun's children made sure it was one of the most civilized and fertile of kingdoms.

Nantu and Etsa

The Shuar of Ecuador were agriculturists, but also a warring people. Their notorious head-shrinking practice was based on the belief that the spirits of their enemy must be trapped in the head of their victim in order to honor their ancestors. This myth is part of an epic tale of murder, lust, and incest, but reveals the powerful influence of the Sun and Moon.

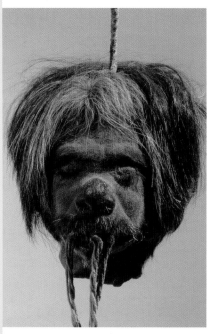

Head-shrinking was thought to trap the enemy's spirit and thus gain control over its powers and abilities.

Etsa was the Sun, Nantu the Moon. They were both created by the creator god Kumpara. Nantu was so beautiful that each night when she appeared, a great bird, the goatsucker, became infatuated with her ghostly beauty. Many times he tried to seduce her, but Nantu would never let him near her. Etsa, too, fell in love with Nantu and followed her around the sky, displaying his love and desire for her. Etsa painted his face to make himself even more attractive than usual, but Nantu climbed higher into her chamber and painted her body so that it was as black as the night. She painted lines on her face and even now you can see the faint markings on the Moon's surface. The goatsucker saw Nantu at her highest in the sky and decided to try his own luck at wooing her by climbing up a thick vine that hung from the starry mantle.

But Nantu cut through the stem, which fell back to the jungle, and the goatsucker went off to sulk among the trees.

Etsa caught two parrots and two parakeets and tied them to his hands and knees. The birds flew up to the Moon and, once he was there, Etsa demanded that Nantu love him. A terrible quarrel began and, full of rage, Etsa struck Nantu. This was the first eclipse of the Moon. Nantu fought back, however, and managed to hit Etsa across the belly. This was the first eclipse of the Sun. Nantu was exhausted by the passionate antics of the Sun and she began to weep. Etsa cried, "See how much stronger and more powerful I am, and look, you can only shed tears!" Now, whenever the face of the Moon is red, it is considered to mean that it is going to shed rain across the land.

Shuar peoples were called Jivaro, *meaning "savage," by the invading Spanish. The word is now considered derogatory in Ecuador.*

Offspring

Nantu finally agreed to marry Etsa, and their first offspring was Unushi the sloth, the first Shuar. The Sun and Moon often meet on Earth to procreate when there is no moonlight. Once Nantu came down to Earth and the goatsucker painted his face and put on his beetle-wing earrings and chased after her. But Nantu fled to the sky again and, unrequited, the goatsucker went back to his miserable lifestyle. This is why on moonlit nights you can hear his mournful love song *Aishiru, Aishiru* ("beloved, beloved") through the canopy of the trees.

269

Ag-Ag and Klang

To the Semang, an indigenous *negrito* ethnic group of the Malay peninsula, this is a simple story of how the Sun and Moon came into being. Like many oral traditions, it's not so much why something is as it is, but rather how it got there that is relevant.

Ag-Ag and his wife Klang lived in a beautiful house built on stilts above the edge of a dark muddy river. Their child Tnong was a dragonfly who flew about, skimming his wings above the water as he buzzed around the mangroves. But one day the vibration of his wings jolted the house off its stilts and it flew up into the sky. Tnong didn't know what to do—he was just a child—so he carried on flying around the house.

Klang was terrified as the house flew into the sky and she fell out through the door. But as she fell, wings sprouted from her back and a beak grew from her head and she became transformed into a hawk. Ag-Ag looked beneath him and saw the river snaking its way across the rainforests like a viper hunting its prey; he saw a hawk soaring on the thermals, and realized it was Klang. He too fell out and became a crow.

The house flew higher and higher toward the west. Tnong still kept circling beneath the house, and eventually after some hours he skimmed through the door as it dropped slowly down to Earth and landed in a cavern of darkness. The house tumbled toward the caves of the east, then emerged again on the other side of the Earth, soaring up into the sky once more. Tnong decided to stay in the house and play in it forever. This was how it became the Sun house.

Tnong always enjoyed his daily games, but was jealous of the Moon, who seemed to have all the stars in the sky with her at night. When Tnong came out to play, all the stars would run away except for two that would come out to peep at him when he rose, but would leave him when he zoomed down into the dark caves.

Designed to resist floods and keep interiors cool in the tropical heat, stilt houses are still built in Malaysia.

Tnong sometimes sends a large moth out at night to swallow the Moon, so that he can play with the stars instead. The people on Earth make a noise and dance and bang drums to scare the moth away, then the Moon re-emerges. However many times Tnong sends the moth to the Moon, the people know that the Moon must return to keep the stars in order. Tnong might want to play with them forever, and then there would be no light from his Sun house in the day.

271

Glooskap and summer

The trickster god Glooskap appears in many North American myths. For the Algonquin peoples, he was arrogant and deceitful, and could be anything he chose—a feather, a rabbit (his favorite guise), smoke, or a stone. But this myth tells how he brought summer to the lands of the north, thus enabling people to cultivate that part of the world.

An Algonquin village c. 1585, centered around a great fire to keep winter at bay.

For many days and nights, through a blizzard, Glooskap had wandered north, reaching ice-covered rock, frozen rivers, and wastes. Through the storm he caught sight of a tiny light and, worried that he might not survive the freezing night, struggled on toward shelter and warmth. He saw a huge tepee, so big that it took up the whole of a mountainside. With chattering teeth he hurled himself through the opening, not caring whether he was eaten alive or thrown back out into the cold. Inside was the Giant of Winter, who invited him to sit beside his icy chair. There was no fire, no warmth, no light, except for a glinting icicle hanging above the giant's head. Winter offered Glooskap his pipe and, as he drew on the pipe, he began to feel warmer and calmer.

Winter's enchantment

The giant had many tales to tell, and as they smoked and chatted, Glooskap didn't notice that Winter was freezing everything around him. Glooskap began to feel drowsy and eventually fell into a deep sleep that lasted for nearly six months. But as the days grew longer Glooskap woke and found Winter had gone. Setting off southward, he soon felt the Sun on his back and went to find Summer. In a mountain glade he saw the tiniest people dancing in sunlight as it streamed through the trees. In the middle was Summer, the tiniest of them all.

Glooskap snatched up Summer and tied a lasso around her diminutive body. With Summer clasped to his chest, he ran back out of the forest and headed north, with the long cord of the lasso trailing behind. The Summer-light people ran after Glooskap, following the trail of the cord to find their queen.

Glooskap's return

He returned to the icy home of Winter. But this time, as Winter told tales, Glooskap began to tell his own tales, too. This heated up the tepee and beautiful Summer's heat produced so much warmth that Winter began to sweat. Winter thawed and the sweat turned to huge torrents of water. The tepee began to melt too, and soon plants pushed their way up through the damp earth. Nature came alive and the birds began to sing. So Glooskap left Summer behind and the Summer-light people found their queen and stayed there for a while to keep the land fertile and warm. Now Summer will always visit the north once a year.

The Moon man

Many Aboriginal peoples recount different versions of this tale of the Moon, a man who lusted after two sisters. Usually happy and carefree, he spent most of the time joking and whistling. But one day he fell into a black mood and felt quite rejected. He felt bad because he had no luck with girls.

Although he was funny, the Moon failed miserably at wooing any of the girls that he met. They saw him as a fool and made jokes about him, and laughed behind his back, because they thought he was dull and fat. Each night he would travel across the land looking for a girlfriend. But his neighbors sent out messages warning of his approach.

One clear night, the Moon was singing a happy tune as he wandered along a river bank, his silver light shimmering across the water. Two girls heard his voice and thought he must be handsome and strong. But when they saw him they were disappointed, so they ran away and jumped into a canoe. The Moon decided to trick the girls and shouted after them, "I need to get across the river, too; please come back for the sake of the Pleaides in the sky!"

The sisters reluctantly went back, remembering that the Pleaides taught that they must never harm any creature and must love all human beings. But on their journey back, the Moon began to tickle the girls and the canoe capsized. The Moon plunged headlong into the river, and as he sank the girls saw his shining face, big and white at first, then paler and ghostlier the further it sank. Eventually it became half his face, then a thin crescent line until it disappeared totally into the blackness.

The raven heard about the fate of the Moon from the girls and sent out a message to all the peoples of the land. "The Moon can no longer shine all the time. He will come from the land of the spirits in the west with only a part of his face shining. Every night more of his face will be visible, then he will gradually disappear into the east and will be invisible for a while. When he comes back from the west, he will peep round the corner at first, because he is ashamed

For many cultures, the moon is associated with a deity; in this tale, it simply represents a lonely man.

of his lust for women. But he will dare to smile once a month and try to woo some girl in the full light of his fat face. Then he will gradually fade away again because he will always be disappointed. That is the true nature of the Moon."

275

How night began

For the peoples of the Upper Orinoco river in Venezuela, Wanadi was the creator god who reincarnated himself many times on Earth. Before humans were created there was only light, and it was only the incompetence of one of the lesser gods that meant night, and subsequently darkness, came to the world.

When the world basked in eternal daylight, Wanadi decided to send his messenger to Earth to create the first people. This spirit messenger was Wanadi himself and on the Earth he gave birth to a race of people and then buried his umbilical cord and placenta in the ground. From the placenta grew a man called Odosha, who was evil. Everything that Wanadi tried to do to help the people, Odosha tried to destroy. He persuaded the humans to kill the spirit Wanadi and as punishment they were all turned into animals. Two more Wanadis were sent down to Earth to deal with the evil Odosha.

Wanadi the second wanted to show that his power was greater than Odosha's and pretended he was teaching the people how death and life were only an illusion. He sat smoking and dreaming in silence, and then dreamed his mother into existence. She was already grown-up and he called her Kumariawa. When Wanadi thought "life," she was born and when he thought "death" she died. Wanadi buried his mother and then left a parrot to watch over her grave in case Odosha came by to see if it were true. "You see, if I can think her into dying, then I can think her into living again. Soon she will be back and I don't want Odosha to find her first."

Wanadi went hunting and decided to leave his shaman's medicine pouch with his nephew Iarakaru for safety. "You must never open this pouch or you will release night into the world," he told him. But Odosha had overheard Wanadi and crept up behind the young god and whispered in his ear, "Open the pouch, open the pouch, or Odosha will come for you." Iarakaru was terrified of the evil Odosha and opened the pouch, then threw it on the ground.

*The people of the Upper Orinoco river were concerned with
day and night and the forces of good and evil.*

Wanadi began to "think" his mother alive again, and as she pushed her arm
up through the ground, the parrot screeched and Odosha ran toward the grave.
Odosha urinated over the reincarnating woman and the poisonous acid
scorched all the flesh from her bones. The parrot screeched again, but when
Wanadi arrived it was too late. Wanadi dejectedly took his mother's bones back
with him to Heaven. Now that there was no light, Wanadi believed the world
was no longer his and that Odosha's evil powers would take over. But it is
believed that a new race of good people will live on the Earth, Odosha will die,
and his evil will be be wiped out. A third Wanadi will then be sent to Earth,
but it will be the fourth Wanadi who will destroy Odosha and finally his evil
will disappear forever.

BEASTS AND MONSTERS

Monsters and strange beasts often appear as secondary characters in a myth and usually result from strange matings between gods and animals, or demons and people, fire and rocks, and so on. There is very little logic involved in the fantastic procession of dragons and monsters throughout myth. But the one thing they all have in common is their horrifying appearance or their bloodthirsty hunger for human flesh. They represent not only fear, but also the fertile imagination of the peoples of the world.

The Serpent and the Eagle

Babylonian mythology is packed with monsters and animals, sometimes as symbols of power and sometimes as totemic forms of the gods themselves. These included a winged bull, the four dogs of Marduk, and the eagle, a symbol of the Babylonian Sun god Shamash.

Eagle and Serpent were good friends who would often hunt together. But one day Eagle was feeling extraordinarily hungry and thought that nothing would be better than a tasty meal of serpents. The Eagle told his family that he intended to eat the children of his friend the Serpent, but one wise young eaglet warned him that if he did, he would incur the wrath of the Sun god Shamash and that Shamash would then punish him. Eagle, however, refused to believe his son and swooped down on the tree where the serpents nested. As he landed on the topmost branches, his weight destroyed the nest and all the tiny baby serpents fell to the ground. Eagle devoured them greedily. When Serpent returned to find all her children gone, she appealed to Shamash for help to avenge the death of her family.

Eagles are symbols of power.

Shamash agreed to help Serpent achieve her vengeance, and gave her advice: "There is a dead ox on the road to the mountains; hide inside the carcass, and soon Eagle will come. When he does, you must circle him quickly, squeeze the life out of him, then bite him with your poisonous fangs. Then you must cast him into a pit."

Hidden serpent

Serpent found the dead ox, split open the carcass, and slithered between the ribs to hide. A few hours later, she heard the cawing of birds and the flapping of wings. Hundreds of carrion crows swooped down to eat the flesh, but Eagle was wary and stayed away until all the other birds had feasted. Then Eagle became hungry and wanted to eat: "There's no choice, we must eat the flesh of this ox like everyone else."

The Chaldean Sun god Shamash was also known as the god of justice in Babylonia and Assyria.

The wise young eaglet spoke up again: "Beware, Father, I'm sure Serpent lies in wait for you inside this corpse and is going to kill you."

But Eagle would not pay attention and laughed. He said that he wasn't scared of Serpent and, overcome with greed for the delectable meat, he landed on the ox's belly. As Eagle ripped some flesh from the corpse, Serpent emerged and seized him between her jaws, coiled herself tightly around him, and then sank her fangs into his neck. Eagle tried to plead for mercy, but Serpent squeezed even tighter until Eagle was suffocated. The dead Eagle was thrown into a pit. From that day on, no eagle has ever dared kill a serpent.

Hindu beasts and monsters

The monsters and beasts of Hindu mythology were usually evil spirits or beings who contrasted or complemented the gods and their various qualities and deeds.

The Nagas

The Nagas were depicted as evil, but they were like humans and behaved ambivalently. Although most were demons, a few obtained immortality by licking up *amrita* (the food of the gods) as it fell to the ground when Garuda rescued his mother Vinata from the Underworld after a family quarrel. Vinata was the daughter of Daksha, who was one of the original lords of creation.

These strange gods could take any human or snake form they wished. At times they were half-snake, half-woman, at other times warriors with snake-like necks. Some had five hoods, some seven. They wore jewels that lit up the Underworld or lived in fabulous jeweled palaces in the sky or under the sea. The Nagas were the servants of Indra and their jewels were Indra's drops of rain.

They often carried the rain on behalf of Indra and could withhold it if they were feeling mean. Some were more virtuous. Sesha, king of the Nagas, was the world serpent upon whom Vishnu sleeps. He lies coiled when the universe is at rest and his seven hoods shade Vishnu from evil.

Sesha is a symbol of the eternal—his tail is in his mouth like the ouroboric snake in alchemical texts and supports the Heavens. Another, Muchalinda, supposedly protected Buddha by coiling around him seven times when he was threatened by a great storm while meditating under the bho tree.

The universal snake who eats his own tail, Ourobouros was known as Sesha in Hindu myth.

The Rakshasas are evil demons, often disguised as grotesque dwarves.

The Rakshasas

The Rakshasas emerge from their mother Night as grotesque demons and creep stealthily around the world in different guises to hide their monstrosity. They can be dwarves or giants, multi-limbed animal horrors or wolves and vultures. Some appear as night demons with red eyes and lolling tongues who bring dead bodies back to life and eat the flesh. There are demons who make men insane, those who attack holy men, and those who haunt men's minds and make them do foolish things. There are also Rakshasis (female demons) who can bewitch and enchant men into frenzies of demonic lust. They can slip in and out of body orifices when least expected and the only thing they fear is fire.

283

The popular Hindu festival Dussehra celebrates the defeat of the demon king Ravana by Lord Rama.

Ravana, the demon king

The king of the Rakshasas, Ravana had originally been a creature of Heaven, but had insulted Brahma and was given the choice of being reincarnated seven times as Vishnu's friend or three times as his enemy. He took the easy way, assuming that Vishnu would prefer to dispose swiftly of his enemies, which would secure himself a place back in the Heavens more quickly.

In his first incarnation as Hiranyakashipu, he murdered anyone who got in his way, and was finally destroyed by Vishnu. In his second incarnation, Ravana, he was particularly nasty—seducing other men's wives, breaking every law, and raping and destroying anything in his path. He was a horrific monster with ten heads, bulging red eyes, twenty arms, and teeth like the gaping jaws of a wolf. He could grow as tall as a mountain and he raged around the world, churning up the sea and hurling around the mountains. Ravana was indestructible by the gods and only Rama, one of Vishnu's avatars who was born on Earth specifically to kill Ravana, finally defeated the terrifying demon king.

In his last incarnation as Sisupala, he was cursed with three eyes and four arms and was more of an irritation to Krishna (Vishnu's ninth avatar) than anything else. After many conflicts, Sisupala insulted a notable king, which led to his death. Sisupala's soul was absorbed into Krishna, and he was allowed to return to Heaven, finally forgiven after paying the price of being the three enemies of Vishnu/Krishna.

Ravana, the demon king, was the most fearsome of all the demons.

Greek beasts and monsters

Throughout Greek mythology there are numerous monsters—some to be vanquished by heroes or gods, others to guard sacred places, and most of them horribly ugly.

Typhon

Typhon's mother was Gaia and his father was Tartarus (see pages 102–103). His name means "smoke" and he was formed out of a misty smoke that grew a hundred dragons' heads. His arms and legs were a thousand snakes, his mouth spat molten rock, and his eyes were flames of fire. He was born to avenge the defeat of the Earth giants—as soon as he was created, he rampaged around the universe and set out to destroy Olympus.

He was eventually defeated by Zeus. Some accounts suggest that Zeus picked up Mount Etna and smashed it down on Typhon, who was forced into the Earth's crust forever; occasionally his angry fumes still rise up through mountains in the form of volcanos. Echidna and Typhon created a terrible brood of creatures: Cerberus, the three-headed hound of the Underworld (see page 290); the Hydra, a multi-headed water snake that lived at Lerna (see below); the ghastly Chimaera (see opposite); and the Sphinx that tormented Thebes (see page 289).

The Hydra

Roaming the swamps of the Lerna, the Hydra had nine snake heads, one of which was immortal. The other heads were mortal, but would regrow if cut off. She had a dog-like body and a dragon's tail that was so powerful it could snap a man in two with one blow. Her breath, urine, and blood were lethally poisonous. Just one inhalation of her venomous odours could end a man's life.

One of Heracles' labors was to destroy the Hydra. With the help of his charioteer Iolaus, he destroyed the eight mortal heads and finally decapitated the Hydra's immortal head with Iolaus' sword. He disemboweled the writhing carcass and dipped his arrows in her blood, which proved to be fatal to any mortal or god, including Chiron.

*The monstrous Chimaera was thought once to have been
the pet of the King of Caria, but escaped to the mountains.*

The Chimaera

The Chimaera breathed fire from her monstrous lion's head, her body was half-snake, half-goat, and she was the most hideous creature alive. For some time she was kept as a pet by the King of Caria, but she escaped to the mountains in Lycia.

King Iobates of Lycia sent for a mortal called Bellerophon and challenged him to a test of strength whereby he had to kill the Chimaera. Bellerophon was terrified and asked the gods to help him. He was given a bow, a quiver full of arrows, and a spear tipped with lead. The gods gave him the winged horse Pegasus and he flew around the Chimaera's cave, shooting arrows at her until she weakened. He hurtled the spear between her panting jaws and she choked to death. Unfortunately, Bellerophon believed that this was the only deed required of him, but it was simply the first among others that eventually led to his downfall. The Chimaera's name was later used for any monster that was improbable or fantastic like herself.

*The Sphinx was Hera's curse on Thebes to punish the city
for having displeased the goddess.*

The Sphinx

The Sphinx, or Throttler, was a monstrous woman with the face and breasts of a female, the wings of an eagle, the body of a lion, and the tail of a serpent. Hera had sent her as a curse on the city of Thebes and she guarded the sole exit and entrance to the citadel. The Sphinx would ask a riddle of all those who passed by; if they failed to give the correct answer, she would throttle or devour them on the spot. The riddle was: "What walks on four legs in the morning, two legs at noon, three legs in the evening, and is weakest when it walks on four?" It seemed that no Theban could answer this riddle and thousands of people were devoured.

Meanwhile, it had been prophesied that Oedipus would murder his father and marry his mother. He was fleeing to Thebes in an attempt to avoid this fate—although he had unknowingly fulfilled part of it already: the stranger he had argued with and ended up killing on his way to Thebes was in fact his father. However, when he came to the Sphinx he remembered the inscription carved across Apollo's temple: "Remember you are a mortal." He shouted up to the Sphinx: "The answer is a man—man crawls on all fours as a baby, walks on two legs as an adult, leans on a stick in old age, and is weakest when a baby." The Sphinx, horrified that Oedipus knew the answer, threw herself off the cliff and smashed to pieces onto the rocks below. As a reward for ridding Thebes of the Sphinx, Oedipus was made king of Thebes, which later led to him fulfilling the prophecy by marrying his own mother, the widowed Queen Jocasta.

Medusa

Medusa was one of the three Gorgons, the other two being Euryale and Stheno. These were monstrous creatures with scaly bodies, bronze hands, and golden wings, tusks like rhinos and hair that was a mass of writhing, hissing snakes. The Gorgons were so powerful that one glance at them would turn a person to stone.

Perseus hunted out Medusa as a gift for his host, King Polydectes. Hermes gave him winged sandals and a sickle made of "adamant," Hades gave him a helmet of invisibility and Athene her polished bronze shield. Perseus used the shield to reflect Medusa so that he didn't have to look at her directly. He decapitated her with the adamant sickle, threw her head in a bag so that he couldn't see it, and escaped her sisters by putting on the helmet of invisibility.

*Cerberus was Hades' loyal guard dog, and allowed only the
dead to enter the Underworld, but never return.*

Cerberus

Cerberus ("pit demon") was the son of Echidna (half-woman, half-serpent) and
Typhon. He had between three and fifty monstrous dog heads and one
hundred serpent tails. He guarded the entrance to the Underworld, and
eternally prowled the gates to stop intruders from entering. The dead were
allowed to pass by him as shadows, but the only way the living could get past
him was by devious means. Orpheus lulled him to sleep with his music, Aeneas
drugged him, and Heracles terrified him.

Heracles' last labor was to bring Cerberus back alive to King Eurystheus. He decided to use his own strength, brawn, warrior skills, and rage to capture the dog. Even the ghosts fled as Heracles stepped off the ferryman's boat; brandishing his sword and casting fierce, war-like glances gave him easy access to Hades' realm. Heracles easily caught Cerberus by the neck and, as he was wearing an impenetrable lion skin, the dog's snarling teeth made no impact on him. Clamping an iron chain round the dog's neck, he led the overpowered animal back to the River Styx and on to the Upperworld. When Cerberus emerged into the light, he began hissing and his saliva gave seed to the poisonous plant aconite. When King Eurystheus saw the terrible monster, he fled and Heracles unchained the dog, which hung its serpent tails between its legs and ran back to the Underworld.

The Harpies

The Harpies (snatchers) were so repulsive that even their own parents were revolted by them and kept them hidden in the deep caverns of the Underworld. With bronze talons, they were half-bird, half-woman, and were originally thought to have been beautiful winged goddesses. Their numbers were indeterminate, but they had names like Ocypete (swift), Aellopus (hurricane), and Celaeno (dark one). They were also known as goddesses of storms and had been reputed to snatch the weak on battlefields or children without warning, hence their name.

Phineus had been blinded by the gods because his prophecies came true once too often, and the gods cursed him with a pair of Harpies as companions. The ghastly winged creatures dropped their poisonous secretions on his food and pecked at his eyes. Jason wanted to know how to recover the Golden Fleece, and Phineus struck a bargain with him if he'd get rid of the menacing, filthy Harpies. The Argonauts feasted with Phineus and immediately the Harpies flew down to snatch the food and peck at their eyes. But Jason sent the two winged sons of the north wind, Calais and Zetes, to chase the Harpies across the sea to the edge of the world. Here the Harpies became whirlwinds that spun so fast they tangled each other up. They occasionally stop spinning when the north wind forgets to blow and then they prey on unwary mortals again.

The *Shanhaijing*

Weird and wonderful monsters and dragons abound in Chinese mythology. Fragments still remain from a book entitled the *Shanhaijing* (*The Book of Mountains and Seas*) that may be more than 2,000 years old; this extraordinary encyclopedia contains strange and terrifying creatures that the ancient Chinese believed existed on Earth.

The *Shanhaijing* was originally written as if the writer had first-hand knowledge and experience of these oddities. Here are some snapshot descriptions of these bizarre beasts.

- There are strange people living in Qizhong whose feet point backward. They walk on their toes because their heels are at the front of their legs, but some people claim they actually walk backward.
- In the southwest there are creatures with foreheads that stick out and chests that rise like great baskets above their heads.
- There are birds called Biyi with only one eye and one wing. If anyone can ride on the back of a flying Biyi, that person will live for a thousand years.

The creatures of Xuanyuan live for at least 800 years.

- In the south are creatures who are half-human and half-bird. They use their wings to support them, as they don't have legs. They wait beside the seashore to catch large shrimp, and it is thought they descended from a man who committed suicide in the South Sea.
- Further west in Xuanyuan there are creatures who exist with human heads and snake bodies. They live for thousands of years, and their snake tails curl around their necks.

- To the east are creatures like monkeys, who eat charcoal while it is burning and carry the embers with them. They are eternally roasting, so no one can touch them without being singed.
- Even further to the east are mutant creatures, who are black from the waist down and hold snakes in each hand. They have a green snake hanging from one ear and a red snake from another.
- In the South China Sea live mermaids and mermen called Jiaoren. They weave their shuttles all night long and can be heard by those who stand on the beach or go fishing on still, moonlit nights. The Jiaoren cry like people, but their tears turn to pearls. They have beautiful skin and wild hair that reaches down to the end of their tails. If they are given wine, their skin turns the color of peach blossom.

The Jiaoren are mermaids and mermen who live in the South China Sea.

293

Fenrir the wolf

Fenrir the wolf, in Norse mythology, was fated to be the beast of Ragnorak. Feared and misunderstood, Fenrir was the bringer of doom to the gods and was known as "an axe-age, a sword-age, a wind-age, a wolf-age before the wrecking of the world."

Fenrir's parents were Loki, the trickster god, and Angrboda, a frost-giantess. He was brought to Asgard by Odin so that the gods could keep an eye on him. Fearing his rapid growth, they realized he could destroy the world with one bite of his gnashing teeth, so Tyr was given the job of feeding him, and Odin decided he would try to tame Fenrir and cure him of his terrible ways.

Odin heard from the Norns (see page 134) that his own fate was inextricably linked to Fenrir. So, fearing for the loss of his immortality, he decided that Fenrir must be tied up for good. The gods first used a strong chain called the Laeding, but Fenrir snapped the chain into a thousand pieces. They tried again with an even stronger chain, but again Fenrir broke through and the gods feared that they would never be able to stop him from a ferocious attack.

The last resort was to ask the dwarves to make a magical shackle, so strong that even Fenrir could not break it. The tether resembled a silken strand and, when they showed it to Fenrir, he became suspicious of its magical powers. The gods promised that it was just another test of strength, but Fenrir was so wary that he insisted one god put his hand between his jaws as a pledge that no magic was involved. Tyr was the only god willing to do such a deed. Of course, he lost his hand when the shackle was placed around Fenrir's neck and the wolf realized he would never escape.

But the gods still didn't trust Fenrir and they bound him to a rock, then placed a sword vertically in his mouth so that he couldn't bite anyone. The blood that gushed out of his upper palate formed a river and his vast mouth gaped so that the lower jaw touched the ground and the upper one the sky. At Ragnarok (see page 133), Odin will be slain by Fenrir, who can at last take revenge on all the gods.

*Tyr was the only god brave enough to sacrifice his hand in
order to restrain Fenrir.*

The fox and the werewolf

The fox is a well-known shape-shifting spirit in mythology, and it is thought that the power to turn into a fox means you acquire immortality. Werewolves have been recorded as far back as 1000 BCE, and have been feared as recently as the 16th century CE.

Fox-woman

In Japanese mythology, the fox creates delusions in men, often taking the form of a beautiful woman to extract a man's semen during sexual intercourse, thus adding to its own potency. The only way to tell if you're in the company of a fox-woman is to watch for her shadow on water; a fox-spirit's shadow will be cast as an outline of a fox, not that of a woman.

One story tells how the Mikado was seduced and bewitched by a beautiful young girl, the Jewel Maiden. After she had left him impotent, the fox-spirit ran away until she reached Nasu Moor. There she lived inside a huge rock and waited for strangers to pass by. One day a Buddhist priest called Genno heard her story. Realizing he was dealing with a demon-spirit, he prayed to Buddha, and the spirit transformed into a fox, then into a beautiful woman who was sucked back into the death-stone forever.

The more men a fox-woman seduces, the more powerful she is thought to become.

Werewolves

Werewolves have been feared up until near-modern times in some parts of the world. In 6th-century Europe they were regarded as emissaries of Satan, and many people were accused of being werewolves, especially if they had hairy bodies, stubby fingers, birthmarks, or sharp nails. This persecution reached its peak in France between 1550 and 1630, when over 30,000 people were tried, and most of them executed, as suspected werewolves.

Werewolf comes from the Saxon word *wer* (man) and *wulf* (wolf). Throughout northern and eastern Europe werewolves were believed to be born to human mothers, but were supernatural. Their most obvious association was with the Moon, and during a full moon they changed into wolf form. They were sexually attractive to women and sexually voracious themselves. Some were invulnerable to weapons, although a silver arrow and later a silver bullet could wound others.

One of the earliest sources for the origins of the werewolf is the Greek tale of Lycaon, the unruly king of Thessaly whom Zeus turned into a wolf after Lycaon had tried to prove he was cleverer than the god.

Werewolves were considered to be supernatural beings born to human mothers.

The Snake Men

One winter's New Moon a party of Sioux warriors returned homeward, hungry and tired after battle. They still had a day's travel ahead, so one of the braves put his ear to the ground and heard what sounded like galloping buffalo in the distance. He told the chief that rather than splitting up and chasing rabbits, they should ambush the herd of buffalo together.

As the rumbling hooves came nearer, the group hid behind a ghostly white tree trunk that lay across the sand. As they leapt up to ambush the buffalo, the chief froze in horror, for what came hurtling toward them was not buffalo, but a huge snake with blood dripping from its fangs. The snake had a rattle larger than a man's head and moved swifter than the wind. The warriors fearlessly aimed their arrows at the serpent and within minutes it lay dead on the ground. The warriors decided to eat the carcass and it tasted as good as any buffalo.

Rattlesnakes are considered sacred, but they are still feared by the Sioux peoples.

Sioux villagers waiting for the return of their chief and hunting party.

One young boy was reluctant to eat the meat and went hungry, and eventually they all fell asleep beside the camp fire.

But during the night, one by one the men turned into snakes. When the Snake Men saw that only the boy was still human, they comforted him and gave him all their skins and possessions. The chief told him to guide them to the top of a mountain and then to return to the village and relate what had happened, promising that the Snake Men would return in the summer to visit their people.

The boy did as he was told—the families cried and the village became ghostly silent. But one day, when the Sun was high, as promised, the Snake Men gathered outside the village. The boy took their families to meet them, and the snakes asked for horses, moccasins, and skins. The boy said, "Don't be afraid of them, don't run away, and no harm will come to you. Give them their possessions and they will leave us in peace." So their families found and gave them their belongings and then watched as the snakes hissed, slithered, and rattled around their possessions in celebration. The Snake Men stayed all summer, but when the winter came they vanished with their horses and were never seen again.

Oceanic beasts and monsters

Throughout Polynesia the bringers of evil and doom were usually ogres. For the Australian Aborigines, there existed a range of oddities, from fairy-like spirits to the grotesque cat-like creature, the Kinie Ger.

Ogres

In New Guinea, stories of ogre-killing children are prevalent. The actual ogres in the stories are usually stupid, deformed, and demonic. One story in particular tells of an island inhabited by ten brothers—all ogres with different numbers of heads. The other people of the island tried to drive them away by blowing conch shells or luring them into bamboo traps; when nothing worked, the people waited in the hope of someone producing an ogre-killing child.

Aboriginal Mimi spirit figurines. The Mimi were thought to have taught the Aborigines about hunting, preparing food, and sex.

Eventually a woman gave birth to a one-legged boy. This deformity didn't impress the people and they decided there was no chance he would ever kill the ogres. But the one-legged boy's thumbnail was actually sharper than a sword and each time one of the ogres came to stir the stew, he sliced off their heads with his thumbnail. Eventually all fifty-five heads of the ogres were hung from the coconut trees to warn other ogres that there was a very smart ogre-killer living on this island.

Mimi

The peoples of Arnhem Land in northern Australia believed in fairy-like beings with elongated bodies called the Mimi, who were so thin that the wind could snap them in half. To avoid this, they spent most of their time hiding in rock crevices. They were generally thought to have taught the Aboriginal people how to hunt, make fires, and prepare kangaroo meat. They were like humans, but lived in a different dimension, and were also known to be raunchy, vivacious spirits who taught people about sex.

Yowie

Confusingly, there are two types of Yowie in Australian mythology—one an unidentified "hominid" similar to the Himalayan Yeti and North American Bigfoot, and the second a more fearsome and ancient mythical beast resembling an ape-man, with ferocious red eyes on the sides of its head and very large fangs. The Yowie emerges at night, lives in the ground, and eats virtually anything or anyone it comes across.

One of the two confusing Yowie of Australian mythology was similar to the American Bigfoot.

The Yowie is also believed to be related to the Bunyip, a devilish creature with many different characteristics depending on regional variations. Sometimes the Bunyip was a lake monster or lurked in billabongs, creeks, and waterholes, and its blood-curdling screams could be heard for miles as it devoured its prey. It was also known to jump out of billabongs in daylight and devour young virgins.

Kangaroos were not only respected warriors in the Dreamtime, but also hunter-gatherers.

Yara-ma-yha-who

Described by various Aboriginal cultures as a short, little, red man, rather like a vampire, the Yara-ma-yha-who had a huge head, no teeth, and swallowed his food whole. His most distinctive features were his fingers and toes, which were like the suckers of an octopus. He would lurk up in the fig trees waiting for unsuspecting victims, then would drop down on a victim and drain its blood with his suckers.

The Yara would leave the victim, exhausted but alive, to take a nap and then return to eat the body whole, after which he usually regurgitated it. This meant that the person was still alive. Each time you were captured, you grew a little shorter, your skin became smooth, and you'd grow more hair and start to turn red. Eventually you became a Yara-ma-yha-who yourself.

Kinie Ger

The Kinie Ger in Aborigine mythology was part-cat, part-human. He was a grotesque evil creature that roamed the night in search of animals or people.

His limbs and feet were like a human's, but his tail twitched like a domestic cat, and had inherited the innate cat nature to kill for the fun of it. Kinie Ger was particularly fond of watching his victims die a slow, painful death.

This much-feared creature was highly respected by kangaroos during the Dreamtime. In fact, a bodyguard of trained warrior kangaroos was sent out on their hunting trips, and elder kangaroos warned the younger ones not to venture out alone.

Other animals still grieved the deaths of their loved ones at the claws of the Kinie Ger, and the owl and the crow set off to one waterhole where they knew the Kinie Ger would come to drink. After sundown the huge cat slunk across the landscape. This was the only waterhole unguarded by kangaroo warriors, and as he drank, the owl and the crow lunged their spears at Kinie Ger, killing him instantly. They burned the huge corpse, and one spark larger than the rest rose to the sky and took its place in the Milky Way as a star. All the other animals came to see the place where Kinie Ger had died. They saw the huge bloodstain on the ground and the heap of ashes. The dingo discovered some tiny footprints that led away from the ashes. They followed the tracks and found a small cat, quite harmless and purring softly, a shy creature who wanted only to sleep all day in the Sun.

After Kinie Ger's death, all that could be found of him were tracks leading to a harmless, purring cat.

MYTHICAL LOVERS

This collection of myths reveals how the tests and trials of love are worldwide concerns. It perhaps also reflects how for thousands of years humankind has sought to reconnect to the soul, to the very source of love itself, via myths that reflect our own personal feelings. Love is indeed a mystery to be lived, and it is only in myth that the mystery can become truly alive and real for many people. Love-relationships and myth go hand in hand, for myth is the most exquisite mirror of all for the reflection of the self.

Ishtar and Tammuz

Ishtar was the Babylonian goddess of sex and was known throughout Mesopotamia by other names, including Astarte, Ashtart, Ashtoreth, and Inanna (see pages 366–367). It is also highly likely that the cult of Aphrodite originated from Ishtar, because Ishtar was, like Aphrodite, identified with the planet Venus, the Evening Star.

The myth that describes her best is perhaps the account of her descent to the Underworld to find her husband, Tammuz. Ishtar was not only the goddess of sex, but also of music and summer. She would bathe in a sacred lake of purity each evening to restore her own virginity. She was highly promiscuous and had many consorts in various guises, but her heart belonged to Tammuz.

Tammuz was a Sun god of spring, who had sacrificed his immortality so that he could live on Earth and concern himself with nature and fertility. It was Ishtar's love for Tammuz that destroyed him, for one summer, as the Sun rose high in the sky, the heat and intensity of Ishtar's love overwhelmed Tammuz in his fresh innocence and his spring-like growth. As he was a mortal, Tammuz died and Ishtar was heartbroken. The only way to restore their love was for her to travel to the Underworld, Aralu, and try to bring him back.

The gates of Aralu

Ishtar threatened to break down the gates of Aralu if she was not admitted instantly. Ereshkigal, Ishtar's sister and mistress of the Underworld, was furious and decided to set her a test at each of the seven gates. At the first gate, the keeper took away her crown, at the second her earrings, at the third her necklace, at the fourth her ornaments, at the fifth her girdle, at the sixth her bracelets, and at the seventh her clothes. Ishtar was now allowed to pass into Aralu and she stood naked before Erishkigal, who showed her no mercy. Ishtar was tortured and imprisoned by the plague-demon Namtar and left to suffer in darkness.

Light and dark

With Ishtar imprisoned, there was no light on Earth and all sexual activity ceased. The very fertility of the Earth was under threat. The gods asked Ea and Sin, the gods of the Earth and Moon, to help them bring back Ishtar. Ea created a mortal called Ashushu, who was sent down to the Underworld to demand her release, but Ereshkigal cursed the mortal and placed him in a dungeon. The gods tried to bargain with Ereshkigal to exchange the mortal for Ishtar. Eventually Ishtar began to head back from Aralu. At each of the seven gates, she was given back all the things that had been taken from her, until she arrived back in the Upperworld. The gods decided to allow Tammuz to return to life once a year to meet his beloved Ishtar, and so he comes to spend each spring with Ishtar, and fertility and love are restored until Ishtar's passion destroys Tammuz again and he returns to the Underworld for another six months.

The story of Ishtar's descent to Erishkigal's Underworld to find her husband Tammuz dates from around 4000 BCE.

307

Kama and Rati

In Hindu myth, Kama is the god of desire and Rati is the goddess of sexual passion. Kama's name was also known in the Vedas and was originally identified as the creative force that grew inside Parusha when he was alone in the cosmic ocean (see page 220). Kama's first emanation was desire itself, his second the power to create desire in others. The *Kama Sutra* was named after him.

Kama carried a bow made of sugarcane strung with rows of humming bees and flew around shooting arrows of desire between mortals and gods. He was incredibly good-looking and swooped around the skies, riding on a parrot, often accompanied by his beautiful wife, Rati, who was just as frivolous as he was.

The gods wanted Shiva to marry again after his first wife, Sati, had thrown herself on her father's fire. The gods decided that Sati should be reincarnated as Parvati and she was sent to the Himalayas to woo Shiva, who had turned to an ascetic, monkish life. Seeing that Shiva was more interested in meditating than being seduced, the gods sent Kama to arouse some passion in the god's loins and heart.

Kama traveled to Mount Kailasa, where he found the great Shiva in deep meditation, impervious to anything around him. As Parvati approached, Kama pulled an arrow from his quiver and sent it hurtling straight toward Shiva. As it struck, lust surged through Shiva's body, but Shiva saw Kama hiding nearby and was filled with outrage. As a punishment, he burned Kama to ashes in a single glance from his eye.

Kama's arrow worked slowly, but Shiva knew he would find no peace unless he married Parvati. Love disappeared from the world with Kama dead, and Rati refused to enflame desire in mortals or gods. Rati went to see Parvati after her marriage to Shiva and they implored Shiva to let Kama be reborn. Reluctantly he agreed and he allowed Kama to return as Pradyumna, the son of Krishna and Rukmani.

After Pradyumna killed Rati's demon husband as foretold by a great sage, the couple were free to marry again. Pradyumna shook off his mortal form and Kama and Rati resumed their original roles as the god and goddess of desire and sexual passion.

Kama swooped around the skies on a parrot, shooting his arrows of desire.

The lovers of Zeus

Zeus was prodigiously promiscuous and lustful, taking lovers among mortals and deities alike, and he provoked enormous anger and jealousy in his wife, Hera.

Metis

Zeus' first love was his sister Metis, who helped him outwit Cronus (see pages 102–103) and win one of the earlier battles between the gods and Titans. Metis became pregnant but Zeus, fearing Gaia's prophecy that if the child were a boy he would one day overthrow Zeus, cunningly tricked her into becoming a fly and then swallowed her. Later, their daughter Athene was born from Zeus' head. Athene never betrayed him.

Hera

His sister Hera was a very different matter; she was unhappy about not having any share in the initial division of the universe, so she skulked off to Mount Thornax where she sulked in the wilderness. For many months she saw no one, then spring came and she found a bedraggled cuckoo. She put it to her breast in a moment of pity, and the cuckoo turned into Zeus, who immediately made love to her. He persuaded her to come to Olympus as co-ruler and be his wife, but Hera was jealous of his wandering eyes and acutely annoyed by the trick he had played on her. She never forgave

Spiteful Hera would often pursue Zeus' lovers and seek revenge on their offspring or on the nymph or mortal herself.

Zeus for his promiscuous wanderings and began to detest him. With the help of Apollo and Poseidon she conspired to overthrow him, but the trap they set for Zeus caused chaos on Earth, and Thetis, the ocean nymph, visited the Underworld and released the 100-handed giants who set Zeus free.

His throne secure, Zeus left the running of the universe to the other gods and spent most of his time in hot pursuit of beautiful nymphs and mortals.

Semele

Zeus was infatuated by Semele, the daughter of Cadmus and Harmonia. He sent her a message declaring his lusting desire and promising her any reward she wanted. But Hera found out about the message, and pretending to be Semele's old servant, she advised Semele to submit to Zeus only if he came to her in his immortal splendor and radiance, not as an ordinary mortal. She sent back the message and Zeus agreed. When he appeared in his divine form he was the Heaven itself. Thunder and lightning bolts raged through Semele's body as he made love to her and she was incinerated in the raging inferno of Zeus' lust. Zeus managed to save the embryo in her womb. This child was Dionysus, who, once he was elevated to the status of a god, placed his mother in Heaven as a star called Thyone.

Hera managed to trick Semele, who was then consumed by the fire of Zeus' divine form.

Callisto

The forest nymph Callisto was Artemis' companion. She loved Zeus and bore him a son, Arcas, but she

311

was transformed into a bear, either by Hera in a fit of jealous rage or by Zeus himself in order to save her from the evil deeds of Hera. Unfortunately, while in bear form, Callisto was shot by mistake by her own friend Artemis. Zeus placed her in the constellations as the great She-bear (Ursa Major) as a sign of his love for her.

Danae

Poor Danae had been imprisoned in a tower by her father, the king of Argos. An oracle had warned him that he would be killed by his grandson, hence her imprisonment. But Zeus took pity on her and came to her in a shower of gold which poured through the roof of the tower. After a night of rampant sex, Danae ended up bearing a son, Perseus. But slaves heard the baby crying and told the king. Fearing his life was in danger, he ordered both Danae and Perseus to be put in a wooden box and tossed into the sea. But under Zeus and Poseidon's protection, the box drifted across the sea to the island of Seriphos. A fisherman found them and took them to live with the King, Polydectes. After many adventures Perseus did end up killing King Argos by accident when throwing a discus in a competition.

Leda

When Zeus spotted Leda bathing in the River Eurotas, he was instantly filled with lust. She was, however, already carrying the Spartan King Tyndareus' child and was known to be incredibly faithful to him. Zeus therefore asked Aphrodite to help him trick Leda; he turned himself into a swan and Aphrodite turned herself into an eagle. Together they soared across the sky like hunter and the hunted, and then Zeus suddenly swooped down near Leda as if he had been attacked by the eagle. Leda took pity on the injured swan and took it onto her lap. As soon as Zeus knew she was happy stroking the swan, he had sex with her, then took off into the air and disappeared. Leda subsequently gave birth to two swan eggs. Out of one hatched Clytemnestra and Helen, out of the other Castor and Pollux. No one knew who was the father of which children, and therefore which were mortal and which immortal. When Leda died she was taken to Heaven and merged with Nemesis, the goddess of retribution.

Leda was already carrying the king of Sparta's child when Zeus turned into a swan to ravish her.

Europa

Europa was out picking flowers with her maids in the fields near the king's cattle. Zeus disguised himself as a bull and let the girls play with his horns and fondle him. Europa precociously dared to ride on his back, but the bull plunged into the ocean with Europa and disappeared to Crete. Zeus raped her on the beach and she bore three sons, Minos, Rhadamanthys, and Sarpedon. She then married the local king, Asterius. Zeus gave him a bronze man called Talos to defend his kingdom as compensation for Europa's lack of virginity.

Etain and Midir

In Celtic mythology, Etain was one of the Tuatha De Danann people (see pages 144–145), the supernatural inhabitants of Ireland and the last gods to rule before mortals took over their kingdoms. This is the tale of Etain's reincarnation and how two beings, a mortal and a god, fought for her beauty and love.

Bewitchment

Midir was the son of the Dagda, father of all the gods. Midir had been married to Fuamnach for some time, but the beauty of Etain bewitched him and he decided to marry her, too. Fuamnach was of course jealous of Etain and so she used her magic to turn Etain into a butterfly. The winds then blew Etain further and further away from Midir.

One day she fell into the drinking cup of the wife of an Ulster chief called Etar. Etar's wife swallowed the butterfly unknowingly, and Etain grew again in the wife's womb. She grew up to be a beautiful mortal woman and remembered nothing about her previous life as Midir's virgin bride.

Secret love

Meanwhile, the king of Ireland, Eochy, was looking for a queen. He heard of Etain's beauty and decided that he would court her. They were soon married and Eochy took her back to Tara, but things became complicated when Eochy's brother Ailill also became infatuated with Etain and ill with love for her. Etain eventually agreed, out of pity, to meet him in a

Transformed into a butterfly, Etain fell into a drinking chalice and was unknowingly swallowed by a Etar's wife.

secret enchanted copse to try to restore him to life, but she had been tricked. Midir had actually taken on Ailill's form for this assignation, and revealed himself to her. "You are Etain, daughter of Danann. You are a goddess not a mortal, come back with me—do you know how much I love you?"

The battle for Etain

Etain shook her head in confusion. But it seemed the only way to ensure that she was not torn between Eochy's love and Ailill's despair was to return to her life with Midir. The long battle for Etain began. Eventually Midir appeared at one of Eochy's feasts in his form as a god, grasped Etain in his arms, and flew away with her to his palace, Bri-Leith. Eochy gathered his armies together and set out to destroy the palace and claim his bride. Midir offered to give up Etain only if the king could find the right Etain out of fifty identical women he sent outside the palace walls. But Etain's mortal love for Eochy shone through her eyes and Eochy immediately took her into his arms. The spell that Midir had cast had been broken. Etain would always love Midir and knew she would be with him one day, but first she must return to Tara to finish her mortal life with Eochy.

Midir tried to take Etain back to the land of the gods, but it was too late— she already loved Eochy.

315

Rakian and the bee-woman

Rakian lived with the Fusan people of Borneo and his job was to gather bees' nests in the jungle. One day he went further than he'd ever gone before; the trees were denser and much taller than those near his village and he could hear the buzzing of bees from the highest branches.

In the canopy of tangled trees far into the depths of the jungle, Rakian was surprised to find a nest of white bees.

Rakian was a good climber so he scrambled like a monkey up to the top of the tree, where there was a nest unlike any he had seen before. The bees were completely white. Rakian began to cut down the nest, but as he hacked through the tangled boughs he heard a strange cry. He frowned, put his knife away, freed the nest with his fingers, put the nest into his basket, and set off home.

He hung the nest over his sleeping mat and the next morning went to work in the rice fields. When he returned, to his astonishment he found some rice and fish cooked for him. This continued for several days, until his curiosity got the better of him and he decided to spy on his own hut to find out what was happening. As he lurked behind a tree, a beautiful woman appeared through his front door on her way to fetch some water. Rakian dashed inside the hut and, worried that she might steal his unusual bees' nest, pulled it down from the rafters and hid with it under the table.

When the girl returned, she stopped and shouted, "Who has taken my sarong?" Rakian emerged from under the table: "What are you doing in my home; are you here to steal my bees?" The woman turned to him, "All my clothes and possessions are in the nest—you've hidden it, haven't you?"

Rakian replied, "Yes, but if I give it to you, you'll run away and then I'll never see you again." The woman thought for a while, and replied, "No, I won't go. I was given to you by my mother because I have no husband among my own people. But you must never tell anyone that you have married a bee-woman."

Boastful Rakian

Rakian promised he would never tell a soul, but after a year he smoked too much leaf one night and boasted about his bee-wife. The villagers were shocked and so the bee-woman ran away. Rakian spent weeks searching the jungle for the sound of bees. Eventually he found a longhouse and heard buzzing inside. It was the biggest nest he had ever seen. Bee-woman

The bee-woman was able to hide her secret for a long time, because she could take on a human form.

saw him and appeared to him in human form, and so did all the other bees who flew down from the rafters and turned into people. So Rakian became a member of the bee-people so that he could stay with his wife, and his own people never saw him again.

The convolvulus fan

Fans have always played an important part in Japanese culture and mythology. The fan that folds up on itself symbolizes life: the rivet being the beginning of the journey and the radiating parts made of paper the road of life itself.

Fans were inscribed with secret love messages and exchanged between lovers. This is the tale of Asagao, blinded by her love for a merchant and how their exchange of fan messages brought them together after many years.

Komagawa the merchant and Miyuki, a beautiful young lady of Kyoto, fell in love. They exchanged fans, as was the custom, and Komagawa wrote a poem on his fan about the beauty of the *asagao* or convolvulus flower. When Miyuki returned home, her parents told her that she was about to be married to someone she didn't know. Heartbroken, she ran away and hurried down to the river where she'd met Komagawa, but even the fireflies had vanished in the cold morning air.

She wept until the salt tears caused her to become blind. Out on the streets, Miyuki refused to beg, but made money with her beautiful singing voice. She loved to sing the poem about the convolvulus and so people began to call her Asagao and her fame spread as she traveled the country.

Chance encounter

A few years passed; Komagawa and his friend Takita stopped at a teahouse to rest and, as he sat cross-legged on the floor, Komagawa saw his own love-poem written on a painted screen. The owner told him that a blind girl had given him the poem because it was her favorite song. In fact, she was in the tea garden at that moment and wouldn't the two merchants like to hear her voice? Asagao sang unknowingly to her lover, but he couldn't reveal who he was because his companion Takita was a friend of her family. When the merchants had gone, the teahouse master handed her a fan that Komagawa had left for her. She realized it was from Komagawa and suddenly, her sight restored, she

Japanese fans were exchanged by lovers both as gifts and as a means of communicating messages.

ran out into a fierce storm to find her lover. All night she wandered in the hail and rain, and then as morning came, she heard her name being called, "Asagao, Asagao!" She turned round and saw that Komagawa was running toward her. The convolvulus flower may not last for long, but for now they are reunited.

319

Bitiou and the clay bride

This ancient bloodthirsty Egyptian tale of love and vengeance dates back to the reign of Rameses the Great in about 1300 BCE. Some sources say it may even be based on an earlier myth dating from about 4000 BCE.

The boy Bitiou drove his cattle to feed every day. One day his brother's wife saw him and asked him to lie with her. He refused, because he loved his brother dearly. She, however, returned home and told her husband that his brother had slept with her. Just before sunset, Bitiou led his cattle into the night shelter, but the lead cow cried, "Watch out, your brother Anapou has a knife!" Bitiou ran as quickly as he could from his brother's attack; the Sun god Ra took pity on him and created a huge river between them. Anapou shouted across the raging torrent that Bitiou had raped his wife and deserved to die. Bitiou was shocked, since he'd never lusted after her, let alone raped her. He was so horrified he cut off his own testicles and threw them in the river.

Anapou was overcome by guilt and ran home in a frenzy, the knife gleaming in his hand. Ra had saved his brother for a reason, but the knife needed a home. Anapou crept back into his house and, before his wife could turn round to face him, he sunk the knife deep into her neck.

Bitiou put his feelings and heart in the trunk of an acacia tree. The potter god Khnum felt sorry for him and made him an artificial bride out of clay. Bitiou fell in love with her and showed her where his heart was hidden.

The girl would wash her hair in the river near the tree and its magical perfume wafted downstream to the pharaoh's palace, casting a spell over all who lived there. The pharaoh wanted to find out who had bewitched him, so he found the artificial girl and immediately asked her to marry him. She agreed because she wanted wealth, and told the pharaoh to cut down the acacia tree because she was bound by its power. The moment he chopped it down Bitiou died, and Anapou, sensing his brother's death, came to find the fallen tree. He placed the last acacia berry in a cup of water and it transformed into a white bull, Bitiou.

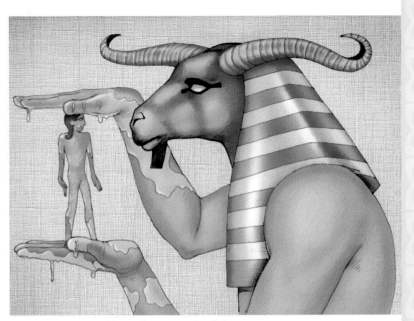

Khnum, the potter god, felt sorry for Bitiou and made him a clay bride.

Sacrifice

As the bull approached the palace, the artificial girl guessed it was Bitiou, so she asked the pharaoh to sacrifice it as an offering to Ra. Its blood gushed across the courtyard and made two seeds from the persea tree grow so tall that people began to worship them as if they were divine. The artificial queen knew that Bitiou's soul resided in these trees, so she ordered them to be cut down. As the woodman axed the trunk, a tiny slither of wood flew between the queen's lips and she conceived a son. She did not know her son was Bitiou and, when the pharaoh died, Bitiou ruled the land. He sent for Anapou and made him prince of the Nile; they brought the artificial girl to trial, telling the people how she had never loved anyone but herself.

Pomona and Vertumnus

Vertumnus was the Roman god of the woodlands. He was shy and seemed doomed to live without love. His job was to turn the leaves brown every autumn, and tell the grubs and worms to burrow and turn the soil throughout the winter.

Pomona was a beautiful wood nymph who lived in the orchards on Palatine Hill. She removed parasites from trees and plants and picked greenfly from the new shoots. Vertumnus loved watching Pomona dancing with the other nymphs, but was too shy to speak to her. Wretchedly, he asked the goddess Pales, the keeper of the pastures, what to do.

The kindly goddess said, "If you can change the leaves from green to brown, then surely you can change yourself from shy to bold? Then Pomona will see you in a different light and you can declare your love for her."

Vertumnus disguised himself as a farmer, a plow-man, then a soldier, but Pomona was not interested in the mortals that paraded before her every day. As a last resort he disguised himself as an old woman and hobbled into the orchard in the heat of the day carrying a cup of water. He offered her a drink, she drank from the cup and then danced away. He went back the next day disguised as the woman again. This time Pomona sat with him on a grassy bank and they talked. "Have you ever heard the story of Iphis?" he asked as she drank from the cup. "No, is it sad?" she queried.

"Very sad. Iphis was a poor peasant boy who fell in love with the princess Anaxerete. But because he was poor she refused to have him, so Iphis hanged himself from a tree. When Anaxerete saw that he was dead, she turned to stone so that her body matched her heart. Don't you think that's sad?"

Pomona replied, "Yes, indeed, but I must tend to my fruit, and you're old and frail and must go home." Vertumnus, believing Pomona would never love him, threw off his disguise and began to walk away through the trees. Pomona turned and, seeing the old woman's clothes on the ground, ran after him. "Who are you?" she asked.

Once she had seen the truth, Pomona's feelings turned to love for Vertumnus.

He turned to face her and she recognized him instantly. "Now I can see you as you really are!" Won over by his eloquence and his efforts to win her, she ran into his arms, and from then on Vertumnus and Pomona were inseparable. They worked together changing the seasons, just as surely as Vertumnus had changed Pomona's heart.

The herdsman and the weaver girl

This is a Chinese myth of how the stars Altair and Vega came to exist. In the sky lived a weaver girl whose job it was to make the clothes of Heaven and hang them as clouds of different colors. This part of Heaven was called the Silver River, and on Earth was a young herdsman who worked in the fields with his ox.

The herdsman meets the weaver girl once a year in the sky, and her tears fall to Earth from the clouds that she paints gray.

When the herdsman Ni Lang came of age, the ox spoke to him for the first time, telling him about the beautiful weaver girl, and how, if he could steal some of her clothes, she would be his wife. So the herdsman traveled down to the bank of the Silver River as darkness fell, and hid among the reeds. Soon the weaver girl and her friends arrived to bathe.

Entranced, Ni Lang watched the girls for a while, then dashed out of the rushes and snatched the weaver girl's bundle of clothes. The other girls ran away, but the weaver girl asked, "Who are you? Come out, I won't harm you." The herdsman crept out, "Here are your clothes, I'm sorry, but my ox told me that if I stole your clothes you would be my wife."

The weaver girl laughed, "Well, you'll have to be my husband now you've seen me naked." Ni Lang looked up and, instantly, they fell in love and were married the next day.

The gods' demand

For some years they lived on Earth, but the gods demanded that the weaver girl return to Heaven or be punished. One day Ni Lang returned home to find her gone. He set off with his two children in panniers across his back toward the Silver River, but the angry queen of the Heavens had moved it far away from Earth so that no mortals and gods could ever meet again. The old ox was dying and told the herdsman to wrap himself in his skin, then he would fly to Heaven. Ni Lang put his two children back in the panniers and flew up to the sky. But the Silver River was now deep and dangerous, so Ni Lang took a ladle from his basket and started to drain the river. The god of Heaven felt sorry for Ni Lang: "You can visit the weaver girl once a year, but that is all I can do for you."

So the weaver girl and the herdsman live on different sides of the Silver River. She is the star Vega and he is Altair. Every seventh day of the seventh month of the lunar calendar the herdsman crosses the bridge and embraces his weaver girl. The four bright stars beside Vega are the shuttles of the weaver girl's loom, and the two stars either side of him are his children. Beside the weaver girl are three bright stars, which are messages from Ni Lang. And when these bright stars are seen in the autumn sky, it is a reminder of the eternal love between the two of them.

Scar-face

Scar-face was one of the best hunters of all the Algonquin tribe, but he was teased because of his ugly scar. Girls refused to look at him, even though the scar was the result of a heroic encounter with a grizzly bear.

Scar-face had fallen in love with the chief's daughter, but most of the warriors wanted to marry her too. He knew he must ask her before it was too late. He found her beside the river pulling rushes to make baskets. "I may be poor, but my heart is filled with love for you. I've no furs or riches, but I live by my bow and spear. Would you marry me and live with me in my lodge?"

The girl looked into his eyes: "It's not necessary for my husband to be rich, but the Sun god has decreed I shall never marry anyone, for I am his Sun maiden. If you can find him and make him change his mind, I will marry you, but he must remove the scar on your face as a sign."

Scar-face set out to find the Sun god, but he was sure the god would never give up such a beautiful girl. For many moons he traveled—a wolverine took him part of the way, but when they reached a huge lake he refused to go any farther. Scar-face nearly turned back, but two swans appeared and he jumped on one and they glided across the lake. At the other side he encountered Apsirahts, the son of the Sun god. Together they climbed the mountain to the god's lodge and Scar-face was warmly welcomed by the Sun god and his wife Kokomis, the Moon goddess.

A wish granted

One day Apsirahts was nearly killed by two bird monsters, and Scar-face came to the rescue and slaughtered them. The Sun god was so grateful he asked Scar-face if he had a request he could grant. So Scar-face told him why he was there and how the chief's daughter could not marry him while she was still under the power of the Sun himself.

The Sun god nodded, "You have saved my son. How can I not grant you this request? Go back to the woman you love and marry her, and as a sign I

Algonquin engravings on a granite rock face at Nephton, Ontario, tell stories from their past.

have agreed this, I will now make you whole again." The Sun god raised his golden hand and instantly the scar on the youth's face disappeared.

Healed, Scar-face left the Sun god and happily made his way back to his home, and when he arrived at the encampment people wondered who this beautiful warrior was. The chief's daughter looked into his eyes, though, and knew instantly. They were married, and Scar-face became known as Smooth-face. Together he and the chief's daughter built a medicine lodge in honor of the Sun.

Island love

For the Ifaluk peoples of Micronesia, Wolfat introduced the art of tattooing to seduce women, while in Haitian and Voodoo mythology, Erzulie was the goddess of love, beauty, and retribution.

Throughout Micronesia, the art of tattooing is symbolic of the sacredness of life and love.

Wolfat's fancy

Wolfat lived in the sky of flowers with all the other gods and sometimes visited Earth in different forms. Each day one god or another would descend to see what was going on and whether Wolfat should get up to any tricks to sort out human or animal behavior.

One day, Wolfat came across the beautiful Iloumuligeriou and immediately lusted after her. In his guise as a mortal he painted his face and body with intricate black designs, made a fire in her house and she was instantly besotted and they had sex. In the morning Wolfat left her and returned to the sky. But he was so filled with sexual desire for the woman that he went back down to Earth again, only this time without his skin decorations. This time the woman didn't fancy him, so he covered himself in tattoos again and returned. And this time Iloumuligeriou welcomed him with open arms.

Wolfat showed all the men how to tattoo their bodies with black soot and a sharp feather from a bird's wing. When they realized it made them desirable to women, they tattooed themselves every day.

Erzulie

In Haitian and Voodoo mythology, Erzulie is the goddess of love as well as beauty, dancing, luxury, flowers, and ideals. She lives in a palace of delights and is always powdered and perfumed. She is generous with her love as well as her gifts, and wears three rings to signify her three marriages. Her husbands were Damballa the serpent god, Agwe the sea god, and Ogoun the warrior hero and smithy god. Rather like Aphrodite, she is also a fickle and jealous goddess, and in her aspect as Erzulie Dantor, she can give love and take it away depending on her mood. In her aspect as Erzulie Ge-Rouge (Red Eyes), she huddles in a corner with tight-clenched fists and knees up tight to her chest, weeping and wailing for the shortness of life and the limitations of love. She then sends out emotional torments, betrayal, and infidelity to punish her worshippers.

The Voodoo goddess Erzulie is still worshipped today, along with the Virgin Mary, in festivals across Haiti.

329

Tristan and Isolde

This myth originated in Brittany and eventually became identified with Arthurian and Celtic legends. As a myth, it shines out from many others in its painful account of betrayal, romantic frustration and self-destruction, although this version provides only the bare bones of the tale.

Tristan was brought up by his uncle, King Mark of Cornwall, and one day he killed Morholt, the giant half-brother of the King of Ireland. Mark sent Tristan to Ireland to bring back the beautiful Isolde to be Mark's queen. On their way back on the ship, Tristan and Isolde mistakenly drank a love-potion, which Isolde's mother had made for her to give to King Mark when she arrived. And so they fell deeply in love.

Mark and Isolde were married, but on their wedding night Brangen, Isolde's maid, took the place of Isolde in the marriage bed, and because the king was so drunk he suspected nothing. The secret lovers could not be kept apart, and they would meet in the orchards outside Tintagel until they took too many chances and were discovered. Growing suspicions and jealous whisperings around the court led Mark to believe the worst. One day while out riding he discovered Tristan and Isolde sleeping side-by-side with a drawn sword between them. Jealous and yet compassionate, Mark exchanged the sword for his own, so the lovers would know they had been discovered. When they awoke they realized the truth, and Tristan decided he must go to Brittany in self-imposed exile and that Isolde must return to Mark as his wife.

Jealousy and retribution

Tristan went to France and married (for her name) Isolde of the White Hands, but he yearned for his true love and couldn't consummate his marriage. He was seriously wounded in battle in France, and his friend Kaherdin was sent to fetch Isolde from Tintagel in the hope that she could heal him. If Kaherdin was successful in bringing her back, he would raise a white sail; if not, a black sail.

For Tristan and Isolde, love became an unbearable test that led to both their deaths.

Tristan was too ill to watch for the boat's return and so he asked his wife to. Isolde of the White Hands, realizing Tristan had never loved her, saw her chance for revenge. As the ship appeared she told him the sail was black. Tristan died in deep despair. When Isolde landed and found his body, she died of grief too. King Mark took their bodies back to Cornwall and buried them side by side, then planted two trees whose branches intertwined forever as they grew.

TRICKSTERS, HEROES, AND QUESTS

Every culture or civilization has produced a hero, great mortal, or semi-divine warrior as well as ubiquitous trickster gods. Whether on a divine quest, the search for enlightenment, the desire for vengeance or fulfillment, the hero reflects our own personal growth. Tricksters, meanwhile, were morally neutral and often helped humankind to understand its corruption and/or its goodness. Heroes and tricksters often merge or their skills overlap, as with Odysseus' cunning and Olifat's heroic quest.

Gilgamesh

This is one of the oldest surviving stories in the world,
dating back some 5,000 years to ancient Mesopotamia.
One version, discovered in the library of King Ashurbanipal
and dating from around 600 BCE, was written on 12 tablets
of clay, each containing 300 lines of verse. Some scholars
believe that Gilgamesh was a real person, a King of Uruk
who ruled c. 2700 BCE.

True character

Gilgamesh is probably the earliest recorded part-mortal to achieve heroic
status. The questing nature of the individual is clearly part of our psyche,
whether more than four thousand years ago or today. Most heroes in later myth
were on a quest for social status, redemption, or glory, but Gilgamesh sought
not only wisdom but the acceptance of his own mortality.

Gilgamesh was the son of the goddess Ninsun and a demon father who had
disguised himself as the King of Uruk. As a young man, Gilgamesh took over
the throne and proved his courage and strength by hunting and fighting, and
later by his determination and stature by building a great wall around Uruk
with 900 towers. However, inside the fortress it was a different matter. He made
men his slaves, he had an insatiable sexual appetite, he raped and gambled and
behaved like a spoilt child. His unruly behavior earned him a bad reputation
and the people of Uruk prayed to the gods for help.

The arrival of Enkidu

Anu, father of all gods, persuaded Mother Earth to create a huge wild man called
Enkidu. The wild man lived in the wilderness and thought he was a beast of
the night. The other gods put an image of the wild animal into Gilgamesh's
mind one night as he lay restless and disturbed by terrible nightmares. That
night he dreamed of a man so wild and untameable that he longed to capture
him and conquer him.

*Sumerian ruins at Uruk. There were many dynasties of
Uruk, one of the first including the hero Gilgamesh.*

Gilgamesh believed this wild man was dangerous, so rather than hunt him
and face the possibility of being killed, he sent a sorceress to lure him out of
the wilderness. Enkidu was enchanted and the sorceress seduced him and
showed him how to wash his body and deal with human civilization. Enkidu
was taken to the great walls of Uruk where the feast of Ishtar was in progress.
Gilgamesh was ready and the people were elated. At last here was a creature
who might match the tyrannical Gilgamesh. But as the two fought they began
to respect each other's power. Eventually, exhausted, they fell to their knees,
kissed and embraced and from that day on they were the best of friends. There
were now two petulant rulers, not one.

The monster Humbaba

So the people again called on the gods for help, and this time they put an image in Gilgamesh's mind to send him on a quest to destroy the great monster Humbaba. The gods hoped Humbaba would kill both Gilgamesh and Enkidu, and Uruk would be at peace again. Gilgamesh knew that if he defeated the monster he would be proclaimed a hero. He did so and returned to Uruk with the cedars of Humbaba's forest to prove it, and he was hailed a great hero. He wore fine clothes and his face glowed with pride. Even the goddess Ishtar could not resist trying to seduce him, but he rejected her. In her anger, she called on her father Anu to send down the bull of Heaven to kill Gilgamesh. Anu reluctantly agreed, but the bull raged through the citadel killing hundreds of innocent people before Enkidu and Gilgamesh managed to tear out its heart.

The real quest

Ishtar took matters into her own hands and arranged for Enkidu to be struck down by the plague. After his death Gilgamesh wailed before the people, insisting they mourn this great hero as one of their own. In his grief, he vowed to grow his hair and roam the wilderness, clad only in a lion skin. However, Gilgamesh wasn't prepared to die like his friend. He wanted to find out how to avoid death.

He found himself (probably at Ishtar's instigation) on a quest to seek out Utnapishtum, the only man to have everlasting life. Utnapishtum explained that mortals could not cheat death, because to be mortal is to live and die. So Gilgamesh set off to find the one flower that, when made into a potion, would give him eternal youth. But a serpent snatched the flower before Gilgamesh could pick it and, devastated, he began his long journey back to Uruk. Yet as he walked toward the outer walls his heart grew stronger, for in losing what he desired so much, he had begun to accept who he truly was. As he approached the great gate of Uruk he thought how beautiful the citadel was with its 900 towers. No one would ever forget his achievement, and that was how he would become immortal. He wrote down on tablets the stories of his travels and placed them on the walls of Uruk in order to share his wisdom and be remembered as the one who came to understand why he was only human.

Gilgamesh and Enkidu quickly killed the monster Humbaba, who guarded the cedar forest.

Hanuman

In Hindu mythology, Hanuman, or Hanumat ("heavy-jawed") is a trickster god and monkey. He was a major character in the *Ramayana* (see page 340) and also appeared as a monkey when he accompanied Tripitaka on his journey from India to China.

Youth

Born to the monkey queen Anjana and the god of the wind Vayu, Hanuman was ravenously hungry as soon as he was out of the womb. Catching sight of the Sun, he thought it must be something tasty, so he chased it up into Heaven. Indra intervened by throwing a thunderbolt at Hanuman, which knocked him back to Earth, smashing and deforming his jaw. Vayu was so angry that he slid into every god's belly and gave them terrible wind until Indra apologized to Vayu and agreed to grant Hanuman immortality.

Some accounts suggest that Hanuman was given immortality because of his loyal support of Rama. Agile and strong, he became an invaluable ally against the demon king Ravana. He could fly at the speed of wind and had the strength to uproot mountains. As a trickster, he could change form and make himself invisible. He terrified enemies with his golden skin and enormous swishing tail.

Feats

One tale from the *Ramayana* tells how Hanuman was sent as a spy to Lanka and also to deliver a message to the kidnapped Sita. Hanuman was concerned whether he could leap across the straits dividing Lanka from the mainland. While pondering the mission, his body began to grow until it was the size of a mountain, and he leapt across the skies, roaring and flashing his red eyes. But a female demon, Sarusa, swallowed him in mid-air and he instantly shrunk to the size of a thumbnail, then swelled up in her belly, bursting through her skin and shattering her into a thousand pieces. When he reached Lanka he transformed into a cat and wandered into Ravana's bedchamber to give Sita the message.

Hanuman was a trickster monkey god, who killed ogres and demons in the epic tale, the Ramayana.

Hanuman was of great service to Rama, and his greatest feat was to fly to the Himalayas to fetch a healing herb for Rama's wounds. Indra tried to make it difficult for Hanuman, but he simply shrugged and tore up the whole mountain and flew back with it under his arm. As he drew near the city, night began to fall and he knew that the moonlight would prevent the herb from working properly. So he swallowed the Moon and delivered the magic plant safely to Rama.

After the battle of Lanka was won, Rama offered Hanuman anything he chose. Hanuman asked to be allowed to live for as long as Rama's name was spoken. Rama's memory lived on and so did Hanuman.

Rama

From the great *Ramayana*, a Hindu epic compiled between the 11th and 6th centuries BCE, comes Rama and his quest to destroy the terrifying demon Ravana and save his love Sita.

Rama's real name was Ramachandra (Rama the Moon). In Hindu myth he was the seventh incarnation on Earth of the god Vishnu. The demon king Ravana had become so invulnerable that the only way to destroy him was to send a mortal, since Ravana had been too conceited to ask for immunity from humans when he claimed his power from the gods.

The demon army

Vishnu volunteered to go to Earth and, in his incarnation as Rama, he married King Janaka's daughter, Sita. Ravana's demon sister tried to seduce Rama, but he rejected her and so Ravana sent 14,000 demons to destroy Rama. However, Rama massacred the entire army so eventually, in revenge, Ravana kidnapped Sita and took her to Lanka.

Rescuing Sita

The monkey king Sugriva gave Rama an army of monkeys, led by Hanuman. The monkeys built a huge stone causeway across the evil waters and a terrible battle was fought at the gates of the city. One by one the demons were killed, and the conflict could only be resolved by single combat between Ravana and Rama. With a magic arrow given to him by a magician, Rama killed Ravana, and all the monkeys that had been killed were brought to life by the gods.

Rama's death

The victorious Rama was unsure if Sita had been faithful, even though she promised that she had rejected Ravana's advances. Rama therefore exiled her for 15 years, and when she returned with his two sons, Sita asked the gods for a sign to prove she was pure and the children were his. Mother Earth split open and swallowed her up. Rama was heartbroken, realizing she had always told

Rama, one of the many avatars of Vishnu, eventually killed the evil demon Ravana in single combat.

the truth, and he longed only to follow her to eternity; not long after her death he walked into the River Sarayu, ending his human life and returning to his divine form as Vishnu. His mortal quest as the destroyer of Ravana had been tragically completed.

Odysseus

Odysseus was the relentless heroic wanderer who has been
portrayed in many forms of literature and legend, but it is
Homer's *Odyssey* that does the hero real justice. Here he not
only faces hardship, adventure, and true suffering, but also
contends with his shadow.

The *Iliad*, on the other hand, portrays Odysseus as an arrogant, heroic
adventurer who has no depth of character and no chance for psychological
growth. Using both these sources it is possible to see that Odysseus
encompasses all facets of human nature, from unscrupulous deceit to the
integrity of a real hero. It is the light and dark of such a character that
illuminates our own particular journey.

Youth

Odysseus (Ulysses in Latin) means "angry." This angry young man was the son
of Anticlea and Laertes, the King of Ithaca, or some say the trickster Sisyphus.
The centaur Chiron brought him up and as soon as Odysseus was old enough
to rule, Laertes abdicated. Like many other young heroes, Odysseus wanted to
marry Helen of Sparta, later Helen of Troy, but unlike most of her suitors, he
wisely married her cousin Penelope instead.

War and Troy

While Odysseus was in Sparta he advised Helen's father to make all her suitors
swear an oath that they would support whoever eventually married her. So when
Helen was abducted by Paris, it was this oath that compelled every Greek hero
to help King Menelaus and subsequently join in the Trojan War.

But Odysseus was so devoted to Penelope that he pretended to be a madman
when recruitment began (although some say he was afraid of an oracle that
had informed him he'd be away for 20 years and would return as a beggar). He
yoked an ass and an ox to the same plow and sowed his fields with salt to prove
his madness. But Palamedes, on his way to the war himself, tricked him by

The Trojans thought the horse would bring them divine protection, but all it brought was Odysseus and his army.

Poseidon turned against Odysseus and ensured that the walls of Troy were rebuilt.

dropping Odysseus' baby in front of the plow. Odysseus stopped immediately and Palamedes declared this act was something no madman would do. Odysseus was now forced to go to war, but he never forgave Palamedes and brought about his untimely death later on.

At Troy, Odysseus used cunning and strategy to help the Greeks. He showed the Greek leaders where Achilles was hiding, he seized the statue of Athene that symbolized Troy's luck and he led the forces that hid inside the Trojan horse. Because of his divided support among gods and mortals, his return to Ithaca took ten years. Poseidon had turned against Odysseus and had rebuilt the walls of Troy that had been destroyed. In fact it was Poseidon who saw to it that he was the last Greek hero to return home. On this epic journey Odysseus faced adventures, conflict, and supernatural forces, all of which he defeated by cunning, bravery, and strategy.

The wanderings

His exact route remains a mystery, but he first set sail for Thrace. He was, however, blown by storms to the land of the Lotus Eaters, an island where the sandbanks altered every time the tide changed and the people lived only in the present, with no thought of the past or future. Some of Odysseus' men ate the lotus fruit and he found them in a senseless daze; they had lost all their will to get home and thought only of consuming the lotus flower again.

Odysseus outwitted Polyphemus, the King of the Cyclopes, whose father was Poseidon. Polyphemus was seeking revenge on all mortals for the loss of his beloved Galatea to a mortal man. When Odysseus landed in Sicily, Polyphemus ate two of his men alive. The next day, Odysseus went to the Cyclopes' cave and left him vast quantities of wine. In a drunken stupor Polyphemus asked Odysseus his name and he replied "Nobody." Once asleep, Odysseus took his olive-wood spear, heated it in the white ashes of the fire and seared out the Cyclopes' eye. Polyphemus screamed with terror, "Nobody's hurt me!" The other Cyclopes could not find anyone called "Nobody." As the ship left Sicily, Odysseus cried out, "Never forget that the Nobody who tricked you is the greatest hero, Odysseus of Ithaca!"

Odysseus tricked Polyphemus, getting him drunk and blinding him in his one eye, so that he and his men could escape.

345

The travelers then arrived at the floating island of the ruler of the winds Aeolus. Odysseus was given a present of a bag of winds. But his men were curious to see inside, and when they opened it, all the winds dispersed and were no use as they blew off in all directions. Odysseus also resisted the spells of the enchantress Circe, and, with the aid of Hermes, he restored his men to human form after she had turned them all to pigs. He stayed some seven years with Circe, delighting in her charms and seductive ways.

Eventually he set sail to the east, escaped the sea-monsters Scylla and Charybdis, and ended up alone after the remaining men became mutinous and deserted him. Odysseus drifted to the island of Ogygia, where the beautiful sea nymph Calypso fell in love with him. He stayed with her for seven years, spellbound, yet longing to return home.

The sea nymph, Calypso, loved Odysseus and offered him immortality, but all he wanted was to return home.

Odysseus disguised himself as a beggar and competed with the other suitors to win back his bride and his kingdom.

The return

Penelope had been loyal to Odysseus for those 20 years, but the pressure on her to remarry was intense; she agreed to marry whoever could fire an arrow through 12 tiny loops of leather tied to the end of 12 axe-heads set upright in the ground. Everyone failed, except an old beggar. This was Odysseus in disguise. With the help of his son Telemachus, he fought a fierce battle until all the suitors were killed. Then he revealed his true identity and was welcomed back as king.

On one of his journeys to the mainland he had consulted the Delphic oracle which told him that his own son would kill him. He immediately banished Telemachus, who went to marry Circe and founded a whole new dynasty. But Telegonus, Odysseus' son by Circe (a son he didn't know he'd fathered) turned up on Ithaca quite by chance with a band of men. Telegonus had been searching for his true father, but had no idea who he was. Odysseus saw them land and, thinking they were pirates, fought them on the shore. Telegonus killed Odysseus with a poisonous spear made from a stingray's spine and the oracle came true. In some accounts, Telegonus then went on to marry Penelope and rule Ithaca.

Loki

In Norse mythology, Loki is both the oldest and youngest god. He existed as a concept before creation and came into physical being through cunning. There are numerous tales about Loki, the god of mischief, lies, and deception. Unlike the rest of the gods of the Norse pantheon, Loki's personality evolves and he has more human traits than any of the others.

Loki ("alluring" or "fire") was also an adept shape-changer. He could be anything from a fish to a fly to a grain of sand. He could even be the frown on a giant's face or the heel on a man's shoe. He occasionally befriended humans who he thought were deserving.

In one story, a peasant challenged the giant, Skrymsli, to a game of chess. Unfortunately the giant's stakes were high. If he won, the peasant must give up his own son to the giant unless he could hide so well, that the giant could never find him. Foolishly the peasant agreed and of course lost. He asked the gods for help, but the gods got bored and so as a last resort the peasant asked for Loki's help. Loki set a trap for the giant, then hacked off both the giant's legs and placed a flint block between the limbs and the body so that the giant's magic was disabled. For once, Loki had helped someone in distress.

However, he wasn't always such a benevolent god, and when Balder, Odin's son, became a threat to Loki's antics, Loki became enraged and jealous of Balder's popularity, and tricked Hoder into killing him. Loki was then banished from Asgard, and his tricks became more and more spiteful.

Eventually, the gods captured Loki and imprisoned him in a deep cave. First they changed Loki's son, Vali, into a wolf and set him on his brother, Narfi. They tied Loki to rocks with Narfi's entrails, and the giantess Skadi hung a serpent above his head so that the venom dripped on his face until Ragnarok. Loki's wife, Sigyn, sits by his side and catches the drips in a cup; when she moves away, the drips cause Loki such pain that earthquakes shake across the world. When this cycle ends, Loki will escape from the cave and destroy all the gods.

Loki was bound to the rocks as punishment for his tricks in killing Odin's son, Balder.

Gassire

The Fasa, an aristocratic people of the southern Sahara, lived around the 3rd century BCE. They displayed courage in combat, but would fight only those who were their equals. Like many mortal heroes, Gassire was a warrior, but desired everlasting fame. However, what was best for him was not necessarily best for his people, and this desire was his undoing.

Gassire's father, King Ngaanamba, was old and Gassire was not young himself. He longed to inherit the kingdom and wished the old man dead. Gassire would ride into battle and achieve honor as a great hero, and would listen to his fellow warriors praise him. Each week he looked for signs that his father would die, and his greed for power eventually turned to rage.

He visited the wisest man in the Fasa kingdom, and asked when his father would die and when he would become king. But the wise man told Gassire that he would never inherit his father's shield and sword, that he was destined to carry only a lute. Gassire was outraged, but the old man shrugged and said, "Your path in life is not that of a king, or hero. When you hear the partridge in the field you will understand the nature of your journey."

The lute

Gassire didn't believe the wise man and stormed off to try to prove that he was the best warrior in the land. He bravely fought the Burdama people until they retreated in fear, and meanwhile his heroic status grew and grew.

One day, he walked into the field and heard a partridge singing how its song will live forever, long after all the heroes and kings are dead. So Gassire returned to the wise man and asked if he could sing a great battle song that would never be forgotten. The wise man nodded, "Long ago the Fasa fought other peoples; the bards played the lute and it was the bards who were remembered, while the warriors were not. You, too, will be a singer of battle songs, but never a king."

Gassire longed for fame, but it was a lute that brought it to him, in a different way than he expected.

Gassire asked a smith to make a lute that would sing, but was told that the only way it would sing was by having a heart, which was achieved by drawing the blood of his deeds and the blood of his sons in battle, so that it became part of him and his people. Every day, therefore, Gassire took one of his sons to battle and each one was killed, blood oozing across the lute as he carried them home over his back. The Fasa people began to realize that Gassire didn't care for his sons and that he was choosing fame over life. No longer praised, he was outcast in his own kingdom.

That night, camping out under the bright stars and wrapped up against the cold desert air, he could not sleep. He gazed upon his few companions and men who slept, and then yearned to touch the blood-stained lute beside him. Then, as he began to pluck the strings, the lute began to play its own beautiful battle song. At the same moment in his home far away, his father, the old king, died. The lute began to play again and this time all of Gassire's anger left him and he wept with both grief and joy. The song that he sang and the music that he played were the most exquisite ever. For the grief was for his dead sons and father and for the real pain of his deeds. The only joy he felt now was that he would be remembered for his battle song long after any of the heroes or warriors were remembered for their valiant deeds.

Coniraya

Coniraya was a trickster spirit who maintained that he was the one and only creator. His main skill was deception and he spent most of his time disguised as a mortal beggar. Scholars believe that Coniraya predates the Incas and was probably one of the earliest tales from South America.

Coniraya was renowned for his seductive skills, but when he saw the beautiful Cavillaca weaving beside a fragrant *lucma* tree, he changed into a bird of paradise and flew to the top of the tree. Pounding some of the tree's fruit into a mash, he mixed it with some of his own semen and dropped it at the feet of Cavillaca. The girl, who was about to have lunch, picked up the fruit immediately and ate it ravenously. Soon afterward she gave birth to a son and resolved to find the child's father.

The child

She summoned the gods and invited all the local suitors to a feast. Coniraya was there, dressed as a beggar and mingling with the locals. Cavillaca put the boy in the middle of the gathering, knowing that he would crawl toward his true father. As the child shuffled toward Coniraya, the men gasped in horror and Cavillaca was horrified that the father of her son was so shabby a beggar. She ran away to the sacred city of Pachacamac, by the sea. Cavillaca was so disgusted with herself as she sat throwing stones into the water that she dived into the ocean and was immediately turned into a rock.

Tricking the god

Everywhere he went, Coniraya blessed those who gave him good news about Cavillaca's whereabouts and cursed those who said they didn't know anything. Arriving at the sea, he discovered that the god Pachacamac had turned Cavillaca to stone for daring to jump into his sacred sea. This sea-snake god was fed a daily supply of fish by his two daughters, and no mortal or god was allowed any of the fish. Coniraya transformed himself into an otter man, seduced the

The archaeological site of the Temple of Pachacamac, with its fish frescoes, lies southeast of Lima in Peru.

elder daughter and returned nightly to have sex with her. The younger daughter changed into a pigeon and flew away, scared by his trickster powers. No longer caring about the serpent, the elder daughter hid all the fish in her cave pool. A week later Coniraya released the fish into the ocean for every man to catch. Pachacamac tried to set a trap for the otter man, but Coniraya changed into a fish, slithered down the stream into the open sea and headed home.

He returned to Haurochiri and resumed his shape as a beggar to play more tricks on humankind. It was far safer than clashing with a god.

Väinämöinen

As a key figure in the epic *Kalevala*, compiled by folklorist Elias Lonnrot in the 19th century, Väinämöinen was the mythical hero and trickster in the struggle between the land of the Finns (Kalevala) and Pohjola, in the north.

Väinämöinen, the son of Luonnator, was born already more than 30 years old. He had magical powers, thawed the glaciers and generally made the countryside farmable. The frost-giant Joukhainen wasn't happy about this and began chanting spells to make the ice return and the vegetation wither away. But Väinämöinen simply sang his spells louder and outwitted the giant by turning his horse into a boulder, his sword into lightning, and his arrows into birds. Joukhainen offered to give his sister Aino to Väinämöinen as a prize. But Aino rejected the already-old hero and drowned herself rather than marry him.

Eternal bachelor

Worried that he was unsuitable marriage material, Väinämöinen set off to Pohjola and the land of the ice-giants to find a suitable wife. He swam for days through icy wastes and, on the point of drowning, an eagle rescued him and placed him on the shore. He arrived at the palace of the witch princess Louhi, who offered him her daughter if he could make a magical device (a *sampo*) that could produce gold, salt, and flour. Väinämöinen set off home to try, but Louhi's daughter caught up with him, and he pleaded with her to marry him without the *sampo*. She agreed, as long as he performed her own set of tests, including peeling a stone and making a boat from a weaving shuttle. But wicked spirits stopped him from completing his tasks and, without thinking, he gave his brother Ilmarinen the smith the task of making the *sampo*. Ilmarinen made one, took it straight to Louhi and married the witch's daughter.

Brave hero

But the marriage didn't last and the witch's daughter was killed by her own cattle after a dispute with a servant. Ilmarinen returned to Finland now a widower,

Väinämöinen was known to be a trickster, shaman, and intrepid explorer.

and even though Väinämöinen had been jealous of their marriage, the brothers were finally reconciled. They decided to steal the *sampo* to ensure the prosperity of their people. With another adventurer, Lemminkainen, the three stole the *sampo* from the palace at Pohjola and set sail for home. But Louhi sent storms to wreck their ship, and as it disintegrated in the icy seas, the *sampo* broke into pieces. Väinämöinen rescued some fragments and joined them together with a binding spell, then blew the breath of light and warmth across the forests of Finland so that when Louhi came to attack them with cold weather, the spring would come to restore life. Very, very old, he sailed away on a bronze boat on an eternal journey between Heaven and Earth. It is said that if Finland ever needs him, he will return.

Rata

There are many versions of Rata's adventures throughout the islands of Polynesia. Rata is a warrior hero with magical powers and is part of the Tawhaki cycle, a great cycle of dynastic myths. In this version from the islands of the South Pacific, it is Rata's quest for vengeance that is told.

Rata was the son of the mortal Matoka and the comet god Wahie-roa. Not long before she gave birth, Matoka had a terrible craving for a delicacy called *koko*, a kind of fat bird with meat as rich as venison. Wahie-roa set off to catch one, but he trespassed on the land of a terrifying giant called Matuku and was killed.

The magic tree

When he grew up, Rata vowed to kill Matuku, but he didn't have a canoe. Only one magic tree in the forest could be made into a boat, but each time he cut it down the tree rerooted itself and sprang to life. Spirits of the forest told him, "This is the sacred grove of the great god Tane; return home and make sacrifice, then we will help you." So Rata offered flowers and chanted songs, and the next day he found a canoe and the spirits helped him launch it to sea.

Revenge

Rata sailed to the land of the man-eating goblin Poua, who chanted spells and hypnotized Rata's men

In Polynesian myth, sacrifices were made to Tane, the ancestor god of all the forests and trees.

into a trance. But Rata had a more powerful magic. He filled the goblin up with food and burning stones from the fire, and the goblin's body burst. Then they landed on Matuku's island and lured the giant out of his cavern. Rata and his men threw a noose round his neck, chopped off his arms and legs and then his neck. Matuku turned into a bittern, and can still be heard across the marshes.

Return of the bones

Rata's father's bones were being used by the Ponaturi wise men to make spells so that no one could defeat them. Rata stole the bones back and used the spells to strengthen his men and weaken the enemy. The Ponaturi fled, and Rata made sure everyone was slaughtered. Any of Rata's men that were killed sprang to life and the bones of Wahie-roa rattled on the sails in the sea breeze.

Because Polynesia is made up of islands, boats and sailing feature prominently in the mythology of the area.

Olifat

Olifat was best known as a trickster whose pranks sometimes caused death, but usually made fools out of mortals. Like many tricksters, he was the son of a mortal woman and a god, in this case the great god Anulap. Olifat's sole concern was to prove he was superior to humankind, as well as avoiding the mortal condition of boredom.

Olifat's birth was highly unusual—his mother's long ebony hair was twisted up in a knot and fastened with a coconut leaf. One morning she released the coconut leaf and Olifat fell out of the knot. He was highly precocious and matured quickly. Anulap had warned Olifat's mother never to let him drink from a coconut that had a small hole, because he feared he would find out who his father was. But Olifat did and, because he had to tip his head so far back to catch the last drop of milk, he glimpsed Anulap in the Heavens.

The trick

Olifat decided to visit him immediately, but he wasn't popular in Heaven. He would sabotage the sky children's games, he gave the scorpion fish real spines, he gave sharks a menacing set of teeth, and the normally docile stingray real stingers on his tail. He plagued many of the gods by upsetting their cooking vessels, keeping them awake when they wanted to sleep, and eventually ravishing their daughters as he grew up and turned from boy to man. When he arrived at the highest level of Heaven, the gods were in the middle of building a spirit house for the dead. Olifat offered to help, but the gods were highly suspicious and he sensed that they would try to kill him if they could. So he hid in a special hollow in the bottom of one of the post holes, and when the post was rammed in, he threw out handfuls of muddy red earth and chewed up green leaves. With the slime spewing out, the builder gods thought Olifat's blood and guts had spurted out of the hole, and so they made sure it was plugged up, convinced he was dead.

Olifat was responsible for putting the spines on the scorpion fish's back.

But Olifat asked the termites to make a tunnel through the post and into the rafters. He then perched on the beams until he saw the builders returning to the spirit house. With a piece of coconut he banged around in the rafters pretending to be a great spirit. On seeing him, the lesser gods were afraid of this spirit, but his father saw Olifat and told him to get down.

Back on Earth, Olifat would sit in the rafters of men's houses and cause trouble by burning holes in the wood or calling on his termite friends to eat the posts. He soured wine, swapped good eggs for bad, and was the biggest seducer of women of all the gods. It was only through death that humans could escape his ridiculous tricks, but the eternal dullness of death only made humankind long to return to life and put up with Olifat's antics.

Bluejay

Among the coastal peoples of Oregon and the inland plateau groups, Bluejay was a trickster god who changed from bird to human form at will. His adventures resulted in many changes in the natural world and showed his skill at outwitting his rivals. Bluejay also appears further south among the Jicarilla Apache of the southwestern United States.

For many Native American peoples, birds such as the Bluejay were sacred tricksters, amoral, but wise.

Bluejay's escapades usually had something to do with his sister Ioi. His favorite tease was "Ioi is always telling lies." Ioi decided it was time Bluejay took a wife from among the dead people. Bluejay liked this idea, but rather than take an old dead wife, he chose a recently deceased chieftain's daughter. Although Ioi scowled, she told him he must take the girl to the Land of the Supernatural to bring her to life.

So Bluejay set off to the Land of the Supernatural, and at each village he asked the people to restore his wife to life. But each village only restored those to life who were one day dead, or two days, or three, and Bluejay was always a day late. Eventually he arrived at a village where the people felt sorry for him. They restored her to life and he became their chief. The couple lived there for a long time, but Bluejay was bored with the Land of the Supernatural. Luckily, his wife's tribe turned up, disapproving of the marriage, so Bluejay turned himself into a bird and soared away.

Ghost world

Bluejay wanted to see his sister again, and discovered that the ghost people had come for her one night. He transformed himself into a spirit and found Ioi surrounded by a pile of skeletons who were also his in-laws. Ioi told him, when there was no one around, how they got up and behaved like normal people, but loud noises scared them and they would crumble back into bones. Bluejay liked the idea of this game and took his cousin fishing. He purposefully sang as loud as he could just so that he could watch his cousin collapse into a heap of bones again.

Diving competition

When Bluejay returned to the land of the Chinooks, the Land of the Supernatural sent a message challenging the Chinooks to a diving competition. The loser would forfeit his or her life. Bluejay agreed to dive for the Chinooks and tricked his rival by creating a breathing hole beneath the water; each time he dived he could breathe, but each time the rival dived, she lost her breath and became more and more exhausted. Bluejay clubbed her to death beneath the water and arose the winner for the Chinooks.

Tjinimin

The myths of the Murinbata peoples of the Northern Territory in Australia include a trickster of the Dreamtime called Tjinimin ("bat"). Like most tricksters, he was energetic and creative, but also amoral and lustful. In one version of the myth, Kunmanggur the Rainbow Snake, a powerful sexual fertility deity, is also challenged by the lascivious antics of Tjinimin.

Tjinimin's favorite sport was attempting to ravish the Green Parrot Girls, the consorts of the Rainbow Snake. He was filled with insatiable lust and had a permanent erection; nothing stopped him from his rampant attacks. But the girls managed to drive him away first with bees, then by pushing him off a cliff onto jagged rocks where he smashed into pieces. But Tjinimin's trickster power meant that he could regenerate himself, and he tested this by cutting off his own nose and then putting it back again. He used a magic spear to destroy the Rainbow Snake who, in agony, gouged out huge rivers and water-holes, kidnapped fire from the world, and then dived to the depths of the ocean floor.

A rock painting of the Rainbow Snake at Dukuladjarranj, Central Arnhem Land, Australia.

Tjinimin didn't know how to make fire, but the kestrel, Pilirin, saved the world by showing everyone how to summon the fire spirits by rubbing together two sticks. Tjinimin only ventured out at night after that and from then on roosted upside down with his eyes on the stars so that he wouldn't be tempted by the fires of sexual desire in the world below.

Simpang Impang

To the Iban peoples of Sarawak, Simpang Impang was a cultural hero. He had no claims to fame or fortune, but managed to tame the wild wind.

During a night of torrential rain a woman had sex with a creeper in the form of a man, and she gave birth to a child who was half-creeper, but with a human arm and leg. The child, Simpang Impang, found some grains of rice and left them out in the sun to dry. But the wind blew up and the rice grains flew to the west.

Simpang Impang wanted his rice grains back. He hobbled through the jungles and across mountains in search of the wind. On his way he found an ancient tree, a lake, a banana tree, and some sugar cane that wanted the wind to come back and help them as well. Simpang Impang finally caught up with the wind, which tested him by

An Iban longhouse in Sarawak. The Iban were a fearsome warring people of Borneo, once infamous for head-hunting.

swirling first across the lake, believing the boy couldn't cross water; but a fish chased after the wind, who thought it was Simpang. The wind whistled through a tiny blow-pipe and an ant scuttled through the blow-pipe in Simpang's place.

The wind didn't have Simpang's rice grains, so angrily he set light to the wind's tail and it screamed out, "Put out the fire and I will make you a whole man!" Simpang dropped the fire stick and saw that he had become whole. In his delight, he made friends with the wind, and the wind promised to unplug the lake and blow off the dead leaves of the banana tree. He couldn't give the sugar cane boughs, though, since after all he was only the wind.

363

DEATH AND THE UNDERWORLD

The balance of light and dark correlates to that of the
Upperworld and the Underworld, the latter a place of
eternal darkness, usually governed by demons or invisible
deities. For most peoples, the gods denied humans the gift
of immortality, so death resulted in either suffering or
paradise. For example, to the Maoris, death was a return
to the womb of the Great Mother; to the Egyptians, it was
the final judgment; and in Norse myth, Valhalla was the
resting place for heroes and warriors.

Inanna and Erishkigal

Inanna is the Sumerian equivalent of the goddess Ishtar, and her tale is a direct parallel to that of Ishtar and Tammuz (see page 306). Inanna's descent to the Underworld and the resulting loss of fertility in the world, leads to the sacrifice of her unfaithful consort, Dumuzi, to her sister Erishkigal. It is also similar to the Greek myth of Demeter. Many believe they are all aspects of an original Great Goddess.

Inanna was the Sumerian goddess of fertility and was responsible for the growth of the land. The shepherd king Dumuzi was her consort, for whom she built the city of Uruk. He is described as being like a wild bull with a beard of lapis lazuli; similarly Inanna's vulva is likened to a "boat of Heaven" or "fallow land," which she urges Dumuzi to plow. Inanna was also the goddess of light. Her twin sister was Ereshkigal, the goddess of darkness who ruled the Underworld.

It is not clear why Inanna decided to visit her sister in the Underworld, but she dressed in her most exquisite robes and arrived at the first of seven Gates of Invisibility. Inanna was allowed to pass through each gate as long as she removed one or more of her garments and jewels. By the time she faced her sister, she was naked. The judges of the dead assumed she'd come to take over Ereshkigal's

Inanna was identified with the planet Venus and was the daughter of the moon god, Nanna.

*Symbols such as palm trees and goats were used to depict
Inanna's role as fertility goddess.*

throne, dragged Inanna off into the darkness and hung her on a butcher's hook
for her corpse to rot.

Inanna's return

While Inanna was in the Underworld, there was no light or fertility on Earth,
and the gods realized they must get her back. Enki, the trickster god, created
three beings with no brains, sexuality, or internal organs and gave them a cup
of immortality to drink so that they could pass through the Gates of
Invisibility. They took Inanna off the butcher's hook and gave her the rest of
the potion to revive her. Ereshkigal agreed that Inanna could return to the
Upperworld as long as she sent a replacement. On her return to Uruk, she
discovered that Dumuzi had neither mourned her nor cared that she'd gone.
Not only had he usurped her throne, but he had slept with her sisters. His betrayal
was enough for Inanna to banish him to the Underworld as her replacement and
thereby satisfy Ereshkigal's conditions. After some time Inanna regretted her
decision and allowed Dumuzi to return to Earth every year for six months as a
god of vegetation. This myth represents the time on Earth when there is no fertility
or growth and symbolizes the cycle of life, death, and rebirth.

The Egyptian Underworld

The philosophical and religious tending of the afterlife played a major part in Egyptian life. Mummification and the *ka* and the *ba* were essential components of their belief system. Osiris mummification was the first to be recorded, the art being perfected in about the fourth dynasty (2600 BCE).

Ka and ba

When a human was created, the *ka* was created simultaneously by the god Khnum on his potter's wheel. The *ka* was a spirit double of the body which could travel out of the body and when the body died, the *ka* divided and became the *ba* (the soul) and the *akh* (the spirit).

The *akh* took the form of a human-headed bird, which flew off to the Underworld. The *ba* lived in the tomb with the body, but was free to come and go as it pleased. As long as the *ba* was on Earth, the *akh* was free to live forever in the Underworld, the great realm of the dead where good spirits mingled with the gods and lived a life of peace and harmony. Should the body be destroyed, the *ba* would become homeless and both the *ba* and the *akh* would die a second death—something much feared by Egyptian people.

If the tomb was robbed or the body destroyed, the *ba* could stay with the statue of the deceased placed in

Osiris was the ideal king, but leaving his sister Isis to reign alone while he civilized the rest of the world was to be his downfall.

the tomb. This statue meant that the *ba* could avoid a second death.

The death of Osiris

A great ruler, Osiris was often away on his travels, so he left his sister-wife Isis to rule, but their brother Seth became envious and plotted his death. Osiris unsuspectingly climbed into a specially made box-bed offered at a great feast, then Seth and his conspirators slammed the lid down and poured molten lead over the box to seal up the cracks. The deadly coffin was thrown into the Nile where it drifted to Byblos. Isis eventually found it in a myrrh tree and took the coffin back to Egypt. With a magic spell she revived Osiris just enough to conceive a child and, as a fugitive, gave birth to Horus in the delta region.

Horus, the son of Osiris, eventually defeated Osiris' evil brother Seth and became ruler of Osiris' kingdom.

Seth found the coffin and cut Osiris' body into 14 pieces, which he scattered around Egypt. Isis reassembled them with the help of Anubis, the god of embalming, and Osiris was eventually brought to life again by Horus. He went to live in the Underworld as the ruler and judge of dead souls.

The cult of Osiris

The mummification of Osiris took as long as 70 days to complete. The Osiris cult carried with it the belief of life after death and continued down through the Egyptian dynasties as a distinct religion. Between 2500 and 1500 BCE Osiris was considered as important as Ra. A festival was held annually at Abydos, the place where Isis found Osiris' head. This became an important location for wealthy Egyptians to be buried in. In the last 600 years BCE, the Osiris cult outshone all others in Egypt and the mystery religion spread throughout the Mediterranean.

The Indian Underworld

In the early Vedic period, the Underworld was considered a fairly pleasant place for the souls of the dead, but in later Hindu mythology, gods of death, such as Kali, were harbingers of doom for those who must enter the dreaded Underworld of Kalichi and its ruler, Yama.

The Hindu goddess of death is usually depicted as a terrifying, naked woman, her bloodthirsty tongue lolling out of her mouth. She had black flesh, fangs, and a necklace of skulls. She was either the personification of one of the seven tongues of Agni, the fire god, or more usually the rage of Durga, Shiva's consort.

One story tells how Shiva sent Durga to fight the terrible demon Raktabija, who had the power to clone himself from any spilt drop of his own blood. Durga also tried the cloning trick, but the demon's power was greater. She became so enraged that Kali exploded from her forehead and lapped up all the demon's blood before it reached the ground. She became so drunk on the blood that she began to dance Shiva's cosmic dance of destruction.

Yama

At the end of the Vedic period between 900 and 550 BCE, Yama was the first man to live and die. He also discovered the road that led the dead to Heaven, and became its ruler. Agni, the fire god, could distinguish good and evil in each mortal by the color of the cremation flames. The ashes that remained represented evil, so the soul was transported in a golden chariot to Heaven to rejoin the purified body and live a riotous and happy life in Yama's kingdom.

Yama passed the time drinking *soma* and playing his flute. This was a place of lightness and music, laughter, and eternal paradise, until the era of rival gods and their own kingdoms arrived. Indra and Varuna had their own more sophisticated heavens, and eventually Yama's became linked with the darkness and he began to be considered a figure of terror. In Hindu belief, Yama evolved as the ruler of Hell, where only the wicked and evil would go. He lives in a

The Hindu goddess Kali's dark, horrifying appearance was a sign of imminent death.

forbidding place called Kalichi. With his book of destiny he writes the time-span allotted to each human, and his recorder Chandragupta reads aloud the virtues and sins of the dead. The soul may be sent to one of his many hells or returned to face another life on Earth. According to one myth, Shiva eventually beat Yama to death and all beings became immortal. But the world became overrun with too many people and life was miserable for those who were good and virtuous, so the gods decided to restore Yama and mortals lost their one chance for immortality.

The Greek Underworld

The Greeks shared the Egyptian belief that the realm of the Underworld lay to the west and the setting sun. They also believed that neither the Underworld nor its ruler Hades was particularly evil in intent. It was just as necessary as the Upperworld, and its reputation as a dark, menacing place probably derives from the myths of Persephone's abduction by Hades and Orpheus' search for Eurydice.

Hades ruled from the shadows and his invisibility made him a particularly reclusive character, although more by necessity than by actual deeds. He only went to the Upperworld when he was searching for a consort and was overcome by lust. He abducted the beautiful Persephone, who eventually became Queen of the Underworld for six months of each year to maintain the cycle of fertility and the seasons.

Tartarus, the Underworld, could only be reached by crossing the River Styx, usually by paying Charon the ferryman to carry the dead soul on his boat. Traditionally, relatives of the dead would leave a coin under the corpse's tongue for that purpose. Charon was the son of darkness and night and he refused to transport the living unless they bribed him. On the far bank of the river lived the fierce many-headed dog Cerberus, who guarded the shore and devoured any mortal who might try to enter or any soul who might try to leave.

There were several regions of Tartarus: Asphodel Fields, where ordinary souls would twitter forever like birds and bats; the

Cerberus is often depicted with varying numbers of heads, ranging from two or three to more than 50.

Charon, the ferryman, takes a coin from Psyche's mouth as payment for taking her across the River Styx.

Pool of Lethe, where souls could drink to wipe out all memory of their lives; and its opposite, the Pool of Memory. There was also a place for evil souls called the Punishment Fields, and one for those who had been virtuous called the Orchards of Elysium.

Hecate's domain

Erebus was the deepest, most inaccessible region where Hecate, the goddess of black magic, lived accompanied by the Furies, who decided the torment for wicked souls. Hecate would dance across the fields of Tartarus with a pack of ghosts howling after her, and some sources believe that when Persephone was living in the Underworld she preferred the company of Hecate to that of Hades.

Nemesis was no stranger to the Underworld either, for she would hunt down the guilty to ensure that the punishment fitted the individual's crime.

Orpheus

The myth of Orpheus was widely retold and became a mystery cult in ancient Greece. Devotees believed that initiation into his cult would guarantee them a free passage from the Upperworld to the Underworld and enable them to cheat death, as Orpheus had done. Fragments of so-called Orphic writings survive, probably part of the teachings of the cult, but scholars have not been able to learn much from them. One of the greatest musicians in the ancient world, Orpheus was the prince of Thrace whose singing voice and lyre-playing made even the rocks sigh with contentment. When his beloved wife, Eurydice, died from a snake bite, Orpheus was so desperate that he went down to the Underworld to retrieve her. Even Hades and Persephone were moved by his music and agreed that he could take Eurydice back, as long as he did not turn round to look at her as he led her toward the Upperworld.

Orpheus readily agreed to this deal, and Hermes led the couple back up through the kingdom of invisibility. But Orpheus could not resist checking to see if Eurydice was still there. As he stepped onto the threshold of the Upperworld he turned round, and Eurydice, following behind but still in the Underworld, vanished before his eyes.

Orpheus spent seven days searching the caverns and tunnels of the Underworld, begging Charon to take him across the Styx, but the old ferryman refused. So Orpheus stumbled back to the Upperworld and went to live in a cave on Mount Pangaeum. People heard that he had returned from the dead and groups of disciples came to his cave to learn his secret. In his grief for Eurydice, Orpheus never slept with, married, or even looked at another woman, and some suggest that he introduced male homosexuality to the human race.

Ultimately, his worship of Apollo and his dislike of women cost him his life. The Maenads, the wild female devotees of Dionysus, were furious that he was no longer interested in women. They raged into his cave one night like a pack of wolves and tore him apart, throwing bits of his body into the sea, and eventually binding his head to the lyre and throwing it in the River Hebrus. The lyre began to play and the head sing as it floated gently downstream toward the sea.

Orpheus' mother Calliope and the other Muses gathered the bits of Orpheus' body from the sea and buried them on Mount Olympus. The lyre floated on to the island of Lesbos, where the islanders buried the head in Dionysus' temple, and Apollo hung the lyre in the sky as a constellation.

Orpheus was warned never to look back at Eurydice or she would vanish forever.

Valhalla and the Valkyries

In Norse myth, Valhalla was Odin's great feasting hall for
the Einherjar, the heroic dead who had been slain on the
battlefield. The Valkyries were the warrior priestesses of Odin.

Valhalla was gigantic—its roof was made with shields and its wall with spears.
It had more than 500 doors and each was wide enough to accommodate 800
men marching abreast. The newly fallen heroes were admitted through a door
called the Valgrind, but before they could do so they had to undergo a series
of obstacles, which included crossing a torrential river of air.

Once inside, the great heroes were cured of their wounds and lived an endless
life of hedonism and fighting. Each morning they would don their armor, go
to the practice ground and fight each other. If killed, they would be brought

*Dead warrior riding Odin's eight-legged horse to Valhalla,
from the Tjangvide 1 Stone, found in Sweden.*

back to life to endure all the agonies they had previously suffered. But each evening they would return to Valhalla to feast on the meat of a huge boar, reincarnated every day. Because the Vikings believed this to be the perfect existence, older warriors who were not slain on the battlefield during their youth or active years would fall on their spears to be welcomed into Valhalla.

The Valkyries

Beautiful yet deadly women, the Valkyries rode over the battlefield selecting heroes for Valhalla and choosing the ones they most desired. They originated from earlier goddesses of slaughter who took delight in weaving tapestries out of severed limbs, entrails, and blood. On the battlefield they were sadistic and terrifying, but in Valhalla they were seductive women to fallen warriors. Each morning, after a night of rampant sex they would be reborn as virgins, wearing white robes and combing out their long golden hair.

They were also assistants to the god of war Tyr and rode on panting white stallions (or sometimes wolves) across the battlefield skies, swooping down to pluck their chosen hero. Sometimes they rampaged across the Earth seizing sailors from ships, then spraying the Earth with frost or early-morning dew that came from the drowning men's soaking clothes or falling tears.

Several of the Valkyries were renowned for their more serious relationships with mortals or gods. Brynhildr was the unfortunate lover of Siguror. She threw herself onto his funeral pyre when she realized that he hadn't betrayed her at all. Freyja (see page 136) was the leader of the Valkyries and also the goddess of sexual desire, and was known to indulge in orgiastic pleasure with fallen warriors.

The Valkyries were supernatural battle-maidens who decided who should live and who should die.

Xibalba, the Mayan Underworld

The second book of the *Popol Vuh*, the Mayan sacred texts, tells the story of two hero gods who venture into the Underworld, Xibalba, to avenge the murder of their father and uncle by the Underworld gods. Many images of Mayan death gods have been found in temples. They are referred to as "Death God L," or "Death God D," also known as Itzamna. Xibalba was renowned for its rotting, sulphurous odors.

The hero gods' ancestors, Hun Hunahpu and Vucub Hunahpu, had played a game of *tlachtli*, a kind of ball game popular throughout ancient Mexico. Unfortunately, they lost the ball down a tunnel that led to the dreadful realm of Xibalba. The lords of Xibalba challenged the gods to a game, but the gods were fooled, then murdered, sacrificed, and buried in the House of Gloom.

Many years later, the twin hero gods, Hunahpu and Xbalanque, met a rat, which told them the story of their ancestors' death. The rat explained about the game of *tlachtli* and where it had been played. So the twins set off to try the ball game, determined to meet the challenge of the demons and avenge their father's and uncle's death. The twins found the tunnel and followed the path that led down to the River of Blood and the entrance to Xibalba.

Tried and tested

Each night they were tested by the lords of Xibalba; the heroes were thrown into the House of Lances, pushed into the House of Ice, survived the House of Tigers and the House of Fire. In the House of Bats, Hunahpu's head was ripped from his body by a vampire bat, and the head rolled across the ball court. But a tortoise crossed the court, touched the head and magically it returned to Hunahpu's body. The game recommenced and the twins won by boasting they could bring the dead back to life and prove they were immortal. First they invoked two sorcerors to help them in their death and rebirth. The lords of Xibalba then demanded that they kill and resurrect the Hound of Death and

Symbolic stone death figures found in the ruins of the Mayan site of Copan.

cut a man to pieces and bring him to life again. The heroes did this and smiled as the Underworld rulers and demons asked if they could be resurrected too. The twins reminded them that they were merely dark shadows and phantoms and their power soon waned and they were forbidden to play *tlachtli* ever again.

The souls of the ancestors Hun Hunahpu and Vucub Hunahpu were, however, sent up to the Heavens as the Sun and Moon, and the heroes returned to the world to remind people of the immortality of the gods and their triumph over the land of the dead.

The land of ghosts

In Bantu mythology, spirits and ghosts of the ancestors live on after the death of the body and influence those who are living. Few of these ghost lands are found above ground and most are hard to access.

There are different classes of ghosts: family ghosts, *kungu* are honored and propitiated throughout the generations until they lose their individual personality and merge into a host of spirits known as *vinyamkela* or *majini*. The *vinyamkela* are friendlier than the *majini*, but both are more powerful than the family *kungu* ghosts. These ghosts are usually invisible but have moments when they can appear with half a human body and nothing on the other side.

The ghost country is found by way of holes and caves in the ground, but variations occur depending on the geographical landscape. On Kilimanjaro, for example, the ghost land is reached by throwing oneself into a deep pool; for the peoples of the Transvaal, the gateway to Mosima (the abyss) is said to be via a great ravine.

To reach the ghost land of Mount Kilimanjaro, souls must throw themselves into a deep pool.

Ghede

In Haiti, Ghede was originally the god of love and sex incarnate. In Voodoo, Ghede is also a term for a family of spirits embodying death and fertility; these spirits are known as *loas*.

From the notorious "slave coast" of west Africa, millions of people were transported to the Caribbean and North America between the 16th and 19th centuries CE. Their original mythology and religious practices merged with the indigenous beliefs of the peoples already there. In Haiti and some parts of North America, this new religion based on an ancient mythology was called Voodoo. The word "voodoo" comes from the west African word, *vodun* (spirit).

Ghede is god of both life and death. When devotees are possessed by Ghede, they become ecstatic and orgiastic to demonstrate that Ghede is also the lord of potency. His

The Haitian Voodoo flag, showing the symbols of death and Ghede.

followers would sweep along in a trance-like dance, called a *Banda*, behind one worshipper who would act out the part of Ghede, also known as Baron Samedi. Originally a phallic ritual, this was later considered to be a dance of death, when Ghede's orgies would end at the boundary of the afterworld, known as Guinee. Ghede could enter, but his followers must die first. He was traditionally depicted dressed in funereal black and sporting a top hat in his other role as psychopomp for the souls of the dead. In more recent times he has been depicted with sunglasses, twirling a long cigarette holder between his fingers or holding a tomato.

The Chinese and Japanese Underworlds

Also known as Di Kang Wang and Ti-Tsang, Di Zang was the Chinese god of the Underworld, while in Japanese Buddhist myth Emma-O was the great ruler of the Underworld, Yomi.

Di Zang

Originally a Buddhist monk, Di Zang was quite a benevolent Underworld ruler. When he first died, he went to the Underworld and stormed around the place demanding the release of his mother, who had been sent to the Underworld for eating meat. With a gang of monks, he made such a noise that eventually his mother was sent back to the Upperworld and Di Zang became ruler of the Dead. Once given immortality, he became a generous ruler and would sit listening to lost souls, teaching them his Buddhist beliefs. Generally compassionate to all, Di Zang's Underworld was very much a parallel world to the goodness and compassion of Buddhist teachings on Earth.

Emma-O

Yomi also meant the darkest part of night, and was originally considered to be a mirror-image world with no light, no beings, just nothingness. Izanami's escape to Yomi brought with it the creation of the demons to live in the Underworld, tormenting all those that had died. Subsequently Yomi became known as a place of torture and ordeal, rather than just a netherworld of formless concept.

As the judge of all who came to Yomi, Emma-O sat at a great desk made of precious metals. He judged the male souls, while his consort and sister would judge the female souls. The souls were transported in chariots of fire or brought once a year across the sea of darkness. Those who were deemed innocent were returned to the Upperworld in a new incarnation. The wicked would be punished before returning to another life. No one could change this unless they were blessed at the last second by the goddess of mercy, Kannon.

*If he met a soul who wanted to repent their sins, Di Zang
would arrange for the soul's sentence to be reduced.*

Polynesian and Aztec Underworlds

Throughout Polynesian and South American mythology, there are many variations of Underworlds. For the Aztecs, the Underworld in general was a place of nothingness, but for the Polynesians, Po was a place of terror.

Po

Po was divided into different regions. The most ominous part of Po was ruled over by Miru, who waited with a huge net in which he caught the souls of lonely people, those who had done something wrong and those who had the misfortune to be killed by sorcery. As the souls "leapt" out of the real world into the Otherworld, he scooped them up with his net and then threw them into his huge ovens where they were totally annihilated. Those who were privileged enough to have friends, or had been through the correct funeral rites, were usually allowed to join their ancestors in the spirit world that mirrored the real world. But some were not so lucky and would be locked in an eternal twilight zone.

Mictlan

The lowest (ninth) layer of the Aztec Underworld was known as Mictlan, where every soul went after death, apart from warriors who had died in battle and women who had died in childbirth. The journey there would take four years, although the souls would be accompanied by the god Xolotl. Mictlan itself was an empty, blank place, where the dead were eternally still.

The rulers of Mictlan were Mictlantecuhtli, the god of the dead, and his consort Mictecacihuatl. Mictlantecuhtli was usually portrayed as a skeleton, sometimes spattered with blood. He had ghastly protruding eyes, disgusting teeth, and a collar of eyeballs, and he lived with his wife in a windowless house. He was also associated with bats, spiders, and owls, the north and the eleventh hour. Worship of him was also known to have involved cannibalism.

Worship of Mictlantecuhtli involved rituals such as the sacrifice every 260 days of a man dressed up as the god himself.

Land of the Grandfather

For the Guarayu peoples of Bolivia, if the soul manages to survive the tests and trials on its long, arduous journey to the afterworld, it may enter the Land of the Grandfather, ruled by Tamoi. There it would join its ancestors to enjoy eternal youth and the kind of paradise longed for on Earth.

Once burial was complete, the soul had to choose between two paths: one wide and apparently easy, the other narrow and dark. If it chose the easy way it was certain to spend the afterlife in eternal darkness.

The soul first crossed a wide and dangerous river, and unless it took with it the bamboo pipe buried in the grave, then the ferryman would refuse to help the soul across. Once across this river, the soul would traverse a raging torrent on an unstable log. If it fell off into the surging foam, it would be devoured by the *palometa*—a fish whose sharp teeth and foul-smelling breath would bring eternal pain.

Once past this, the soul had to deal with dangerous torrents and a worm-judge, pick one million feathers from darting hummingbirds, and offer them to Tamoi as his headdress. Yet more dangers faced the weary soul: crashing rocks, inspection of the soul's correct face-paint by the gallinazo bird, being tickled for a day by a monkey without laughing, walking past a speaking tree without listening, and finally gazing upon the thing the soul desired most in its past life and not wanting it. If the soul survived all these tests, it would be welcomed to bathe in a pool of eternal youth and live life much as it had done in the "real" world.

Souls must pluck one million hummingbird feathers to offer to Tamoi.

Dubiaku

Dubiaku is a trickster hero of the Ashanti people of Ghana, and was the only mortal to outwit Death. Being the 11th son of a poor family, his mother pleaded with the sky-spirit to ask Death to come and take some of the boys away.

Sky-spirit sent the boys to Death's hut, where she welcomed them and set out 11 sleeping mats, which they would share with her own children that night. Her plan was to eat each of the boys, but Dubiaku stayed awake and tricked Death by sending her out to do things. Finally, the boys sneaked out of the hut and left their bundled clothes on the mats. When Death came back to find the children asleep it was her own offspring that she ate.

Enraged, Death ran after the boys, who climbed trees to hide. Dubiaku urinated on her head, and she shrieked out a spell to make them fall down and one by one the boys fell to the ground and died. Dubiaku had already leapt to the ground so, when Death climbed into the tree to see where the last boy was, Dubiaku called out the same spell she had used on the boys, and Death herself dropped dead to the ground. Dubiaku then threw Water of Life across the boys' faces to wake them, but some drops also splashed on Death's face and so she too was revived, like the boys.

The Ashanti (also known as Asante) people of Ghana have a colorful, lively oral tradition of storytelling.

She chased them all to a river and the boys began to swim across the raging torrent. But Dubiaku couldn't swim and, as Death approached him, he turned himself into a stone, which she threw at the boys on the other bank, and so they all escaped.

Purukapali

For the Tiwi peoples of Melville Island in northern Australia, Purukapali was the son of Mudungkala and the first man on Earth. Originally an immortal creator ancestor in the Dreamtime, Purukapali was responsible for bringing death to the world.

Purukapali was married to Bima, later known as Wai'ai, and they had several children: Jurumi and Madati who created fire; and a third child, Jinaini, who was only an infant when Bima used to carry him out to the forest every day to gather seeds. But Bima was having an affair with Purukapali's brother, Tapara. And one day as they made love beneath the trees, they forgot about the sleeping infant. As the Sun moved further across the sky, the baby was soon lying in the full heat of the midday Sun and was burnt to death.

The bird Tokampini wept and ran to Purukapali with the terrible news. Bima ran away, chased by some angry pelicans that hissed and pecked at her. Purukapali found his brother and fought him, knocking him to the ground. But Tapara ran away to the Moon, their mother, who protected him and told Purukapali that she would bring the child to life again, but only at the times of a full Moon. Mad with rage, Purukapali snatched the child's body and vowed that henceforth all humans would die.

The Tiwi peoples decorate their totemic poles to look like the person who has died.

Funeral posts are planted at Tiwi pukamani *ceremonies.*
The posts are then left to disintegrate.

He made the first *pukamani* (funeral) ceremony for his son, then waded out to sea and drowned, creating a huge whirlpool across the ocean. Bima turned into a curlew and as a bird she still roams at night, wailing with remorse and grief. Tapara became the man in the Moon, and you can still see the scars on his face from his struggle with Purukapali. He is the only one who has outwitted Purukapali's omen of death. When he appears in the sky he greedily eats all the flesh of the mangrove crabs, and after two weeks he is so bloated that he's about to burst. But because he's eaten so much he gets ill and then dies. Then his mother brings him to life again, and each time he eats too many crabs and the cycle continues forever.

The Tiwi peoples looked upon the silvery crescent of the waning Moon as the skeleton of Tapara, and the quarter-Moon waxing phase as his reviving spirit.

Annwn and Arawn

Annwn (also known as Anfwn, Affan, and Anghar) was the Otherworld or Underworld in Celtic myth. A mirror-image of the mortal world, it was, however, timeless and formless.

To begin with, there were two rulers of Annwn called Havgan and Arawn. All the inhabitants of Annwn were spirits, demons, or fairies who were of no substance and were only apparent in form when they traveled into the "mortal" world to trick, confuse, or harm the humans they encountered. Annwn later on became Christianized and identified with a land of departed souls.

In the *Mabbinogion,* Arawn wanted to destroy his rival Havgan and become sole ruler of the Otherworld. He knew he wasn't strong enough to win, but Pwyll, the King of Dyfed, was. One day while out hunting, Pwyll's own pack of hounds chased off another pack that were killing a stag. The owner of the other pack was Arawn, and as recompense for this insult, he persuaded Pwyll to rule the Underworld for a year while he, Arawn, ruled Dyfed. During this time, Pwyll easily killed Havgan and a year later they returned to their own kingdoms. As the sole ruler of Annwn, Arawn was from then on seen as a rather tame and gentle ruler. In a much later myth, Annwn was ruled by Gwyn ap Nudd, who led a pack of supernatural hounds and escorted the souls of the dead to the Otherworld.

Grail myths

The *Book of Taliesin*, an ancient Welsh manuscript, contains a poem in which King Arthur and his knights travel through Annwn in search of the Cauldron of Plenty, the eternal source of the Otherworld's delights and immortality. It is possible that this is the precursor to the later Grail myths. The text dates back to the 10th century CE, but scholars believe that most Welsh myth was passed on orally, and thus the poem could be from as far back as the 6th century CE.

Annwn is said to be accessible at the mouth of the Severn River near Lundy Island or from the top of Glastonbury Tor, near the town of Glastonbury in the southwest of England.

Glastonbury Tor in England, revered as a sacred "Isle of the Dead" and a possible entrance to the Otherworld, Annwn.

Index

Acknowledgments

Commissioning Editor Sandra Rigby
Editor Amy Corbett
Executive Art Editor Mark Stevens
Designer Janis Utton
Illustrators John Higgins and Dean Spencer
Senior Production Controller Linda Parry
Picture Researcher Giulia Hetherington

Picture credits

AKG Images 24, 25, 39, 152, 323; /Alfio Garozzo 368; /Bildarchiv Steffens 72, 148; /Electa 37; /Erich Lessing 15, 32, 116, 170, 189, 214, 347, 376; /Jurgen Sorges 355; /Nimatallah 79; /Ullstein Bild 61. **Alamy**/Alaska Stock LLC 208; /Anna Sherwin 205; /Bill Heinsohn 174; /Black Star 16; /blickwinkel 162; /Bruce Coleman Inc 359; /Carlotta 179; /Christian Ostrosky 199; /Content Mine International 183; /Danita Delimont 184; /Deco 180; /imagebroker 138; /Interfoto Pressebildagentur 2, 367; /J Marshall/Tribaleye Images 50, 319; /Joan Wakelin 302; /John Cancalosi 242; /John Warburton-Lee Photography 226; /Juniors Bildarchiv 316; /Karsten Wrobel 159; /Lebrecht Music and Arts Photo Library 345; /LOOK Die Bildagentur der Fotografen GmbH 275; /M Timothy O'Keefe 379; /Martyn Vickery 44; /Mary Evans Picture Library 66, 121; /Mike Goldwater 201; /Mireille Vautier 268; /Murray Cohen 241; /Nik Wheeler 357; /Paul Panayiotou 68; /Rachael Bowes 172; /Robert Estall Photo Agency 327; /Robert Harding Picture Library 36, 140; /Rolf Hicker Photography 185; /Terry Whittaker 243; /The London Art Archive 90, 113, 137, 281; /The Print Collector 35, 272; /travelib ireland 145; /William Laman 360; /Worldspec/NASA 17. **Bridgeman Art Library**/Bibliotheque Mazarine, Paris/Archives Charmet 120; /Bonhams, London 235; /Bradford Art Galleries and Museums, West Yorkshire 331; /Brooklyn Museum of Art, New York/Museum Expedition 1905; /Museum Collection Fund 237; /Galleria degli Uffizi, Florence 313; /Nationalmuseum, Stockholm 132; /Private Collection/Archives Charmet 343; /Private Collection/Peter Newark Western Americana 299; /Private Collection/The Stapleton Collection 311; /The Stapleton Collection 53, 54; /Trustees of the Royal Watercolour Society, London 119; /Victoria & Albert Museum, London 52. **Corbis** 380; /Charles O'Rear 246; /Fine Art Photographic Library 373; /Jaipal Singh/epa 284; /Richard T Nowitz 245; /Yves Gellie 168; /Adam Woolfitt 126; /Alexander Burkatovski 304; /Ali Meyer 43; /Araldo de Luca 6, 122; /Art on File 388, 389; /Asian Art & Archaeology, Inc 263; /Bettmann 11, 232, 234; /Chris Hellier 103, 271; /Christophe Boisvieux 42; /Danny Lehman 171; /Davis Factor 158; /Diego Lezama Orezzoli 194; /Frans Lanting 166, 173; /Hinrich Baesemann/dpa 188; /Homer Sykes 391; /Hubert Stadler 195; /Hugh Sitton 328; /Jane Yeomans 255; /Jim Sugar 265; /John Henry Claude Wilson/Robert Harding World Imagery 251; /Julio Donoso/Corbis Sygma 353; /Karl Kinne/zefa 161; /Kevin Fleming 186; /Lester Lefkowitz 211; /Michael & Patricia Fogden 298; /Michael S Yamashita 67, 97; /Mimmo Jodice 112; /Neil Rabinowitz 277; /Nico Tondini/Robert Harding World Imagery 88; /Nik Wheeler 335; /PBNJ Productions 14; /Penny Tweedie 300, 362; /Pete Saloutos 210; /Peter Adams 46; /Peter Adams/zefa 40; /Roy Morsch 165; /Stapleton Collection 253; /The Art Archive 89; /Theo Allofs/zefa 154; /TongRo 71; /Underwood & Underwood 269; /Werner Forman 385, 387. **Fotolia**/Daniel Rajczak 303; /Jean-Yves Foy 69; /Jenny Solomon 144. **Getty Images**/AFP 219 above; /David Madison 267; /Ed George 239; /Karl Weatherly 98; /The Christian Science Monitor Archive 163; /Thony Belizaire 329. **istockphoto.com**/Jim Jurica 207; /Klaas Lingbeek-van Kranen 41; /Serdar Yagci 351. **Mary Evans Picture Library** 31, 38, 102, 136; /Edwin Wallace 150. **NASA**/Human Spaceflight Collection 177; /NASA/JPL-Caltech/ J. Hora (Harvard-Smithsonian CfA) 13; /NASA/JPL-Caltech/S Stolovy (Spitzer Science Center/ Caltech) 212. **National Geographic Image Collection**/Tim Laman 363. **Octopus Publishing Group Ltd** 204. **Photolibrary Group**/Brigitte Merle 224. **Picture Desk**/Eileen Tweedy 93. **Photo Scala, Florence**/Bildagentur für Kunst, Kultur und Geschichte, Berlin 63; /Egyptian Museum, Cairo 75; /Egyptian Museum, Vatican 12; /Louvre, Paris/C M Dixon/HIP 91; /Monte dei Paschi Collection, Siena 125; /Museo de America, Madrid 193; /Museo delle Ceramiche, Deruta 18; /Musee du quai Branly/Hughes Dubois 356; /National Archaeological Museum of Cagliari 34; /Photo Spectrum/HIP 153. **Shutterstock**/Mark Atkins 223; /Sam DCruz 48; /Saniphoto 10. **TopFoto**/ImageWorks 381. **Werner Forman Archive** 78, 156, 230, 240; /British Museum, London 191, 264, 367; /National Library of Australia, Sydney 181; /Private Collection 157; /Schimmel Collection, New York 27; /Statens Historiska Museum 377; /Tishman Collection, New York 160. **Wikipedia** 92, 292.